A Scandalous Request

by

Micki Miller

A Scandalous Request

Cover Art by *Rae Monet, Inc.*

The Wild Rose Press, Inc.
PO Box 708
Adams Basin, NY 14410-0708
Visit us at www.thewildrosepress.com

Publishing History
First Tea Rose Edition, 2018
Print ISBN 978-1-5092-2227-8
Digital ISBN 978-1-5092-2228-5

Published in the United States of America

"Are you all right? Did he hurt you?"

His deep voice cut through the night with the swiftness of a warrior's sword, and though his words were kind, his tone was not. In fact, he sounded downright angry.

"Yes. I mean no. I mean…" She straightened her bent bonnet as best she could before saying, "I'm fine." It was hardly the truth. While she suffered no more than a few bruises, her heart pounded a wild tempo against her ribs and her body shook to rattle her bones.

Lord Darington seized her then, his hands like steel bands around her upper arms. His grip was firm, angry, but not painful, though it no doubt could be should he choose to make it so. He was holding back. The man could snap her like a winter twig if he so desired.

"Have you no sense at all?" He spat. "Do you have any idea what could have happened to you out here?"

Rose tipped her head back. She wished she hadn't. But for a slight tick, his face could have been stone, inset with glaring eyes as dark and turbulent as a tempestuous storm. Intensity radiated from his powerful physique in waves she could swear were tangible. Lord Darington wasn't just angry. The man was furious.

Dedication

To Ashley, Bill, Lila, Lawton, Keegan, and Keller. You keep love in my heart.

Previous Releases

The Marshal's Pursuit

The Darkest Sum

Chapter 1
London, January 1812

How she wished it was not her birthday.

Rose squirmed to free herself from the lecherous grip of her sister's husband, but Baron Piers Rutherford held tight, forcing himself against her petite frame with deliberate indecency. The excess of his soft body molded around hers, making her entrapment complete.

Panic clawed at her insides. Then Rose remembered her sister, older by twelve years, sat but a few feet away. Piers would rein in his lascivious behavior in front of his wife, wouldn't he? Edwina's presence, if not her protection, is what kept Rose safe in the past.

The man was shameless. He took advantage of any circumstance he could forge into an excuse to touch her, or to brush his body against hers in the dining room or the corridor when there was plenty of room to pass. And as the years ushered her into womanhood, his advances had become not only more frequent, but also bolder. This blasted birthday was but another excuse for him to put his filthy hands on her.

Finally, as an icy gust threw snow against the window, the white, lacey specs a sharp contrast to the black night, Piers loosened his grip. Rose took such a quick step back, she almost tripped.

It was no small struggle to keep her revulsion

hidden. The cool temperature of the room hadn't stopped Piers from perspiring, profusely, as was her brother-in-law's normality. The man always carried a dose of humidity with him. It was but another accentuation to his foulness.

Rose had a powerful desire to run upstairs and into her room, tear off her now damp gown, and scrub her skin raw. Instead, she maintained her composure and took another step back.

"I can't believe our little Rose is twenty years old! Can you, Edwina?" Piers didn't wait for his wife to answer before continuing. "Why it seems only yesterday you were but a poor, tiny waif on our doorstep with nowhere else to go, no one else to turn to, and now look at you, all grown up!"

Piers then lunged, throwing out his blubbery arms and wrenching her in for another moist hug.

His indecent behavior was even more disturbing than the deliberate arrow to her pride. She long ago thickened her hide when he hurled those spears. She had to. Her choice was to either numb her pride or drown in her humiliation.

Neither her brother-in-law, nor her sister, ever missed an opportunity to speak of her circumstance. They often reminded her how she was indebted to them for every stitch of her simple clothing, every morsel of rationed food that made its way to her mouth.

Rose allowed herself an inward groan as she thrust herself away from her brother-in-law once more.

At her age, she really should be married and in a home of her own. She'd had several callers. One young man, Callum Overshire, even approached Piers and made a formal request to court her. Piers turned him away. It left her both aggravated at his control over her life, and relieved he'd not forced her into marriage.

Callum was a pleasant enough gentleman, but marriage to anyone, well, the thought alone could cause Rose a full shudder. The very idea of a man pawing at her as Piers did, and worse, having the right to because he was her husband, caused her stomach to roil and her head to pound. In this house, at least, was trouble she could handle.

Or rather, it had been. Of late, her sister's husband had grown more audacious, and Eddy's presence was becoming less of a deterrent.

Piers ran his tongue across his plump, bottom lip, gawking at Rose as if her simple, demure clothing hid nothing from his lustful eyes. Rose shot a glance toward her sister. Edwina returned her silent plea for rescue with a glare so full of hatred and blame, Rose shrank with despair.

Using one hand, as the other held an empty glass; Edwina heaved her thin body up from her favorite seat positioned close to the stingy fire. Rose lowered her eyes to the ruby cushioned chair where her sister had been sitting. The contrast between this room, the modest-sized parlor where they receive visitors, and the rooms upstairs, was extreme.

The furnishings down here, the green sofa and Edwina's button back armchair, the two, orange floral tall backs, were all of quality and in good condition. The imitation Moorefield carpet showed not the least bit of wear and the heavy wood sideboard and tables always gleamed with fresh polish.

Their private rooms upstairs in the baron's home, however, were ever meager and threadbare. The only bit of luxury at all was the fine, chintz drapes hanging over the windows, as they could be seen from the outside.

Almost immediately upon rising, Edwina listed to her left and it took a precarious moment to gain her balance. Experience taught Rose it was best to ignore her natural instincts and not offer help. Her sister had more pride than dignity and her temper swelled larger with each drunken tumble.

Just as Edwina steadied herself, the empty glass in her hand slipped. She tightened her grip, though, hugging the glass against her heart before it could fall.

Rose gazed at her sister, appalled at how skinny Eddy had become over the last year or so. Her bodice was loose and her slate blue gown hung askew upon her bony shoulders. Edwina's hair, once as golden and thick as Rose's, now gave the impression of loosely bound straw. Puffs the color of stormy skies sat in bags below her dull eyes. What had become a permanent scowl pinched the gray tinge of her face.

After following her body's lean toward the flat-paneled sidebar, Edwina sloshed cheap brandy from the fine, crystal decanter into her glass. She tipped a long sip, and then another. Finally, she turned toward Rose and managed to focus her glossy eyes. Rose cringed as Edwina's narrowed gaze ran a slow, condemning inspection of her from top to bottom.

"Yes. Our little Rosalind has grown into quite the thing, hasn't she?" Each word Edwina spoke slurred into the next. A powerful coughing fit overtook her then, evoking heavy barks from deep within her chest. When it was over, Edwina shot a brittle smile to Rose and added, "Happy birthday, sister dear."

"Thank you," Rose murmured. She took a few steps to stand by the paltry fire that did little to keep away the chill of the night. Rose stretched her hands out hoping to catch what little heat it offered. Without guests in the house, Piers would keep the cost of warmth down to the barest minimum.

"I've had cook prepare a special meal for tonight," Piers said. His happy leer bespoke his anticipation of gratitude. "With some of those sugary cakes you like so much for dessert."

Rose mumbled another quiet thank you without turning from the fire. Piers had walked up behind her and she did not want to give him a chance at another lewd show of affection. Her imagination provided a moment of entertainment while she stared at the andirons. In the privacy of her mind, she hefted one of them, spun around in a trail of sparks, and shoved the heavy piece into his bloated belly.

Rose suppressed a smile at the image, and then lost it altogether when his sour breath wafted over her shoulder and across her face.

"Tomorrow we shall take a nice stroll in the park, as I was otherwise occupied today and unable to take you on an outing for your special day. I know how you love the outdoors."

"That's not necessary," Rose said, slipping away from Piers, and the small bit of warmth the fire provided. "I understand you're a busy man. Besides, tomorrow I'm working with Lord Sennett on the Foundling Project. He's had some wonderful ideas to raise money for the cause. We'll be quite busy the entire day."

"Just you and the Viscount Sennett, working alone

together?" Piers said. His tone darkened and the joviality drained from his voice. "That's highly improper, my dear. I'm afraid I can't allow it."

"Of course we won't be alone," Rose responded, spinning around to face him. "Lady Emory will be there, as well as Lady Brimsford."

After an interminable pause, Piers said, "It seems the viscount has gathered quite the little brood of hens all for himself."

Rose bristled at the insinuation leveled at her good friend and didn't hesitate to come to his defense. "Lord Sennett's intensions are nothing if not noble, I assure you."

"My dear, you are much too innocent to understand a man's intentions."

Not so innocent. Not since you set out to grope me at every possible opportunity.

The words were on the tip of her tongue. Her well-honed sense of preservation kept them there. She forced a reasonable tone and said, "He's been a great asset to the cause, both with his money and with his influence. Ashton is a very kind and generous man."

"Ashton, is it?"

Rose winced inwardly at her slip, knowing it was impossible for Piers to understand a pure friendship, free of clandestine motives. "We've become good friends. Nothing more."

The baron's steady gaze held still on her for a long time before he said, "You will remain here tomorrow."

"I told you, Lord Sennett and I won't be alone. Lady—"

"Yes, you told me. They are married women, not innocent young chits like yourself. It would be nothing at all for Lord Sennett to corner you alone and take advantage of you."

"He would never do such a thing," Rose said, her temper rising. Unable to keep the jab from her tone, she added, "Lord Sennett is a *true* gentleman."

Though she could tell Piers caught her intent by the way his eyes hardened, be it ever so brief, he did not give her the satisfaction of acknowledging it. "I said I forbid it."

"Oh, let her go, Piers," Edwina said from her place leaning against the sidebar, an unkind smile twisting her pursed lips.

Piers ignored his wife and focused his address on Rose. "The matter is closed."

"I'm a grown woman," Rose said, her voice escalating as she fought to keep her anger in check. The older she got, and the more troublesome her brother-in-law became, the more difficult it was to achieve such.

The work the group was doing mattered. If they could get this new foundling home built, the lives of those orphaned and abandoned children would know a vast improvement. And, on a note of pure selfishness, working on the project gave her good stretches of time to be away from the house.

In a strained, but reasonable tone, Rose said, "What we're trying to accomplish will make a significant difference for all of those children. I'm sure you can understand the importance."

Linking his fleshy fingers across the broad expanse of his belly, Piers said, "I've already said no, Rosalind. You'll do as I tell you. Do not forget your place in this house."

Rose's anger and frustration came untethered from

her good sense and she shouted, "You cannot confine me here as if I was your pet!"

At her insolence, Piers' eyes flared with outrage, and then something else flashed across his face, something Rose could not define with any accuracy. A dark entity prowled in his shallow depths, incited, vile, and very, very frightening. Rose had the distinct impression she had roused a horrible beast.

Piers lowered his arms and stepped toward her, the gleam in his eyes shone bright above the tilt of his leering grin. His jaw twitched beneath heavy jowls. At his sides, his thick fingers pulsed into fists. The pace of his breath had accelerated, deepened, and she detected a slight tremble when he sucked in a gulp of air.

Rose had never been more afraid.

Before she could react and protect herself, Piers slapped her hard across the face. Her head snapped back, and she had to shuffle her feet to keep from falling. Her sister's laughter penetrated the ringing in her ear.

Rose pressed her hand to her cheek. Her skin burned against her shaky palm. Without looking at either Edwina or Piers, she ran from the room, bolted up the stairs, and didn't stop until she slammed her door shut. She smashed the flat of her hand against the wood panel and wished there was a lock to turn. A dozen locks would be better.

After lighting the candle sitting on the scarred table beside her bed, Rose paced through the chill of the room with furious steps. She knew every inch of the small chamber, as it had been hers since she was twelve years old, when her mother and father were lost at sea. She thought of them now. Sometimes, like tonight, she missed them so much the ache in her heart twisted fresh.

On the table beside the candle stood the golden amber pig her parents had commissioned for her twelfth birthday, two months before they died. It was a beautiful piece they had made just for her. As long as her flattened hand and three inches tall, she loved the way it transformed flecks of light into living versions of its own amber color.

The solid, carved pig gifted her with comfort every time she saw it, more so when she held its solid weight.

She snatched up the heavy pig and clasped it against her in a tight grip as she paced off her rage and frustration across the oval carpet so ancient it was unraveling. Outside, fat snowflakes clung to the window. Others flew by on the cold breath of winter.

In the habit of saving her precious allotment of wood for bedtime, Rose did not yet light what was in her small hearth. She was too upset to pay much notice to how chilled the room was anyway. Besides, her endless pacing was enough to keep her warm.

From the door, to her narrow bed with the rough, plank headboard. To the window, crusted with snow, and back to the door. Over and again while her mind sought possible solutions from her impossible situation.

Sometime later, when she tired and her steps slowed, a heavy breath left her, carrying off the last of her energies. She crawled upon her bed. With the amber pig still cradled in her arms, she wept while the cold wrapped around her like the dungeon of her circumstance.

****

Rose awakened to a knock at the door.

As she sat up, fully dressed atop her covers, the memory of the evening's wretched events returned. At another knock, Rose swiveled her head toward the door. It was Edwina. Her sister was distant and unsympathetic, more so with each passing year. However, Eddy was her blood and her husband had gone too far tonight. Rose crossed the room, opened the door, and found Piers on the other side.

Before she could react, Piers said, "Rose, I'm sorry about what happened tonight."

Rose said nothing. She wanted to believe her brother-in-law was speaking the truth, that he was sincere in his regret for striking her. She was not a greedy woman. All she'd ever wanted was a peaceful life.

"I lost my head tonight," Piers continued, his plump hands gripping each other atop the round protrusion of his stomach as if to plea. "I promise you, it won't ever happen again. I've been sitting alone downstairs for hours. I can't go to sleep without your forgiveness. Please, Rose, say you'll accept my apology."

Unsure as to his sincerity, yet not in a position to do anything else, Rose nodded. "Of course. We'll just forget tonight ever happened and start fresh in the morning."

"Thank you, Rose," Piers said on an exhale. His lips made two motions as if he would say more, but then he glanced off to her right, peering into her room. "Here, let me light the fire for you. You must be freezing."

"Thank you, but I can—"

"No, no, I insist."

She stepped to the center of the room and stood as he lumbered into a kneeling position before the small hearth and made a fire for her. With some effort, he got to his feet and turned around, brushing the dust from his hands.

"Thank you," Rose said.

Piers nodded, saying nothing as he passed her. She heard him close the door and wilted in her relief. She then swiveled around, only to find he had closed the door, from the inside.

"Piers?"

"Rose, you've no idea how lovely you are, do you?"

He stepped toward her. Rose stepped back. "Piers, you have to go."

"It's torture, torture I tell you. Every day I see you around this house, looking as you do. You're so innocent, and sweet, yet so fiery. It's intoxicating. I've spent these years watching you grow into this beautiful, desirable woman I now see before me. You couldn't even begin to guess the desperation of my need for you, Rose."

Rose attempted to be discreet as she stepped sideways. If he would not listen to reason, perhaps she might dash around him and make it to the door, and get to Edwina.

"You shouldn't say such things, Piers. You are my sister's husband."

His hardened distaste lasted the duration of his first sentence, before he again focused on Rose. "Edwina is a cold fish. But you, you are so much more than you even know. If you'll but allow me to teach you how to be a woman, your life here in this house could be so much more enjoyable."

Less discreet now as her fear grew, Rose took a longer step to the side. The shift gave her a direct and open route to her door. Then, Piers shifted his girth over a step, once again blocking her exit.

"Piers, you must see how this is outside the bounds."

"I've wanted you for so long now, Rose. I have to have you."

"Piers…"

Her brother-in-law said not another word. Instead, he took action. Piers lunged for her. Rose trotted backward until she ran up against the wall. Her sister's husband was but a half step away. Before she could make another maneuver and escape him, Piers clasped her upper arms, squeezing her in a painful grip.

Perspiration ran from his temples, down his jaw, and dripped to the floor. Teardrops of whatever honor the man once had. His nostrils flared. His head made a slight tilt to the right when he spoke. And he shook her a bit, emphasizing his words.

"I'm mad with desire for you, Rose. Can't you tell? I know you must feel it for me, too. You're just too young to understand your own desires."

Words ran through her head as she tried forming new, more effective arguments. Fear stunted her thoughts at every turn. Swinging her around as if she weighed nothing, her brother-in-law threw her down on the bed.

"Piers, no! Eddy! Eddy!" she shouted, two seconds before he dropped on top of her. His heavy girth quashed her breath and doused her shouted pleas in the fluid mobility of his excess.

He grabbed her breast, squeezing hard, and she cried out again as loud as she could raise her voice under his weighty suppression. Piers used his other hand to clamp down over her mouth. Rose struggled beneath his heft. She shoved with all her strength, but her brother-in-law outmatched her in every way.

Piers lowered his face. She twisted her head away as his sloppy kiss dragged across her brow.

Then, with her face pressed against the worn counterpane, her eyes caught sight of the heavy, amber pig still lying on the bed.

She ceased her useless effort to shove away her brother-in-law, and instead made a grab for the pig. Her fingertips brushed the cool surface of its head, but it was too far away for her to get a grip.

Piers shifted his body so he could maul her other breast. The slight movement allowed her to squirm a little and get closer to the pig.

Rose caught a fingernail on one of its small ears. She was able to scoot it toward her a tiny bit before her fingernail slipped. Stretching her shoulder, arm, and fingers out as far as she could, she almost had it. Yes, yes, she caught hold of its head.

A moment later, she had its solid body secured in her grip.

As hard as she could, Rose smashed the heavy pig against the side of Piers' head. Blood immediately gushed from the split in his scalp just above his ear. His eyes widened with shock. He lifted himself up to his knees. For a moment, he froze in place. Then his eyes rolled back in his head and he fell over, dropping to the floor with a heavy thud.

Trembling from head to toe, her breath coming in

sharp gasps, Rose leapt from the bed and spun around on shaky legs to stare at her sister's husband. He lay on his back perfectly still. Blood streamed from his head in a condemning red, flow. It formed a small pool on the unpolished, wooden planks of the floor.

"Piers?"

He didn't answer. She couldn't even tell if he was breathing. Maybe he was dead or would be soon. She had to get Eddy. But would her sister help her, or condemn her? Or worse, leave her fate to Piers.

Rose spun around to run from the room, but then stopped, her head swiveling to look back over her shoulder. The pig lay in the center of the bed. In the spin of her mind, the one, solid point was the comfort of her precious pig. She wanted it in her hands. She needed it, now, first.

On quick and quiet steps, she walked back and leaned over the bed on her left leg, hand stretching out to retrieve her precious pig.

"You ungrateful bitch!" Piers shouted as he grabbed hold of her ankle.

Rose struggled to get away, but his grip was like a leg-iron. With eyes bulging, Piers stretched his neck, his mouth opening, lips peeling back. She gaped in helpless horror as he shoved her skirt aside with his other hand and sunk his teeth into her calf. Rose cried out before lifting her right leg, and with all the force she could marshal, stomped her foot down into the mound of his soft belly.

Piers' hand snapped into a flex and shoved Rose away at the same time his vicious bite released her. When his mouth gaped open, lips peeled back, smears of her blood showed on his teeth. He bellowed an angry, painful cry. The entirety of his expelled breath muffled the sound like a windstorm over a howl.

Rose swallowed a scream and grabbed her amber pig. She dashed from the room. Without a pause, she ran down the stairs, out the front door, and into the cold, cold night.

Chapter 2
London, May 1812

No, he could not have heard right.

Burke Darington, Third Earl of Blackwood, raised one dark brow and peered over his snifter of brandy into the clear eyes of Viscount Ashton Sennett. Between the music and chatter of the soiree, the sound of the man's words must have jumbled. Sennett couldn't possibly have made such an outrageous request.

Three violinists positioned at the other end of the hall filled the room of sixty or so of the Viscount's guests with soft, pleasant arrangements flowing with ease from one to the next. On a portion of the marble floor cleared for dancing, several couples dressed in their colorful finery bowed and stepped in a graceful minuet.

Crystal glasses clinked, silver forks tapped on Creamware plates with scalloped edges. Laughter accentuated the already jovial mood. Conversation ebbed and flowed, but never ceased beneath the candle glow of a half-dozen, multi-branched chandeliers.

The tidy young viscount chuckled. After straightening the crisp, white ruffle at his cuff, he slid a hand back against his fresh-trimmed, blond hair and said, "Yes, you heard me right."

The earl set his glass on the varnished, tulipwood

table and folded his hands beside it as he leaned back. The evening had been pleasant enough, the music, fine brandy, some of the company he even found tolerable; the young viscount with whom he now spoke, for example.

Lord Sennett had earned his respect. Over the last two or three years, they'd done business. Burke had come to know the viscount was a man of integrity who could be trusted to honor a verbal contract, yet was wise enough to get everything in writing.

Still, Burke was far from a social enthusiast. He cared naught for Society's endless gossip, or more precisely, the ever-active hypocrisy lurking behind it. As far as he was concerned, most of the *ton* could waltz straight into the Thames.

This particular invitation, however, had intrigued him. Or rather, it was the note Sennett had written on the back of the invitation.

The viscount implored him to overlook his aversion to social events and attend the soiree. He wrote there was a matter of great importance he wanted to discuss with him. As Lord Sennett was not given to dramatics, Burke's respect and curiosity was roused enough to make an appearance.

Burke swept a brief scan of the room. Most of the faces he knew. Several of the women he'd known intimately. Lady Prudence Hortence, whose husband had died in a shooting accident nearly four years ago, had already whispered an explicit invitation into his ear. Burke fully intended to take Pru up on her offer.

His appearance at her door would be quite late, though, as she was not a woman with whom he enjoyed a preamble of dialogue. Of course, he could say so about most. His experience with her particular traits included knowing Lady Hortence was a spoiled, sharp-tongued, chatty bit of baggage. The woman did have one pleasing forte, however. She was adept at putting her mouth to better uses than distributing the latest gossip.

Returning his attention to Sennett, Burke said, "You must admit, it is a most bizarre request. I'd be willing to bet the first of its kind."

"Without a doubt," Ashton conceded with a smile holding both amusement and self-deprecation as his eyes shifted. With a nod, he directed Burke to where his gaze rested, upon his lovely wife who stood not far away. "She is a beauty, Darington. Do you not agree?"

Burke followed the viscount's line of sight. Lady Rose Sennett was indeed an attractive woman. Her features were delicate, with eyes such a vibrant blue he could see the color from where he sat. Her slender body hosted all the right curvatures. She wore her gold and honey hair in a thick braid wrapped around her head in a coronet, a crown over a fair and well-sculpted face.

He found himself wondering what her hair would look like down around her milky shoulders, teasing portions of which were exposed and complemented by her emerald gown. The snug cut of the bodice was perfect for her. It accentuated her narrow waist and the gentle flair of her hips. Her *modiste*, whomever the woman was, had excellent instincts on relation and design, but for one piece.

Covering a good portion of her décolletage was a white, lacey fichu. The piece was at odds with the gown, as it leant a rather modest touch to her appearance. Modesty was not a feature that drew him.

"Your wife is indeed a beautiful woman."

Burke pivoted his attention back to find the viscount leaning forward a bit, an expression of expectancy on his boyish face. The man didn't appear to be drunk, nor had he ever given Burke the impression he was less than in full control of his mind. Yet, what other explanation could there be for such an outlandish request?

"Well?" Ashton prompted.

"You can't be serious."

"I assure you, I am most serious. I've given this matter considerable thought and sifted through a great many candidates before I settled on you. You can't tell me any man wouldn't find her attractive."

"As I said, your wife is a beautiful woman," the earl agreed.

"And you are a man who has known many."

Burke's brow rose once again.

Lord Sennett raised a placating hand. "I meant no offense. In fact, it's one of the reasons I chose you."

"I don't understand why you would choose anyone. She's your *wife*."

"Rose is my friend, my dear friend. And in that I love her with all my heart."

"And yet you put this absurd request to me?"

"That is *why* I put the request to you," Ashton said. "Through our business dealings I think we have developed a sort of friendship."

"We have."

Until this moment, Burke would have sworn to Ashton's honor and sound mind. The viscount had married several months ago in a very private ceremony. Word of the marriage, like all other gossip, spread posthaste throughout Society. The recently wed couple had been making the rounds of parties, balls and other social events of the Season. Since Burke avoided such activities, tonight was the first time he'd seen Lady Sennett.

Burke had heard not a scrap of gossip in regards to either one of them. At least two of the women with whom he had enjoyed bed play kept him apprised of the goings on of Society, whether he cared to know or not.

"While the gossipmongers have pinned you with a reputation as a bit of a rake," the viscount continued. "You are also discreet. It is only by way of whispers anybody even knows that much about your...private activities. Some even claim your exploits are nothing more than rumor, so fine is your discretion. Yet another reason I chose you."

The explanation was far from complete. Burke slanted another glance toward Lady Rose Sennett. Lady Emory, the tall, dark-haired woman to whom she was speaking, leaned in and whispered something into the dainty shell of her ear. Lady Sennett's entire face lit up with a dazzling smile, and then she laughed. The sound was musical, carefree, and full of joy.

For one envious moment, Burke wondered what it would be like to feel so light of spirit.

He kept his eyes on Lady Sennett as she pressed her slender fingers against her lips. An effort to maintain decorum, Burke assumed. He found the move utterly adorable. But as with modesty, adorable was not a quality to which he was drawn.

Lord Sennett cleared his throat and, after a discreet glance around, lowered his voice. "Along with your exploits and your discretion, I've heard at least one woman praise you for your, um…talents."

Burke did smile at Sennett's comment. "My talents?"

"Lady Brimsford wears her desires on her sleeve whenever you are in the vicinity. It doesn't seem to matter Lord Brimsford has taken her to wife. She still…speaks well of you."

Burke knew Lord Sennett worked with many women on the Foundling Project. At least a couple of those women were well aware of his 'talents'. Had some of the women he'd enjoyed actually bragged to another man of their exploits?

Burke flicked a glance to the other side of the room where earlier he'd spotted said former paramour. He and Lady Brimsford, Lady Harcourt back then, had enjoyed a tumble or two during the three years of her widowhood. Perhaps women attach more commemoration to such things than men.

Lady Brimsford was in a heated discussion with her new husband. She did have a temper, he remembered. When she realized Burke was dead serious about never taking a wife, that, against all social mores, he cared not if he produced an heir, and she would never become mistress of his mansion, her screeching fit sent the very tapestries on the wall into a shiver. She now stood before her husband appearing to be on the verge of another fit.

Apparently, Viscount Brimsford did not approve of the breadth of skin his brazen wife was showing. Burke treated his eyes to the good amount of cleavage her cream-colored gown exposed, remembering well how her generous breasts overflowed from his hands.

"I'm surprised she confided in you such

intimacies," Burke said to Lord Sennett.

"Lady Brimsford has done some work on the Foundling Project. She and I have also become friends. After a second glass of wine, the lady's confidences become rather open."

As do her thighs, Burke recalled, with a grin he didn't show.

"You maintain quite a close friendship with a number of women, it seems," the earl said, lifting his glass in what one might perceive as a toast before taking a sip of brandy.

"I enjoy the company of women."

"Does that include your wife?"

"Most especially my wife," Ashton answered with great emphasis. "She's a dear woman, kind and strong. Her mind is agile and she possesses a measure of perceptiveness one rarely finds. Any man should consider it an honor to even know her."

"High praises with one breath, an outrageous request with another, which brings me back to my original question."

"You want to know why I have asked this of you," Ashton said, casting a brief but adoring glance at Rose.

"Our marriage is one of convenience. I needed a wife, to help with certain matters of the home, as an asset in my business dealings, to maintain a particular appearance. Rose was in a terrible situation. She showed up at my door late one night, bruised, weeping"—the viscount smiled a little then—"and furious." The smile soon vanished. "Her brother-in-law, the detestable Baron Piers Rutherford, struck her, and then attempted to rape her. The bastard actually *bit* her."

"Dear God." Burke shifted a more assessing look toward Rose Sennett. She was a mere slip of a girl. Baron Rutherford was soft, but taller than she was and of considerable bulk. In a match of physicality, she wouldn't stand a chance.

"How did she manage to get away?"

"She escaped him after whacking him on the head with a pig."

Burke swung his attention back to the viscount. "A pig?"

Ashton nodded. A glint of pride accented his sly grin. "An amber pig her parents had given her. Quite a lovely piece, really."

"Handy, too, apparently." Burke realized he was also grinning. He didn't even know the young woman. There was no reason at all for him to feel pride in her mettle. He did, though. Maybe it was just the concept of the oppressed and improbable opponent emerging the victor giving him gratification. It was by far his favorite theme.

Without realizing it, Burke brushed his right thumb against the palm of his left hand. He could still feel the hard thud of his father's fist when at last he'd grown big enough and brave enough to catch the thrown punch before it landed. In his mind, Burke could still see the stunned expression on his father's face when he learned his son would no longer be the outlet for his anger.

"She still sleeps with the pig beside her bed," Ashton said. "It came through the ordeal undamaged. Baron Rutherford, however, had quite a gash in his head. It cost me a small fortune to gain his assurance of silence so as not to feed the gossipmongers and damage Rose's reputation, and to keep him from having her dragged off to Newgate."

"Her own brother-in-law would dare to have her arrested when *he* was the one who attacked *her*? Quite the protector she had there."

"The man is a lecherous scoundrel," Ashton replied, his distaste for Rutherford scrunching his face into a scowl.

"What about the baron's wife, Rose's sister?"

"Calling for the authorities was Edwina's idea. Her relationship with brandy is more affectionate than her relationship with her sister. Rose had no other family to protect her. Her parents died when she was twelve. She was alone and without funds. Anyway, her situation was intolerable. We spent hours talking, and by sunrise we'd come to an arrangement which has worked well for both of us."

"Marriages of convenience are hardly unusual," Burke said with a shrug. "You care for each other. Such a situation is more than many can claim."

"We do care for each other, very much so. But our relationship, well, it is but a friendship. A very close one, I'll say, but it will never be more, I can assure you. My interests…lie elsewhere."

The viscount then flicked a subtle glance to his left before casting hooded eyes down at his half-gone glass of brandy. He lifted his drink halfway to his lips, but set it back on the table without taking a sip.

Burke searched the direction the viscount had looked. A small gathering of men and women were involved in a discussion. Sennett could have been referring to any one of the three women in the group. Perhaps he'd fallen in love with another before he married Rose. If such were the case, though, why had he not married the woman? He was a man of means. It would not have been a strain for Sennett to help his friend.

"The fact is," Ashton continued. "Rose and I would no more share a bed than we would if we were born siblings. We are simply not attracted to each other as lovers. It would be…beyond awkward, for both of us."

"Are you telling me you two have never so much as consummated your marriage?" Burke asked, astonished at the very notion.

Ashton gave him a level look and said, "My wife remains a virgin. I find my carnal enjoyments elsewhere. Rose deserves the same. She deserves to know the pleasures of a woman. She is yet too innocent to understand what she is missing."

Sennett paused then, perhaps giving Burke time to absorb his words. It made no sense. Friendship or not, she was his wife. Burke spared another glance toward the gathering where Sennett's lover must be standing. Perhaps he was faithful to his mistress. The whole set of circumstances was beyond strange.

"By the bye," Ashton continued. "Rose knows nothing of this proposal I've put forth to you. If she knew, I fear she would be humiliated, and I will not have that. And," he said with another one of those self-deprecating smiles, "she would be past furious with me, I can tell you. She must never know about any of this, regardless of your decision. I'll have your word."

Burke gave his solemn agreement with a nod. As Sennett reiterated, Burke shifted his gaze to Lady Sennett.

"So, I will submit my request once again, Darington," said Lord Ashton Sennett. "Will you seduce my wife?"

****

Rose was still smiling when Lady Emory spun away in a swirl of pink and white taffeta to go and find her husband. Adele told her if she didn't get some food down his gullet to join the wine he'd already consumed, she would need at least two footmen to load him into their carriage. Rose shifted her attention to the soiree Ashton had been so astute in arranging.

The guests all appeared to be having a splendid time. The servants were at their best, their uniforms fresh and crisp, diligent in making sure there was plenty of food and drink, and every single one of their guests wanted for nothing.

Even Stefon, Ashton's curt butler, made an effort to be pleasant toward her. It was pure performance, but who was she to complain? Fortunately, Stefon was the only member of the household staff who was having trouble accepting her in residence, but he had many subtle ways of making her aware of his displeasure. Not tonight, though. The party Ashton had planned down to the last detail was perfect.

Rose cast her gaze about the elegant ballroom, thinking to pluck up her husband for a dance before the musicians took their respite. Her dear, sweet Ashton had expended much effort, seeing to it she was well versed in all the dances. He'd been more than generous at making up for the various lessons her family should have provided. They'd had a great many laughs at her early attempts to learn all the steps.

Ashton, bless his big heart, never once complained about the bruises she must have left on his poor toes. She'd learned all the moves, though, thanks to his endless patience and persistence. Now it was time to try out her new skills on the dance floor. The presentation would do well for the evening. After all, it was part of the reason they'd married.

With her first cursory search, Rose caught sight of Ashton sitting nearby. She took only brief note of her husband before her eyes met and locked onto the other man at the table, a man she'd never seen before. At this point, Rose believed she had met all of London's aristocracy. She was positive no one had ever introduced her to this man. He had not the appearance of a man a woman would forget.

He was broad shouldered, and tall, taller than any other man in the room, she guessed. Even seated, he had a strong, powerful look about him. Ashton appeared almost childlike across the small table from him.

Although the stranger wore a very dignified, crisp white lawn shirt and black tailcoat, his white cravat starched to perfection and tied with impeccable care, he still bore an underlying, untamed quality. He reminded Rose of a story her mother used to tell her when she was a little girl, a story of the wolf who came to supper.

His midnight hair was a bit longer than customary, the dark ends disappearing against his black coat. It added to the feral quality inferred by his size. Unlike most of the men in the room whose faces were pale, the sun had given this man's skin a tint of bronze. The coloring lent a harsh feature to his appearance. Or maybe it was the force of a characteristic showing through.

Between his strong jaw and straight nose was a mouth curved upward in a very slight grin, directed at her.

Rose didn't understand what could have possibly brought that on, but she had a sudden desire to slip from the room. It was the stranger's eyes, dark and intense, holding her in place as firmly as a solid grip. It took a tremendous effort to wrench her fascination away from the man and shift her gaze toward her husband.

Ashton was smiling at her, though she wondered at the mischief tinging his countenance. She'd seen that look before, like the night he proposed their marriage. Her husband's expression left her somewhere between laughter and wariness. She never knew what kind of outrageousness would spring from his mind.

The gown she wore, for example. It was elegant, beautiful, and well-fitted, flaring at her hips to show enough of her form, but not too much. The emerald flattered her hair, so said Ashton when he helped her choose the fabric. According to him, the cut was a fine compliment for her figure.

Their disagreement came with the fabric in the front of the gown, or rather, the lack of fabric. It was so low it was near to indecent. She fixed it, though, with a fine, Brussels lace fichu. Her placement of the fichu rankled Ashton, but he didn't make a fuss about it. By then he was worn out from the difference of opinion they'd had over the first gown he had made for her to wear this evening. Now *that* was indecent.

The silver gown, far too snug over her hips, with endless gossamer flounces around the skirt and a deep show of décolletage nothing short of scandalous, would never leave her armoire.

When Rose smiled back at her husband, she made sure she drew her brows together in the slightest and tipped her head just a bit to the side so he could see her unspoken question. *Who was this man, and why was he staring at her so?*

Ashton stood then and held out his hand.

As she approached the table, the other man rose. Standing, the stranger was even taller than she first thought. His shoulders were broader up close, too. His body had a clear, solid build, without any excess of flesh she could see. In combination with features one would be just in calling him ruggedly handsome. He was by far the most masculine man she had ever seen.

Rose dragged her gaze upward. His eyes were as green as her dress, but several shades darker. She could see flecks of gold sparkling in the depth of color. When he focused them on her own, with an intensity close to overwhelming, an odd quiver rolled through her stomach.

"Darling," Ashton said to Rose upon her arrival at the table. "I'd like you to meet Lord Darington, Earl of Blackwood. You've not met, but you have heard me speak of him."

"Yes, of course, Lord Darington," Rose said, greeting the man she thought she never would meet.

It was no secret Lord Darington's brilliance made him a great success in his business dealings. Rose also understood he was a bit of a recluse. It was considered a boon were he to appear at one's function. Other than those two things however, she knew near to nothing about the man. Even the most profuse of gossips had little to say about him.

"Lady Sennett," the earl said in a voice as rich and as smooth as Ashton's finest brandy. Lord Darington took up her offered hand in his and brushed a light kiss over her knuckles.

Her hand all but disappeared in the mass of his hold. Though the earl's touch was gentle, Rose found his sheer size, coupled with his mystique, left her a bit unsettled. She wished she'd brought a cup of punch with her, as her mouth was suddenly dry.

Rose gave herself a mental shake. She was being silly. Lord Darington was just a man, and Ashton had seen to it she was forever safe from all men. Rose folded her hands in front of her, noting how warm her fingers were where Lord Darington had touched her.

"Please, sit with us, love," Ashton said, scooting out one of the carved, high-backed chairs for her.

She hesitated for a bare moment before sitting. Once the men seated themselves, Rose said, "You have quite the reputation, Lord Darington."

In an instant, a grin curved his sculpted lips and he said, "Do I?"

"Oh, yes. Ashton has nothing but praise for you and your aptitudes."

The subtle glance the two men exchanged made Rose wonder. Then, from the corner of her eye, she was sure she saw Ashton respond to the earl with a small, confounded shrug. What a curious thing.

She continued to speak to Lord Darington. "My husband once told me your skills are the best."

The earl's smile broadened and he appeared to be amused, which made no sense at all. Nothing she said was the least bit humorous. Then, her husband was stuck with a sudden bout of coughing she could swear covered a laugh.

"Ashton, are you all right?" she asked.

Her husband cleared his throat and said, "Yes,

dear."

Rose returned her attention to Lord Darington. "My husband also said you have the sharpest business mind he's ever come across."

"Ah, business aptitudes," Ashton said, clearing his throat again over what sounded very much like a chuckle.

"And skills," Lord Darington added.

"Yes, yes that's true, love," Ashton said.

"He's very kind," Lord Darington replied.

She could swear the man repressed a smile. Ashton shared a similar expression. Before she could question her husband, Ashton said, "Lord Darington and I were just discussing the merits of an open mind."

"An open mind?"

"Yes, love. Wouldn't you agree it is an advantage for one's life experiences to be open to, well, life's experiences?"

Addressing Lord Darington, Rose said, "My husband is a bit of an adventurer. He's traveled to a great many places already."

"And you?" Lord Darington asked.

His smooth voice was coarsened with a trace of gravel. The velvet roughness brushed up her spine.

"I take my comforts in hearth and home," she said.

"Yes," Ashton said. "Rose is happy to spend her days working with the children at the foundling home, as well as reading and walking through the gardens. She has a great fondness for nature."

Lord Darington nodded. "I too enjoy the outdoors. There's nothing like fresh air to clear one's mind."

Rose smiled at him. "I quite agree. Too much time indoors suffocates the soul. Besides, every season has so much to offer. The colors of autumn are always breathtaking. I love a walk in the brisk winter air, and when the roses and the buttercups are in bloom and the trees begin to flower, well, I think nature is just wondrous."

"At least you're now remembering to carry your parasol," Ashton said. To Lord Darington he said, "She tends to freckle, so fair is her skin."

Blushing, Rose changed the subject. "Lord Darington, I hope you are enjoying yourself this evening."

"Your party will get rave reviews, I'm sure."

"Thanks to Rose," Ashton said.

"Oh, don't let my husband fool you. He can plan an event better than anyone in all of London."

"My wife flatters me. It is her influences that beget warmth and welcome." Facing Rose, he said, "You'll be happy to hear the earl has pledged a hefty donation to the Foundling Project."

"Oh, Lord Darington, how very kind of you," Rose said, clasping her hands before her. "The building in which the children now reside is dreadful beyond repair. They are so young and have so little. At the very least, they deserve a decent place to live. Your contribution will hasten the construction of the new building we have planned. Thank you."

"I'm happy to see my money put to good use."

"If you'll excuse me," Ashton said, coming to his feet. "I see Lewis waving at me. I'm afraid I've been putting off Lord Da Ville all evening and he's insisted he has some matter, brief, but of great importance to discuss with me. I'll be back shortly." With a final glance at Lord Darington, Ashton strode away.

Rose stared at her husband as he left and thought to box his ears later for abandoning her with a man she'd only just met. At the insistence of good graces, she gave her attention back to Lord Darington.

His clean-shaven chin rested on the back of his fingers of one hand as he leaned back in his chair, elbow on the armrest. Aside from being such a large man, she found his gaze disconcerting. He gave the impression there was more to the workings of his mind than polite conversation, as if he had many thoughts churning at once. Yet, his sharp attention penetrated it all to focus on her. It took some focus of her own to gather herself enough to speak.

"Thank you, Lord Darington," she repeated. "Your donation will do much good."

Brushing past her gratitude with the slightest of nods, Lord Darington asked, "Have you chosen a place to build?"

"There is a perfect plot of land on Vant," Rose told him. "It's vacant of any structures and overgrown. The owner seems to care naught for it, yet he is being rather stubborn about selling."

The earl lowered his hand to the glossy table and tapped a forefinger a couple of times. "Are you referring to the acreage near Wexler Street?"

"Yes, that's the one. It's far enough from the factories so the air is free of soot. And a good distance from any tavern. Their young eyes have already seen more than children should. Even with the building on the land, there would still be plenty of room for them to play outdoors. They have very little space where they are now. I so had my heart set on that parcel of land. The sad truth is, I'm beginning to lose hope he'll sell."

"That land is owned by Lord Cavendish, I believe."

"Yes. He told me it's been in his family for ages. He claims to be indecisive about letting it go. I've a strong feeling the stubbornness to which he is clinging isn't due to any sentimentality, but rather the prospect of squeezing every possible shilling from us. And it's such a worthy cause," Rose said.

A beat later, she continued in resignation. "I suppose I'll have to give in to my husband's offer and let him try to bargain with Lord Cavendish. I wanted to handle this matter myself. But the man seeks to take advantage of me because I am a woman, I just know it."

"Most women wouldn't have attempted to strike a business deal on their own to begin with."

Fire flashed within Rose, igniting the rise of her temper. Before it overrode her good manners, the earl spoke. He said the last thing she expected to hear, from him or any man.

"Why don't you try him again?"

Rose blinked. "I beg your pardon."

"Make your proposal once more. I just so happen to know Lord Cavendish is at present in need of funds."

"Is that so?" Rose said, her words churning out slow and distant as her contemplations prompted the development of more.

Lord Darington tipped his head. "But a man has his pride."

"Perhaps if I approach him again," Rose continued after a good stretch of thought. "But this time, play to his heartstrings in regards to the children instead of trying to bargain hard, as a man might. It would soothe his male pride; bolster it, even. Perhaps bestowing on him a feeling of benevolence may guide him toward accepting a woman's business proposal."

Lord Darington smiled at her. The expression touched the depths of his eyes, making the gold flecks glitter within the green. She couldn't help but smile back.

Rose leaned forward a bit, her fingertips resting on the table, her attention full on him now. "Lord Darington, you are a genius. Lord Cavendish will have bragging rights as to his kindness, and he'll have money, and we'll have our property."

"As much as I'd like to take credit, it was you, Lady Sennett, who figured out the answer. All you needed was a bit more information."

"Well, we make a fine team," Rose said with a small clap of her hands. Her excitement bubbled and her mouth ran off before she considered her words. "We could use someone like you on the committee for the Foundling Project."

As soon as the words were out, Rose wished she could yank them back. Her impetuousness was going to be the death of her.

She'd already flirted with scandal by going alone to meet with Lord Cavendish. But the property was so perfect, and both Ashton and Lewis had been busy elsewhere. Rumors were circulating about another offer near to proposal for the very parcel of land they wanted.

Thinking about it now, Lord Cavendish himself could have started those rumors to gain the advantage. She hadn't considered such a ploy at the time. Panic had set in and she'd gone to the home of Lord Cavendish uninvited and unescorted.

After that, she pledged to be more cautious so as not to damage Ashton's good name. And here she'd

Micki Miller

gone and thrust her cause in the face of a powerful, and notably reclusive, lord.

"I'm sorry, Lord Darington," Rose rushed to say. "That was far too brash of me. When it comes to the Foundling Project, my emotions sometimes run off with my manners. Please pardon my exuberance."

"Not at all. I find your enthusiasm inspiring."

She'd quite blatantly overstepped the boundaries of politeness, and he was kind enough to spare her feelings. It seemed Lord Darington was far more genteel than his appearance implied. However, the way he now gazed at her encroached on the borders of gentility. The intensity of his regard overwhelmed her. Unable to hold it, she let her eyes drift elsewhere.

****

Burke stared at the woman across the table, confident what he'd said to her was true, and not blithe flattery. So in depth were her feelings for those children, her passion overrode propriety. Not always a bad thing from his perspective. Different, no doubt dangerous if she carried it too far, but not a terrible quality.

The kind of enthusiasm he was accustomed to in women had always been confined to many a lady's bedchambers. Not that he was complaining. Seeing some pluck put to a worthy cause, however, was indeed refreshing, and somewhat disturbing.

Burke continued to study the viscount's wife.

Her eyes were as blue as the sapphire draperies hanging in his bedchamber. She had delicate features over a small but sturdy core, soft skin, soft heart, and was a resilient champion of the underprivileged. He held few people in great esteem. Lady Sennett had managed to win his admiration, and in rather swift time.

She swiveled away then, perhaps out of shyness now that she'd drawn attention to herself rather than her cause. Instead of introducing a new topic, as he could, and should so as to ease her embarrassment, Burke took the opportunity to view her other notable features.

Between the swirls of white lace stretching from her neckline to the top of her evening gown, teasing morsels of fair, luminous skin gave longing to his fingertips. Her breasts were not excessive, but high and plump and enough to fill even his large hands. He hoisted his gaze to Lady Sennett's face.

Her high cheekbones colored before his eyes. She was well aware of his gaze on her. She didn't excuse herself, though. Nor did he cease his visual perusal. It would have been the polite thing to do, yet Burke, quite literally born of impropriety, did not shift his attention away from her.

A tendril of her golden hair had come loose from the coronet of her braid and furled around her delicate ear. For a reason he couldn't begin to understand, the swooping curl had him transfixed. He liked the way its glossy tip caressed the long, sleek column of her neck. Then he wished she would brush it back, so he could see in motion the feminine hand he'd so briefly touched.

When he'd held her small hand in his, he liked the expressed pressure of her slender fingers, gentle, but existent, unlike the ladies who flaunt their surrender. He liked the way they'd curled into his when he touched his lips to the soft skin just above her knuckles. Such a subtle interchange, yet seductive in her innocence. And he liked the faint scent of rosewater he'd detected. It reminded him of his beloved gardens.

Her hands remained in her lap, though, and Burke's eyes lingered a moment more where the white lace ended and the creamy skin of her throat began. It took a force of will to drag his attention away. When he did, his eyes shifted only the short distance to view her profile.

There was a subtle upturn to her small nose. It paired well with the stubborn jut of her chin that even now dared him to continue his inspection, which was exactly what he did. The pink flush dusting her cheekbones intensified. Still, she did not cower. She was modest, but not weak. The combination was intoxicating.

Burke took in the fullness of her lips. They bore a hint of color reflecting her given name and made him wonder at their taste. He shifted, uncomfortable now in his seat as her beauty caused unfortunate and unwanted changes to his man's body.

Her husband's request crossed his mind. It was more than tempting, he mused, as he sat gazing at the lovely creature across the small table. With more than a bit of chagrin, Burke concluded Lady Rose Sennett was too damned alluring for her own good, not to mention his.

Lord Sennett returned to the table then, with a pleasant smile for both his wife and their guest. "Pardon my hasty exit," Ashton said. Then to Burke, "Sometimes a matter is in dire need of attention."

"No need for apologies," Burke said, ignoring the viscount's true meaning.

At the archway at the end of the hall, Burke caught sight of Lady Hortence, who was staring at him with direct intent. Her dark hair was piled high above her gaze and catlike grin. Once she had his attention, she rotated in a slow pull and exited the room, an extra wiggle in her hips.

Burke shifted his eyes back to Lord Sennett. "I found your wife's company quite charming."

Ashton's smile was both satisfied and relieved.

"I'm afraid I must be going now," Burke said as he stood. "Lady Sennett, it was a pleasure to meet you."

"I'll walk you out," Ashton said.

As they waited at the bottom of the stone steps of the Sennett townhouse for a footman to bring the carriage around, Lord Sennett said, "Well?"

"She is lovely. Your description was correct, lacking even, one could in all fairness say. Your wife possesses intellect, beauty, and a benevolent heart."

"All true."

"In regards to your request," Burke said, and then paused as his body and conscience engaged in a brief scuffle. *I will not foul her. She deserves better.* "I'm afraid I'm going to have to decline."

Lord Sennett's face showed a mix of surprise and disappointment. Burke offered no explanation.

At the sound of horse hooves clopping on cobblestone and the clanging approach of his black, lacquered carriage with his family crest of a lion on a shield on the side, Burke swung his attention away from his host. A footman liveried in black and gold opened the door. Burke bid farewell to Lord Sennett and climbed inside, settling himself against the red squabs.

In the dark solitude of the carriage ride home, where he already planned to collect his sorrel stallion and leave again, Lady Rose Sennett's sweet face played into Burke's mind.

Her entire being had been alight with joy over the good his money would do for the children at the foundling home. The sum he pledged was indeed generous. On the morrow when he directed Perkins, his man of affairs, he would double his pledge.

Settling the matter of his charitable donation in his head, however, did not settle his mind. Burke leaned his head back against the lush cushion and closed his eyes. The image of Rose at anyone's mercy clouted him with a sudden desire to ride over to Baron Piers Rutherford's home and pound her brother-in-law into the ground. Cavendish deserved the same.

Opening his eyes, Burke peered out of the carriage window. Still, all he could see was a delicate young Rose, bruised, alone, forced into a violent defense while she lived under Rutherford's tyranny.

As if by their own will, his hands tightened into fists with wishful anticipation. It had been quite some time since he'd had the urge to land a punch. It ate at him, now, though, and caused him to change his evening's schedule. He best forgo the long ride he'd planned and head to Pru's house straight away so he could deplete his energies, lest he get himself into trouble.

Chapter 3

Burke glanced at the candle on the bedside table, burned down to a fat, sloping stub. The size gave him a good estimate of the time. It wouldn't be more than an hour or so before the sun crept through the window to light Pru's over-frilled, over-laced, over-perfumed bedchamber. He would be gone by then.

Beside him, Lady Prudence Hortence lay as still as a knoll. Their night of sex had been robust. After which, Pru had fallen into such a solid sleep, she wouldn't even know he'd gone until the morning passed into afternoon. Nor would she be displeased to awaken to her valued privacy.

Pru preferred to face no one until after her maid fussed over her and had her primped and styled proper from head to toe. He rather enjoyed seeing a woman mussed, especially if he were the one who'd caused her to be in a state of such disarray.

This early, sleepless morning, however, he cared naught if he was there when she awoke. Not that he cared much any other time, either. Tonight, though, any inkling he had toward seeing Pru in the morning light fled the moment she fell asleep, as something was eating at him. What made it worse was he couldn't identify the blasted problem.

They'd both gotten what they'd wanted, and he should be equally exhausted. Pru, if nothing else, was an enthusiastic lover. On her skills between the sheets, he'd not fault her. Yet, although he'd had her several times throughout the night, Burke could not claim satisfaction. At the very least, he should be fatigued, but he wasn't. Slumber did not even whisper his name.

He considered waking Pru, of having her once more before going home to his own bed. Perhaps the problem was a matter of not exhausting his appetites in full. He found neither the idea nor the uncomplicated ease of it appealing.

Rising up on his elbows, Burke regarded the naked woman stretched out beside him atop a rumple of sheets.

Pru lay on her back, her voluptuous breasts only inches from his hand. She would welcome him again, he'd no doubt. Pru was insatiable. It occurred to him that her sexual prowess was one of the very few things he actually liked about her. Prudence was spoiled and selfish, and unless otherwise occupied, the endless, inane prattle flowing from her lips could drive a man to distraction.

But the reason he'd answered her bawdy offer by appearing on her doorstep had not been for conversation. In fact, until his discourse with the delightful Lady Sennett last eve, he couldn't say he'd ever before enjoyed a conversation with a woman.

In all fairness, Burke conceded, he never put much effort into one past the general social expectancies and the necessary matters of seduction. Frankly, it was an aspect of life he'd never considered exploring.

Prudence released a brief moan in her sleep and then flopped away from him to lie on her side. He took an appreciative glance at her bare arse before casting his gaze into the darkness.

Perhaps his mind was too inundated with distractions to sleep. Or rather, one particular distraction. Blast Lord Sennett and his ridiculous request. Yes, of course it was haunting his thoughts. How could it not?

The night had been an unusual one. He'd stayed at the Sennett's longer than he normally would have. It was a rare occasion for him to attend a social event in the first place. He had accepted the invitation based on the special entreaty for his presence Lord Sennett had himself written on the back.

As if out of his control, Burke's mind delved into the viscount's absurd request. Sennett's suggestion was, without a doubt, the cause of his restlessness. He should have realized it sooner.

Lady Rose Sennett, to be sure, was a fascinating woman. From her daring to strike a business deal on her own, to the flare of ire in her eyes when she had failed, and the determined tilt of her cute little chin when it came to helping the children. She could fight off her lecherous brother-in-law and host a party with equal success. Rose Sennett was the most dimensional woman he'd ever met.

She was also an innocent and deserved far better than a sordid affair with a tainted man.

Good god, how could Lord Ashton Sennett solicit him to seduce his own wife? If such a lovely creature were his, he would strangle any man who dared to even think of touching her.

And then Burke envisioned it, another man putting his hands on her, undressing her, taking her virginity. He wondered if Sennett had made a list. He then wondered who was next on the list. Would Sennett tolerate some muttonhead who would treat her as little more than a by-blow, which was essentially what he'd requested?

His jaw tightened for a moment before he could shove away the unwanted image. None of it was his concern, Burke reminded himself. He'd do well to keep his distance from the confounded complications of others. It's what he'd always done in the past, what always worked in his favor.

His entire life had taken place on the outer edges of Society, delving little into their private matters. Business mandated a certain degree of association, of course. He kept it at a minimum. In return, gossip, and all the ugliness that grows from it, had kept *him* at a distance.

The *ton* thrived on gossip, and it could be an invasive and vicious fiend. Unfair, too. If word of his involvement with a married woman hit the rumor mill, Burke would suffer little for it. His title, wealth, and gender provided a sufficient barrier. Lady Rose Sennett, however, would pay a hefty price. Had her husband not considered such?

Again, it was not Burke's concern. The last thing he sought was to insert himself in the private affairs of anyone else. His life's circumstances had left him with the secret of his own social weight to bear, and he'd done so quite well. No one knew the truth about him.

It was cruel in the oddest form. This world could so often forgive a man for his chosen actions, but not for his lineage, for which he had no choice at all.

The only reprimand his bed hopping had ever earned him was but a few sly, knowing grins from the aristocracy. However, if they knew of his mother's indiscretions, knew he was actually her get from other than her earl husband, Burke's lofty status would diminish.

He'd learned not to care. He'd long quit wondering who his real father was, what he was like, if the man even knew he had a son. As a child, these were but a few of the sharp, jabbing points of Burke's suffering. A mother who cared naught and a false father who resented what Burke's existence signified were the rest.

Long ago, Burke had erected his barriers to keep away the pain, and they remained strong.

Of the man who had raised him for no other reason than to salvage his pride, the earl who everyone believed was his father, the man was deep in his grave. No matter his wants, though, Burke could not ever forget his childhood.

He would never be able to evict from his mind the earl's scorn and disdain, his mother's blind indifference, and certainly not the beatings he received from the earl until he gained enough size and fortitude to fight back. But he could keep it all within a heavy casing, in the darkest corner of his mind. It was his shame to bear, and no one else would ever know.

His parents were both dead now; his mother succumbing to illness, his father to the bottle, both dying too late in life by their son's jaded estimation. Before they'd even passed from this world, Burke had decided he would never marry; never beget a child to be his heir and inherit the title. He was the last in the line. His chosen act of revenge was to let the earldom die with him.

Burke lay back down on Pru's bed, letting his head

sink into the soft pillow. He drew in a deep breath through his nose and closed his eyes.

The aftermath of sex still hung pungent in the air, mingling with Pru's strong perfume and her overuse of rice powder. Beneath the soiled layers of their night, however, Burke could almost swear he detected the untainted fragrance of rosewater. He inhaled through his nose again, but the enchanting scent was gone before he could latch onto it with any real success, if it had ever been there at all.

Prudence snorted in her sleep before releasing a contented sigh. Opening his eyes, Burke stared not at the nude woman beside him, but into the dimness where his mind could see a fighter, a survivor, a dealmaker, and an advocate for children, all encompassed in the form of a beautiful, innocent woman named Rose.

After a moment or two, he used quiet stealth to slip out of bed, even though the caution was unnecessary. Pru was out of this world and well ensconced in her dreams, but Burke had a sudden and strong aversion to waking her.

He dressed and quit the room with the silence of a shadow waiting to grow in the coming light.

Chapter 4

"Good morning, milady," Cora said upon entering Rose's bedchamber.

Rose had already tied back the long, floral chintz drapes from her windows on what promised to be a glorious day. Gold-soaked light illuminated every corner of the spacious cream-and-coral colored room with sunny warmth.

"Good morning, Cora."

Cora straightened her mobcap and shook out her brown linen skirt. "I swear I'll never get used to a lady rising so early. And making up your own bed, no less!"

Rose, wearing a white night rail and a matching, soft cotton wrapper tied at the waist, a silver-backed brush in hand, rotated on her padded stool at her dressing table. She smiled at her lady's maid.

The stout woman was about ten years her senior with full, rounded cheeks and a jovial disposition. Previous to Rose's arrival, Cora was in Ashton's employ as one of the housekeepers. She had been delighted with her new position as lady's maid to the mistress of the house, and put forth every effort to shine in her role.

She and Claude, the Sennett's cook, had been married for close to ten years. The couple had worked in the household for almost eight. Their loyalty and discretion in regards to the goings on of the home well secured their positions.

"I don't think I'll ever get used to having someone to help me dress," Rose told her maid. "And I've only been up and a short time. I thought I would sleep in today, but I awoke at my usual time and could not drift off again. Tonight, I'm certain sleep will come early for me. I stayed up quite late last night with our guests, and then playing cards with my husband and Lord Da Ville. Are they up yet?"

"The both of them are just heading down to the breakfast room," Cora said as she opened the wide, rosewood armoire and studied the selection. "What have you planned for this fine day?"

"I'm going down to the foundling home to visit with the children."

"Ah, how about the blue day dress, then?"

"The muslin? Yes, that will be fine."

Cora removed the dress and laid it across the foot of the bed, smoothing out the skirt with her broad hands as she spoke. "They're a fortunate brood, to have a champion like you, they are."

"I feel like I'm the fortunate one," Rose said, running the brush through her hair. "I so enjoy spending time with them."

The maid opened a drawer in the marble-topped dresser and removed stockings, garters, and a simple, white chemise. While laying out the items, Cora said, "You'll make a fine mother someday." She spun around then, sudden, sucking in a loud breath as if she could draw the words back with it.

Rose set the brush upon her dressing table, but didn't move to stand.

"I'm so sorry, milady, I didn't mean to upset you. I

just meant…I was only…"

"It's all right, Cora," she said, raising merciful eyes to her maid. "It was a kind thing for you to say."

Under conventional circumstances, it would of course be a normal thing to say. Although this living situation worked well for everyone involved, it was a far cry from typical.

Cora lived in this house and she was no fool. The woman kept a liberal mind and a closed mouth, respecting both the privacy of her employer as well as her own prudent reputation. Rose liked her very much and she would of course forgive a slip of natural thinking.

Cora helped Rose dress, and then brushed and tied her hair back in a quick, simple chignon. In no time at all she was ready to meet Ashton and Lewis for their morning meal.

"Milady?" Cora said as Rose opened her door to leave.

Rose half-twisted back toward her maid. The apples of Cora's cheeks were washed a fair beet color over her worry and she fussed with the folds of her skirt. "Yes, Cora?"

"Mayhap I'm out of turn here, but, well, you shouldn't despair. You're a young woman. You never know what might happen. The future is ever full of wonderful surprises. You could yet become a mother."

Rose rotated in full to face her lady's maid. The woman had shown her kindness from the start and Rose had already come to think of her as a friend.

"Thank you, Cora. The fact is, overall, I'm very happy with the way my life is now. I am more than fortunate to be here, and Ashton and Lewis, I mean,

Lord Da Ville, are angels. This marriage has granted me more safety and freedom than I could have ever hoped for. If not bearing a child is the one small sacrifice I have to make, then I will make it without regret."

Her statement to Cora was rather sugar coated. The sacrifice was more than a small one, but there was no way around it. She kept herself busy so she wouldn't think on the void of it too much. At least, she tried not to dwell on it. Every so often, though, an ache of longing twisted at her heart. Knowing she would never become a mother was indeed a sacrifice.

She'd considered speaking with Ashton about taking in a child from the foundling home. They had all nestled close to her heart. However, the realities of bringing children into this house, of raising them here in such an uncommon circumstance where they would spend their lives forced to keep secrets, dashed the suggestion before she even made it.

Besides, how could she ever pick a single child from the group to come and live with them, and leave the others hurt, wondering why they were not chosen? No, nothing about the idea would work other than to satisfy her own selfish wants.

Cora accepted her reasoning, though, and nodded until the ruffles of her mobcap bobbed around her face, where her knowing smile had faltered.

****

Rose's husband, Ashton, and Lord Lewis Da Ville, came to their feet when she entered the sunlit room. Lewis set down the delicate teacup he was holding as he stood.

Paint, the color of vibrant, yellow daffodils,

brightened the walls. Ashton told her he'd chosen the color because he wanted the room to look like morning even on the dreariest of days. His concept succeeded, too. No matter the weather, morning in here was always a bright affair.

The round breakfast table, covered with a stiff, white cloth, held one of Ashton's Meissen teapots in the center. The three place settings included tangerine napkins edged with matching lace, silverware bearing a perfect polish, and three plates covered with shiny silver domes. Steam rose from both the men's teacups.

"Good morning," Ashton and Lewis said at the same time. Even if the sunny color of the room didn't brighten the mood, the happy greeting she received each morning from these two men would.

The two of them were dressed similarly in fawn breeches and blue waistcoats. The cut of Ashton's ensemble differed but in the slightest and was two shades darker than Lewis's. Ashton held out her chair to see her seated before the men once again took to their seats.

"Good morning," Rose answered. "I hope you two haven't been sitting here hungry waiting for me to come down."

"Our dishes have just been placed on the table," Ashton said. "We were only going to wait a minute or two to see if you would to join us. We had a bet as to whether you might sleep in this day and miss breakfast, as we kept you up so late last night."

She giggled a bit. "And here I believed you were enjoying my company, as well as the challenge of my card playing skills. All the while the two of you were contriving yet another wager."

"Rose, dear," Lewis said, retrieving his teacup. "You know we adore your company. The bet was but a fortunate offshoot."

"And which of the two of you is the winner of this fortunate offshoot of a bet?"

With a bit of chagrin, Lewis scooped a coin from his pocket and slid it across the table to Ashton, who plucked it up and slipped it into his own pocket. The bet was lost and paid with the same good humor with which Rose was certain it had been made.

Ashton and Lewis bet on things all the time. Whether the rain would fall on a particular day. What member of Society would be the next to make the scandal sheets. Why, once they'd made a bet on how long it would take a snail to cross a paving stone. Luncheon had to be delayed by three quarters of an hour while they all waited for the snail to make its trek. If she was in the vicinity, they invited her to join in on the fun. The bet she made on the snail was her first win.

"My apologies, Lewis," Rose said.

"Ah, no need, love. I'll get it back. I believe the next rain we get shall leave us with a brilliant rainbow in the eastern sky."

Both Rose and Ashton chuckled. Ashton said, "I'll take you up on that bet. I believe I'll take the western sky for a rainbow's appearance. Rose, care to place a bet?"

"Hmm. I've a feeling the appearance of our next rainbow will be in the southern sky."

"Wonderful!" Ashton said. "We have a wager."

"I trust you gentlemen slept well?" Rose said while her husband poured tea into her cup.

"Oh, yes," Lewis answered.

Lewis was a petite man, just two or three inches taller than Rose, with golden eyes and thick, reddish hair always brushed low on the left side of his forehead to hide the crescent-shaped scar his father had given him.

Ashton set down the teapot and nodded to his butler, Stefon, just three, or maybe four years older than her husband's twenty-four years, tall and slender as he stood in stoic formation in the corner of the room. At Ashton's unspoken command, the butler glided to the table.

"Last night was a grand evening, wouldn't you all say?" Ashton said as Stefon lifted the silver dome from his plate. "Thank you, Stefon."

"Milord," the butler answered with a stiff nod.

Pomade flattened Stefon's dark, slick hair to his head. Comb lines placed each hair in perfect order. His thin lips, ever compressed, gave his narrow face a pinched appearance. Rose had never once seen the man smile.

Stefon took a step toward Lewis and removed the dome from Lord Da Ville's plate. He then walked past Rose and her domed plate without so much as a glance, and exited the room on quick steps.

"I'll speak with him again," Ashton said as he shot an angry glare toward the doorway. Lewis closed his mouth, which had dropped open at the butler's insolence, and sent a hard, favoring nod to Ashton.

As her husband lifted the silver dome from Rose's plate and set it aside, he said, "Or perhaps I should let this be Stefon's final mistake. His treatment of you, my wife, has grown to intolerable."

"I appreciate your concern, Ashton, and of course,

your defense of me," Rose said. "But I think your butler just needs a little more time to adjust to a woman residing as mistress of this house."

"His contemptuous behavior is not acceptable, Rose."

"Ashton is right," Lewis said. "Regardless of our unique situation, you are mistress here and should be treated, at the very least, with civil regard. Stefon should understand when he shows disrespect to you he is showing disrespect to the master of the house. Also, he ought to appreciate the value of your presence in this house."

"I don't want to be responsible for the man losing his position," Rose said.

"You're not," Ashton said. "He is."

"Allow me a bit more time to win him over, and let this be for now. Please, Ashton."

Her husband paused a moment before his face softened, just a bit. He tipped her a nod of acquiesce, reluctant, but given. "As you wish, my dear. Stefon had better adjust soon, though. I will not much longer tolerate him snubbing you so, no matter your kind wish."

"Thank you," Rose said. "Both of you." She wondered if her two gentlemen considered the trouble Stefon could make for them should he be dismissed from his position. After all, the man held their secret, and the gossip he could stir would be horrendous.

Perhaps Ashton and Lewis did indeed understand the troubling possibility, and it was the reason they conceded to her wish without more debate. They'd all put forth a great deal of effort to avoid such problems. She would have to double her efforts to win over

Stefon's respect.

As she and the men enjoyed their breakfasts of currant buns, berries, and hot tea, Rose steered the conversation to the weather, to the fresh bloom of crocuses, and a summary of the wonderful turn out for the soiree. Burying Stefon's rudeness took a bit of effort. Her two special friends were ever protective of her. However, by the time they were halfway through their meal, their good humor had returned.

Sunshine poured through the spotless, mullioned windows and warmed the room with more efficiency than the small fire in the grate. The day would be a glorious one, perfect for the children at the foundling home to be outside playing.

"Yes, Rose, everything played out quite as we'd planned last night," Ashton said. "And you, my love, were the perfect hostess."

"Thank you. But you're the one who arranged everything. All I did was follow your lead."

Lewis smiled broad enough to reveal the small chip on one of his lower teeth, another gift from his father. Like with Rose, his past was a different life, a grim life, a life before Ashton.

The revealing wash of sunshine made Lewis's light spray of freckles more pronounced upon his fair skin. Rose always thought they made him appear younger than his twenty-three years. His customary temperament gave the same impression. Most of the time, Lewis was a cheerful soul, kind, accepting, playful as a fun uncle. Most of the time.

On the rare occasions when he indulged in a third brandy, however, Lewis's past would creep over his mind's ramparts to haunt his mood. He would become sullen and quiet. It was as if Lewis was once again beaten down by this world's cruelty against his particular stripe.

Sometimes Rose wondered if Lewis possessed an inner fear, a threatening terror that would have him believe his past was a living thing, one with the strength, will, and the ability to reclaim him. She held the suspicion because on occasion, the same terror invaded her sleep. In her nightmare, Piers came for her, and no one had the power or desire to stop him.

Lewis's gloomy mood never survived the night, thank goodness. By morning, he had the darkness locked back into its proper place, history. They all thrived in this new life, and any threatening entity would have to fight very, very hard to take it away from them.

To Rose, Lewis said, "Yes, I think the reviews of last night will be stellar. Your addition to this household has made everything much easier. Ashton and I are ever thankful."

"I am the one who is thankful. I've never been happier," Rose said, though a small ache in her chest reminded her of the one imperfection in this life she now lived. To never have a child of her own to hold, to teach, to raise with love and understanding. The lacking could pick at her should she let it.

How could she complain, though? Ashton and Lewis were dears. The household staff, with the exception of Stefon, treated her like royalty. Outside the occasional nightmare, she didn't even dwell on her brother-in-law's attack. For that night, the last night he would ever touch her, Piers had chased her from a dismal life and into one where she no longer knew fear, cold, or despair. She would pay the price and not grieve over the cost.

"I'm going to the foundling home today," Rose told the men. She couldn't have a child of her own, but she could still be amongst children, still know a certain degree of fulfillment.

At Ashton's expression of concern, she said, "Don't worry. I'll take Big Bart as my driver. I'll be perfectly safe." Her husband was in the habit of accompanying her to the foundling home, either he or Lewis, as the structure stood in a part of town where danger thrived. As good fortune would have it, they both enjoyed the children, and the children adored both of them.

After a moment, Ashton said, "Actually, I'd like to go with you. My business will be finished early this day, and it is always great fun seeing the little tykes."

Rose brightened. "Oh, they'd love that, Ashton. The children so enjoy spending time with you. And, according to Hester, your lessons in proper etiquette are starting to show. The boys love playing gentlemen. Well, when they're not teasing the girls. Lewis, would you care to join us? You know the children love you, too."

"I have matters to attend to all day," Lewis said with a touch of regret as they were finishing their meal. "I'm afraid I won't return till supper."

"I should be home before one o'clock," Ashton told Rose, setting his napkin beside his plate and coming to his feet.

Fifteen minutes later, Rose bid the men farewell, receiving a kiss on her cheek from both of them. She pivoted on the gold-veined, white marble tile of the foyer and made her way down the corridor to Ashton's study.

Pale green paint on the walls contrasted well with the long, burgundy drapes. The rich fabric color carried over to the square cushions on the two chairs across from Ashton's varnished, teakwood desk and the round pillow on the dark green settee across the room.

He personally chose the décor here, as he had for all the rooms in the house. He'd surprised her, shortly after their hasty marriage for which he'd obtained a special license, forgoing the usual posting of banns. Lewis had taken her out for a long day of shopping. Upon their return, her chambers were decorated in full. He told her if she didn't care for his choices, she was free to make any changes she liked. Ashton's tastes were exquisite and she hadn't wanted to change a thing.

At the ordered desk, she opened a drawer and withdrew a piece of foolscap and a stick of graphite. She spent the rest of the morning in Ashton's study, drawing ideas for the new foundling home, both fortunate and confident her opinions would matter.

It wasn't until her stomach grumbled and she glanced over at the porcelain-faced clock on the mantel, did she realize how much time had passed. She tucked away her drawing with the notes and returned the graphite stick to its proper place. After washing the marks and dark dust from her hands, Rose made her way to the kitchen.

A big iron kettle sat upon the stovetop. Whatever was in it bubbled and steamed, filling the room with a warm, comforting aroma. At the long, wooden worktable, Cora's husband, Claude, chopped a row of three thin carrots with a long knife and swift efficiency.

His kitchen whites were clean, except for one green smudge on his apron. His dark curls were damp at his temples. Rose could not identify the tune he whistled, but it was a happy one and Claude bopped his head to the music he made.

Claude rotated toward the stove and stirred the pot, moving well for a man whose size bespoke his love of good food. While returning to his worktable, he spotted Rose standing in the doorway. His middle jiggled a little with his sudden stop.

A smile as broad as his girth split Claude's steamed-flushed face before he spoke. Deluded a degree or two by a full generation living in London, Claude's French accent added flavor to his speech without confusion.

"Good afternoon, my lady! Today I have potato pasties fresh from the oven. Where would you like to eat this afternoon?"

Rose smiled back at him and tipped her head, though at this point, his question and her shy response was more a game between the two of them than it was a formality. They both knew where she ate her mid-day meal when both Ashton and Lewis were away.

Claude, his dark hair curling from the steam, dragged a tall chair to the other side of his worktable. By the time Rose settled into her seat, he'd set a simple white porcelain plate out for her with three plump strawberries and a hot, flaking pasty.

"Thank you, Claude. It looks wonderful."

"These are especially good, if I do say so myself," the cook said with humble pride.

Piercing the delicate crust with her fork released an aromatic rush of Claude's talent with seasonings. After the first bite of soft, chunky potato, Rose was honest when she told the cook his accolade was an understatement.

She ate her meal and listened as Claude told her more stories about his childhood on a farm while he worked across from her. When he rotated back to the stove for a moment to stir his pot, she reached over and stole a carrot round. Claude caught her, scolded her in French, giving her a mock scowl, and making her laugh before placing two more slices of carrot on her plate.

After she finished the last delicious bite, Rose thanked Claude and once again praised his culinary skills. She then left to pace the oriental carpet in the front parlor while waiting for Ashton to return. It was already half past one, and they were losing precious time.

The cozy room, decorated in peach and pale blues with a white marble fireplace at one end, usually had a calming effect. Today, past the time morning had relinquished the day to afternoon, Rose's impatience to get going only grew.

When the sun seemed hurried, as if it wanted to finish the day before something marred its perfection, Rose stopped her pacing. She knelt on the powder blue settee and peered out the clean glass of the front window.

A curricle drawn by two horses rolled past the house. The driver had drawn back the hood, taking advantage of the day's sunshine. A man and woman, both in dove-gray day clothes, strolled by arm in arm. There was no sign of Ashton.

Something had detained her husband and there was every chance he might not be back in time to make any good use of this glorious day. Or what yet remained of it. She could not let that happen. If he arrived home early enough, he could ride to the foundling home in another carriage and meet her there. She would not waste any more of this afternoon waiting. Rose marched through the house, out the back door, and straight toward the stables.

Following the slate walkway, breathing in spring's fresh air, Rose cursed herself for waiting so long to take the day in hand. Her steps were brisk, but not so much that she couldn't soak in the splendor of her surroundings.

Glimmering, golden rays poured from the sky and wrapped around her like a hearth-warmed blanket. Birds chirped and twittered from high atop flowering trees. The scent of lilacs Ashton had planted all around the house floated on a subtle, balmy breeze. Yellow and white crocuses all but glowed along the curving walk, drinking in the gilded warmth like an elixir.

The air cooled the instant she entered the shadows of the stables, and sweetened with the smell of freshly turned hay and the animal musk of the horses.

"Bart?" she called out. "Is anybody here?"

Strolling past the stalls, her favorite horse, Winnie, nickered and nodded her big head. The darling mare, a deep chestnut color with white socks, and a streak of white on her nose, was a wedding gift from Ashton. After everything he'd already done for her, installing her with a proper chaperone until they were wed, and then giving her a wonderful home and a wonderful life, seeing to her every need. The man was a gift from heaven.

"Of course, I remembered to bring you a treat,"

Rose said as she stopped to pet Winnie's velvety nose. From the pocket of her skirt, she scooped out an apple she'd taken from the kitchen on her way out, and held it in her flat palm for her horse. Winnie chomped the apple down in but a few bites.

"'Ello, milady." Rose recognized the voice of Horace, the skinny young stable lad with a thick mop of coffee colored hair and an ever-present smile. The hand was nineteen-years-old, but his baby face and thin body made him look much younger.

"Hello, Horace. How are you today?"

"Fine, milady, thank ye for asking. 'Ow couldn't I be on such a lovely day?"

"Indeed."

"Are ye and the misters' takin' a ride this afternoon? Tis a fine day for a trot through Hyde Park. Or mayhap ye'd prefer to take an open carriage."

"I'll be taking a carriage today, but not with either Lord Sennett or Lord Da Ville. Is Big Bart around?"

"'E just left. 'Ad to go see the smithy about some ironwork, won't bore ye with the de'ails. We was up 'alf the night tryin' to fix the problem ourselves. Finally gave up." Horace puffed out his narrow chest with pride as if he wore fine livery instead of his down-at-the-heels stable clothes. He lifted his chin and said with a nod, "I'm in charge while Bart's away. I can 'elp ye with anythin' needs doin'."

Rose considered it for a moment. She'd told Ashton if she were to go without him, she would take Big Bart with her, as she normally did. Ashton worried for her safety. Of course, the rascal should have been back by now and if she waited much longer, the beautiful day would be nothing more than a memory.

"I was going to have Bart drive me down to the foundling home," she said, looking around the stables as if she missed Big Bart on her first pass.

"'E won't be back for at least a couple of hou's. I can drive ye," he said, muffling a yawn.

Horace didn't weigh much more than she did. No matter the want, his good intentions would not satisfy Ashton's concerns for her protection. Rose flicked a quick glance behind her. In just the few minutes since she walked out of the house, it appeared as if the sun had taken on weight and was sliding down the sky.

After but a moment's consideration, Rose said, "Yes, Horace, that would be wonderful. Thank you."

Horace jumped to, readying the Berline carriage for her. While he did, Rose dashed back into the house to retrieve her reticule, her small, straw bonnet, and a light wrap, should the air grow chill later. When she returned, Horace had the closed carriage ready to go and he helped her in with gallant grandeur. Moments later, they were off.

Rose stared out the window at the scenery, then at its change.

They passed elegant homes fronted with maintained lawns and flowerbeds tended with meticulous attention. Cared for in kind, was the park. The paths full of riders, while other paths hosted walkers in their neat day clothes, governesses watching from iron benches as children laughed and frolicked about. Many Barouche and Calash carriages with their open or partial tops covered their distance at a slow roll, allowing the well-attired occupants to see and be seen.

Her regret at taking a closed carriage came and went without pause. She was already traveling alone, and her familiarity with the territory ahead forbade such recklessness. Even young Horace knew enough to pack her within and not leave her exposed.

In a little while, when they would leave this scenery of maintenance and decorum, an open carriage would do naught but invite trouble for her and her skinny young driver. For now, she satisfied herself by lowering the window and breathing in deep the fresh air.

When she got to the small, high-walled yard at the foundling home, she could be outside with the children then. The air wouldn't be so fresh there. But with the way things were moving along with the growing funds for the Foundling Home Project, she had every confidence the children would be moving to a better home.

Nearing the edge of the park, they rode beneath a long row of Oriental Planes lining the street on both sides. Their bushy leaves tall overhead created an intricate patchwork of shade through which they passed.

Eventually, they rolled by London's most elegant shops. The street bustled with gentry, aromas, and a cacophony of sound. Horses, people, drivers, and all manner of carriages maneuvered their way through the busy streets.

Men and women in their tailored garments strolled along the walk while footmen helped ladies with their packages. Voices rose up over the braying of horses and the clomping of their hooves, carriage wheels over cobblestones, the jingle and clank of riggings, and the shouting barks of coachmen.

A well-dressed man stepped from the sidewalk,

and then shouted as a horse and rider nearly trampled him. The horse reared. For a moment, Rose feared the rider would take a hard fall to the street where he might be trampled himself. The man held tight, though, and was efficient at calming his horse.

The other man, the one who had to jump out of the way, waved his fist while swearing a string of solid oaths at the rider before crossing the street, much more careful of his route.

Rose caught a whiff of sweet treats and baking bread, and scooted across the tufted seat to lower the other window. Yes, there it is. They were passing a bakery. Aromas of every kind of pastry and bread wafted through the carriage. Right then, Rose would argue with anyone that it was indeed possible to smell warmth.

Beside the bakery sat a blue-painted, brick front of a clockmaker's shop. A man walked out holding bucket-sized packages in both hands. He wore fine clothes and a pleased expression. The next business over was a bookseller with a large front window displaying his latest arrivals posed upright on cloth-covered blocks.

After a while, a notable lessening of formality reformed the scenery outside the carriage windows.

Goods sold in shops became goods sold by street merchants. A thin man with a bushy, black mustache stood at his apple barrow. A grizzled old man wearing rough-spun garments and a very august bicorn hat leaned against his one-horse cart, from which he sold brooms and woven blankets in a variety of colors. From other carts, handbarrows, and makeshift tables fashioned of boards and barrels, sellers offered everything from shoelaces to second-hand clothes.

The carriage made a turn just past a berry vendor. In less than a block, the number of merchants trickled down to none.

The landscape slid into quick degeneration. Buildings sat in forlorn abandonment, awnings sloped over broken windows behind which lay a thick darkness even the bright day couldn't light. Farther down, the odor of open sewers, desperation, and sour rot permeated the air.

Rose closed both windows. She was almost there.

Horace stopped the carriage in front of the tall, crumbling stone walls of the foundling home. Beyond the ancient barrier with the old, iron gate in the center, lay a treeless, dirt courtyard too small to accommodate the needs of the two dozen or so children who called the place home.

The building itself, formed of the same stone as the wall, was soot-stained from the nearby breweries and textile factories whose smoky output left the skies above the foundling home ever gloomy. Untainted sunlight rarely made an appearance here, though enough got through today to add a small glimmer of cheer.

Each new patch of mortar holding the structure together had faded to different degrees in accordance with its age. To look at it now, the face of the downtrodden home appeared fatally stricken with pox.

Through the iron bars of the gate in the center of the wall, Rose caught glimpses of about ten of the children who lived there playing out in the courtyard. Some were orphans, others abandoned at the gate as if they were nothing more than yesterday's trash. They were too old for the foundling hospital, who seldom took children over twelve months old. Without this poor old building, and the women who worked here, they'd have no hope whatsoever.

Their good fortune came by way of the women who resided here with the children. They were kind and caring, doing the best they could to make a home for all of them from the decrepit old building. A small handful of charitable organizations were its lifeblood. The Foundling Project, started by Ashton almost a year ago, set out to build them a more suitable home.

Before a yawning Horace even had the front gate to the home opened all the way, the children were upon her like hummingbirds to nectar. The smiles and hugs, and shouts of joy surrounded Rose in a crush of love she savored. She took in all they wanted to give and returned it tenfold.

"Miss Rose, Miss Rose," little Brennan shouted when the initial excitement settled a bit.

Marion, all of four years old with yellow hair and a smile to charm anyone who saw it into instant love, threw her arms around Rose's neck as soon as she knelt. The little girl hugged her with a laugh and a happy, disjointed story that made no sense at all.

"Miss Rose, Miss Rose," Brennan repeated.

Finally, Rose gave sole attention to Brennan, seven years old, dark hair a bit shaggy, all smiles in his drab clothing which fit a little too big. His small arms were crossed in front of him. No, not crossed, but nestling something. Already kneeling on the ground, Rose leaned toward the boy. Held in a secure grasp against his body, Brennan cuddled a puppy.

"Well, who is this?" Rose asked the boy.

"His name in Raisin, cause he's all black, 'cept for the patch a brown between his ears."

"The little guy just wandered in here one day through the front gate." This from Ellen, the boisterous twelve-year-old who fancied herself as a bit of a mother figure. "We're not supposed to have pets here, but Miss Abigail says we can keep him long as he don't make no trouble."

"Doesn't make any trouble," Rose said. Ellen had asked her for some polish for her grammar. The girl was a quick study and retained corrections with minimal repeating.

"Doesn't make any trouble. Thank you," Ellen said. She then repeated the sentence several times, committing the words to memory.

"I sang to him," Brennan said. "And he came right to me." The boy held the puppy out for Rose to take, brows raising high over his soft, brown eyes. "You can hold him if you wanna. He's real friendly."

Rose took the squirming ball of black fluff. As she held him, several little hands reached over to pet the pup. He was clean and plump; signs the little guy endured extreme care ever since he had the good sense to wander onto the grounds. By the soft feel of the pads of his little paws, Rose wondered if the pup's feet ever even touched the ground.

"Well," Rose said. "I do believe Raisin is the cutest puppy I've ever seen in my whole life."

The children all smiled their joy at her approval of their new friend. Word must have spread she was there, for a sudden stream of children poured from the open door of the home in a flood of cheers and smiles, a sharp contrast to their plain clothing.

For the next couple of hours Rose played games and sang songs with the children. Later, she made some private time for a couple of the older girls who had questions and comments about their developing bodies.

Hester, a motherly woman with a big heart squeezed into her reed-thin body, came out to chat a while. Rose filled her in on the funding progress and told her of the new hope for procuring the land. Hester offered a few wonderful ideas of her own for the new building and Rose promised to incorporate them into the plans.

Too soon, the day wound down. One of the women would be calling the children in for their supper soon, and if she didn't get herself home by the time Stefon served their evening meal, Ashton would be in a tizzy with worry. As she made her round of goodbye hugs, Brennan burst through the crowd, tears streaming down his frantic little face.

"Brennan, love, what's wrong?"

"He's gone. Raisin's gone! Someone left the front gate open and he got out."

"Are you sure he got out?" Rose asked. "Maybe he went inside."

"No. I was up by the door when I seen him run out. I ran to the gate, but I didn't get there in time to grab him, and we ain't allowed to go outside the gate. I seen him run that way," Brennan said, pointing a small finger to the left.

Rose spun around toward the gate. It was indeed open about a foot. She was always careful to close it when she entered so none of the little ones would wander out. But the love of the children had swallowed her before she even stepped all the way through. Had she forgotten to close the gate behind her? Yes, it must have been her, as she was the last one to use it. The puppy was gone, and it was her fault.

"Don't worry, Brennan," she told him with a fierce hug. "I'll go find Raisin."

The little boy sniffled. "Miss Margaret says it's dangerous out there."

"I'll be careful. Don't worry. I'll bring him back," she promised, hoping it was a promise she could keep.

Rose closed the gate behind her, noticing how the children had tied cross rows of string on the bottom to keep Raisin from getting out. Even at their young ages, they understood there were perils outside the walls of this home. Another wave of guilt washed over her.

She went right and walked the few steps to the front of the carriage. Horace lay on the seat curled on his side, his head pillowed atop his skinny arm, fast asleep. Well, if she didn't find the pup in a few minutes, she'd wake him up and get him to help her.

Crouching down, she looked for Raisin beneath the carriage. Even though Brennan had seen him run to the left, she hoped he'd come back and was hiding. But the pup wasn't there.

She peered down the gloomy street, empty of traffic both ways. After calling his name a few times and getting no response, Rose directed herself left and took several steps, calling for him as she went. At the gate were dozens of worried eyes, some trying to hold back their tears, others, like Brennan, gave up the fight and let them flow. She *had* to find that puppy.

Half a block past the high wall of the foundling home, a narrow alleyway separating two abandoned buildings tunneled off to the left. It was quite a bit dimmer than the street. Between the tall buildings and the sooty, late day air, light struggled to give her a clear view of what lay down there.

Varying sized piles of rubbish littered the ground like random tombstones. The odor of rotting garbage and sewage assaulted her sense of smell. Rose used her hand to cover her nose and mouth, but it did little against the foul stench of destitution slithering from the alleyway.

"Raisin," she called.

The grimy brick walls on either side caught the sound of her voice, and kept it, stubbing it out before it had a chance to resonate. Rose stood still and waited some more. She called again. Nothing down the alley stirred.

A glance back toward the home showed her a row of little faces three and four deep, squeezed as far as they could through the bars of the gate. She shifted her gaze over then, to where the sun burned low on the horizon. Not too many more minutes of the day remained, and only meager traces of light made it into the dingy alley. There was no hope for it, though. She couldn't go back without that puppy.

Rose took a few steps into the dimming maw of the alley.

"Raisin," she called, and then crept further in before calling out the pup's name again.

She skirted several piles of debris, much of it unidentifiable. A battered old shoe and the filthy sleeve of a man's blouse, both gleaming wet with something. She didn't even want to think about what it might be. To her right lay a damp clump that may have been food at one time. Flies buzzed about the thing, loud in the compressed silence of the alley.

Her foot skidded on something slippery, but she caught her balance and stepped away, not giving too close a look at what it was. She walked in a bit farther, taking a furtive glance up.

The tall brick walls on either side of her became towers melding and capped with the descending night, as if to imprison her in this festering pit. Refusing to give it more than a peek, more than a fleeting thought lest she run back an empty-handed coward, Rose leveled her herself. Onward, forward.

The alleyway ended at a brick wall, high piles of junk and reeking refuse stacked against it. There were plenty of places for a puppy to hide in the mess.

"Raisin, if you're in there, you come out this instant."

She stood still after the command, but the wait was fruitless. Not so much as a tiny sound came from the pile. Perhaps he wasn't even down here. The little thing could have passed by the alley or gone in the other direction.

"Raisin," she said, one last time before she would search elsewhere. This time she heard a noise.

It came from behind her.

Rose spun around to see the shadowy shape of a man at the end of the alley, blocking her exit. He carried little girth, but he was tall, maybe six feet, with broad hands flexing at his sides.

In the gathering darkness, the way the man hunched, conjured thoughts of ogres and monsters, a shadowed fiend. With an awkward lumber, the man started straight toward her. After a few steps, he stopped, twisted just enough to look back over his shoulder, and then turned himself toward her again.

An icy chill crawled up Rose's spine and tightened her scalp. Without thinking, her hands grasped for her cloak before she remembered she left it in the carriage, along with her reticule. She rubbed her arms with her hands as the man took two more steps in her direction.

"Hello," Rose said in a trembling voice. "I...I'm looking for a puppy. Have you seen him?"

A few more steps and the man paused. He was only about ten feet away from her now. His hair hung to his shoulders, stingy, matted against his head. Wiry whiskers poked out from his dirt-encrusted face. His fingers tapped a light tempo on the torn fabric of his trousers as his watery eyes focused on her.

"Well...if you haven't seen him," she said, drawing hard to suck air into her lungs as her chest had tightened. "I'll...I'll have to look elsewhere."

Keeping her head down, Rose sidled close to the wall on her left where she could pass him. He leapt over so he was in front of her. She stepped right. He did the same, blocking her way once again.

Only about two feet separated them now. Rose resisted the urge to cover her nose again. The man stank of the alley, of body odor his filthy clothing could not contain, of life rotting away.

"Please, I only want to find my puppy."

Rose tilted her face up. His heavy eyes enlivened right before her, glistening with the pungent fervor of malice in the bony framework of his face.

For a moment, he held himself still as death. That was exactly who he appeared to be. With frightening ease, she could imagine this the skeletal entity exposed, relieved of his cloak and scythe, revealing his true image to the condemned before the moment of death.

Beyond the alley, more so within, the night's hunger swooped in, taking greedy laps of the last residues of light.

With nothing but panic to guide her, Rose lunged left in a desperate attempt to run around him. She barely took a step when he snatched her arm in a vicious grip and jerked her back. She screamed as he grabbed hold of her other arm and shoved her hard against the rough brick wall.

She fought against him, kicking at his legs, using all the strength she could muster in a vain attempt to escape his hold. None of her efforts fazed him in the least. He leaned in, his face approaching hers as if to kiss her.

Rose twisted her head until her cheek squashed against the rough wall and her straw bonnet bent around her head. She squeezed her eyes shut. It was Piers all over again. No, she wouldn't let this happen! But the man was so much stronger than she was.

"No!" she screamed. "No!" Her words, her strength, her anger and fear, did nothing to help her. She continued to fight, though, kicking and twisting. It was all she had.

And then, in the space between beats of her pounding heart, the man was gone.

A solid thud resounded within the walls of the alley, fist to flesh. Her widened eyes focused just as the shadowy man hit the ground, where he lay as still as the torn shirt sleeve near which he landed.

Rose shifted her attention to the second man. Even in the weak traces of remaining light, she recognized the breadth of his strong shoulders, the fine shape of his nose, the strong cut of his jaw. Although she couldn't clearly see the eyes staring down at her, she knew they were a deep, sea green.

"Lord Darington."

"Are you all right? Did he hurt you?"

His deep voice cut through the night with the swiftness of a warrior's sword, and though his words were kind, they didn't sound that way at all. In fact, he sounded downright angry.

"Yes. I mean no. I mean..." She straightened her bent bonnet as best she could before saying, "I'm...I'm fine." It was hardly the truth. While she suffered no more than a few bruises, her heart pounded a wild tempo against her ribs and her body shook to rattle her bones.

Lord Darington seized her then, his hands like steel bands around her upper arms. His grip was firm, angry, but not painful, though it no doubt could be should he choose to make it so. It was quite obvious he was holding back. The man could snap her like a winter twig if he so desired.

"Have you no sense at all?" He spat the words. His jaw scarce moved when he spoke. "Do you have any idea what could have happened to you out here?"

Rose had to tip her head back to take in his full countenance. She almost wished she hadn't. But for a slight tick, his face could have been made of stone, inset with glaring eyes as dark and turbulent as a tempestuous storm. Intensity radiated from his powerful physique in waves she could swear were tangible. Lord Darington wasn't just angry. The man was furious.

"I...I have protection. Oh, that's right," Rose said,

with a shake of her head. "I left my reticule in the carriage."

"So?" he asked, letting go of her and stepping back. He shoved both hands through his hair before jamming them on his hips and pinning her with a questioning glare.

"Ashton gave me a pistol for protection not long after we were married. He taught me how to use it. I left my bag on the carriage seat."

"Good," Lord Darington growled. "You likely would have been killed with your own weapon."

She considered arguing his point, but after a brief glance at the still lump of a man on the ground, she had to concede Lord Darington was in all likelihood right. Pride, however, would not allow her to admit it. So, in an effort to salvage her self-respect, as well as giving her a moment to gather her wits, Rose changed the subject.

Clasping her hands in a tight hold before her so Lord Darington wouldn't see she was shaking, Rose said, "What on earth are you doing here?"

She could make out his profile in the folding dusk. The man didn't answer right away, and she'd lay coin it was because his jaw was too tight to speak. Even in the dim light, the tick was evident.

After he took a full breath or two, his head swiveled in her direction, and then he turned full toward her. The man cut an intimidating figure, whether or not such was his intent. Shoulders as broad as a building, tall, commanding, and after seeing what he did to the scoundrel who'd accosted her, Rose had no doubt of his ability, as well as his willingness, to set his muscles to use.

"After our talk last night, I wanted to see the place for myself," he said. His acceptance of the change of topic was a slow grind. He did, though, and she was grateful. She pitied anyone who dared to drive this man's temper to the limit.

"You were right," he continued. "They need a new building. The one they're in isn't fit for anything but demolition."

He glanced around. On the lookout for more danger, perhaps. Danger beware. "Come on," he said. "Let's get out of here."

Lord Darington snatched up her hand and tugged her toward the exit of the alley. Before taking a step, however, he swung back around to her.

"Your hands are freezing," he said, taking both of her hands and encasing them within the warmth of his, giving them a rub and a squeeze. "And you're trembling."

The revelation softened the flinty edge of his anger. Relief allowed Rose to take deeper breaths. For a reason her mind at present found unfathomable, she didn't like him being angry at her. Perhaps it was the fright she'd just suffered. It must have left her with a need for calm and her thoughts too shuffled to comprehend any further.

Posthaste, Lord Darington peeled off his jacket and draped it over her shoulders. Rose hadn't realized how cold she was until the heat from his jacket made her chilled skin prickle. He wrapped one strong arm around her shoulders and said in a gentled tone, "Let's get you home."

"I can't go back," she said, stepping from his protective embrace with a startling degree of reluctance.

"I have to find Raisin."

"Raisin? I take it that's the puppy the children were crying about."

"Yes. He's just a little thing, and he's out here all alone. I can't go back without him. I promised the children."

His head rotated in a swift yet thorough inspection of the alley before he placed a thumb and forefinger to his lips and released a shrill whistle. Within seconds, Raisin trotted out from the pile of refuse against the wall.

"Raisin!" Rose cried as she scooped the puppy into her arms and held him close. "Oh, the children are going to be so happy to see you. Don't you ever frighten us like that again, you naughty little pup."

She wasn't sure, but Rose could swear she heard Lord Darington grunt.

Together they left the alley, giving a wide berth to the man on the ground who was making moaning sounds as he climbed back into consciousness, and walked back to the home. At the gate, the children erupted into cheers and gratitude at the sight of Raisin in her arms. She and Lord Darington entered the yard. Rose knelt on the ground so the children could see for themselves that Raisin was all right.

When the shower of gratitude slowed to a trickle and everyone could hear her, Rose said, "Actually, it's Lord Darington you must thank." Rose nodded to the man standing off to the side all by himself. "He's the one who rescued your pup." *And rescued me.*

As one, the crowd of children swung around. Rose willed the man to smile, but Lord Darington remained as stony as the wall before which he stood, aloof, formidable, a mountain too big to climb.

****

Burke stood as still as an oak tree on a breezeless day, transfixed at the sight of Lady Rose Sennett.

She knelt on the ground, not caring a wit she was without doubt sullying her gown. He knew women who would sooner use peasants for steppingstones than risk soiling one of their gowns. The woman before him appeared not to care for anything apart from the joy on those small, adoring faces crowded around her.

Under his usual circumstances, he would not have been here to witness or wonder at such a thing. And the fiend who'd had her at his mercy would have…no, it was too horrid to think about. Burke thanked every bit of fortune come his way this evening that he'd gone against normality and had arrived in time.

The last fifteen minutes echoed in his head like a sentient haunting. Her terrified screams, a man twice her size throwing her against the wall with intent despicable beyond her chaste understanding. Icy talons clawed at his gut at the knowledge of how very different this day would have turned out if not for mere chance and miraculous timing.

His intent had been to send a bank draught for the cause. While all of his worthy instincts told him the Sennett's had not exaggerated the need for a new foundling home, he'd never been a man to send money without verification of how and where it was to be used. Under most circumstances, he would first have his man of affairs investigate, and then, if all was in order, see to the details of his donation. He hadn't even considered assigning the task.

He should become more involved with worthy

causes. Maybe even take a personal hand and volunteer some of his time. Just because he wasn't passing on the earldom to an heir, didn't mean the title had to die a cold death.

These are the justifications Burke put to himself, and once considered, found viable respectability. Up until this very moment, however, he was deliberate in remaining obtuse to the true draw that brought him here. It was far too foreign. The state of those particular emotions lay beyond the boundaries of his accepted existence. But that didn't make it any less accurate.

He'd traveled to the foundling home in hopes of seeing Lady Sennett.

He wanted to speak with her, though in truth they had nothing further to discuss. He would make his donation. The Sennett's would see the money put to good use. And that would be the end of his involvement, as with the charitable contributions he'd made in the past.

Never had he personally occupied himself with a cause. Of course, his previous donations had never passed through such an alluring woman, a woman whose husband had requested from him a seduction.

It was simple curiosity, Burke told himself. Lady Rose Sennett fascinated him, beautiful, to be sure, charming, too, in her dedication, in her courage, her fortitude, her purity of body and heart. She had conquered a situation in which most women, in his experiences, would do naught but succumb. And when her circumstances vastly improved, when she could have become a lady of leisure, she instead dedicated herself to a worthy and vital cause.

Members of the aristocracy often volunteered their

efforts, on a level not quite superficial enough to forbid grand posturing. They supported almost any cause with enough feasibility to provide a humble excuse for their merrymaking. A charitable ball, a costumed affair, and even the most proper of ladies might attend something as barbarous as a boxing tournament, if the proceeds were for a good cause. It was their version of a sacrifice.

But would any of them dip their pampered hands into actual involvement? No, of course not, it was unheard of.

The only exception he ever witnessed knelt on the ground not ten feet from where he stood, pawed by little hands. If anything, she became more joyful with every touch. And the children, the children in their simple clothes and lackluster lives could be the offspring of the aristocracy, in line to inherit fortune and privilege, for all the contented bliss they expressed in her presence.

For a moment, fleeting, but as sharp as a rapier and maybe as scarring, an ache stabbed at his chest and regret climbed in the wound. Never for one instant had he any second thoughts about his decision to not produce an heir. It was his sworn vengeance against his father, long ago chiseled in granite with every blow of his father's hands.

Seeing Lady Sennett laughing, the children giggling along with her, Burke suffered a vision of his lands, enriched with his own joyous offspring. He saw it. He actually saw it. Fair-haired girls full of their mother's heart. Their brothers, taught to be men through guidance and proper example instead of fear.

A sensation so foreign, yet at the same time deeply

innate, brushed against his heart with the loving touch of a harbinger angel. It left behind a tender void, weeping for the loss.

Burke blinked in the sudden quiet. Every face in the small yard tilted up to his. Had someone asked him a question? Their eyes were focused on him like an audience at the pinnacle of an opera. A little mop-haired boy, about six or seven years old, holding the puppy, took a few tentative steps toward him.

"My name is Brennan. Thank you, sir, for saving Raisin. I love him," the boy said, rubbing his cheek against the puppy's fur.

Burke stared down at the child. Since he'd grown into manhood, he'd not actually been this near to one. The boy was so small, so fragile, and as open as he was innocent. Burke resisted the impulse to lift the child, to speak with him, to tease him, as Lady Sennett had a moment before so he could see the little boy laugh. Would such a thing be allowed? He didn't know.

Burke cleared his throat. He did not bend toward the child for fear of frightening him. The boy was so *small*. He cleared his throat a second time as his mind worked to form a response. What does one say to a person so young? How extensive were his language skills? Burke hadn't a clue. "…You're welcome," was the best he could supply.

"Children," a woman's voice called as she crossed the yard. "It's time for dinner. Rose, you and your friend are, as always, welcome to eat with us."

Taken aback at the informal address to Lady Sennett by someone not of her station, Burke observed the thin woman dressed in simple garb as she neared them. Perhaps they were old friends. Or perhaps Rose had given her leave to address her so. Highly unusual, given the difference in their rank, yet he found the reasoning quite easy to believe.

"Thank you, Hester, but I must get home before dinner," Lady Sennett said to the woman. "Lord Darington, this is Hester Cress. She is one of the angels who lives here and cares for the children. Hester, may I present Lord Darington, Earl of Blackwood. He's the man I was telling you about, the one making such a very generous donation toward the building of the new home."

"Your lordship," the woman said with a respectful bow of her head. "I can't thank you enough. As you can see, the need is great."

Burke nodded, a little off put at the gratitude. Never before had he received such in person. A drawer in his desk contained a stack of hand-written thank you notes from charitable organizations, some from individuals. They never personally called on him. People, for the most part, considered him unapproachable. Before today, he always considered that fortuitous.

"It gives me pleasure to see my money put to good use," he said to the woman before shifting his attention back to Lady Sennett. "We should be going."

If Miss Cress believed anything untoward about Lady Sennett leaving alone with a man who was not her husband, she showed no sign of it. After giving the children time for their goodbyes, always one more hug, one more kiss on her cheek, the woman shuffled them in for their dinner.

Lady Sennett waited until the last child passed under the wooden, chain-hung sign reading 'Foundling

Home' in white paint. The little boy named Brennan, still holding the puppy, was the last one to go in. At the door, he gave her a final wave. The child then shifted toward him. He lifted one of the puppy's paws and waved it at him. At his nonresponse, Lady Sennett shocked him by poking him in the ribs with her elbow.

So, in an odd mix of affront, warmth, and silliness, Burke raised a hand and waved back to Raisin the puppy.

This must have pleased the little boy, for he smiled wide before he went into the house, singing to the puppy, and the door shut. Rose pivoted away from him in the quiet yard, almost a full rotation until she faced the gate. Was she giggling at him? He had the urge to do the same. Good lord, he'd just waved goodbye to a puppy.

After stepping through the gate, they both double checked to make certain its closure was secure. He crouched and ran his fingers along the woven sting making a barrier along the bottom. It was crude, but sturdy. As long as the gate stayed shut, little Raisin would remain within the walls of the yard.

Burke woke her sleeping driver with a hard slap to the carriage, ignoring Lady Sennett's gasp at his harshness. The imbecile coachman was taking a nap when he should have been seeing to the safety and well-being of his charge. When Lord Sennett heard of this, the fool would no doubt be sent packing for sure.

Burke ordered her driver to return to the Sennett home alone and said he would personally escort the lady back. The young man actually had the gall to look to Lady Sennett for confirmation of his order. Would the strangeness of this day ever cease?

"Thank you, Lord Darington," she said to him. "But there's really no reason..."

"We have matters to discuss."

"Milady?" the young man on the driver's bench asked before taking action.

With the agility of youth, he bounded from the carriage bench and positioned himself near his mistress. Her coachman, who wasn't long from his mother's apron strings, puffed out his scrawny chest, as if he carried bulk and muscle to intimidate. He shot hard glances at Burke that should have earned him a reprimand from his mistress, if not Burke himself.

The whelp was not even discreet in his insolence. Nor was his attire anywhere near to proper. By his appearance, one might mistake him for a low-ranking groom she'd plucked from the stables.

"It's all right, Horace," Lady Sennett said. "We'll be right behind you."

Her driver paused, and for a moment, Burke had the distinct impression the young man would actually argue the command. In the end, though, he climbed back onto his bench and set the horses toward home. Burke placed his hand on the small of Lady Sennett's back and guided her to his carriage, lacquered and buffed to a flawless shine. His family crest of a lion on a shield adorned the side. His driver, in full black and gold livery, awaited at the open door.

Burke followed her into the carriage. Instead of sitting across from her, as would be proper, he sat beside her. She hurried to scoot over a bit.

Once the carriage was in motion, Burke found himself at a loss. He already had words with her about the dangers of being out in such a place by herself. Not that she needed a scolding. No matter her courageous veneer, what had happened in the alley back there, and the vile likelihood that hadn't, must have scared the life out of her. It certainly did him.

When he'd seen her in the clutches of her attacker, a violent rage the likes of which he never before experienced blinded him to all but the loathsome creature he wanted to slay. His fists barely registered the two hard blows that felled the villain. If not for the urgent need to see Lady Sennett was unharmed, he may well have killed the man.

Beyond the window through which he stared, a low, half-moon shed a fair glow to landscape better left unlit. Decrepit buildings rife with all varieties of filth, long ago and rightfully abandoned, made a perfect refuge for malevolence. Even with a proper escort, the lady should not have been anywhere near to this section of town.

"Ashton doesn't need to know about...about what happened," she said, her voice breaking into his maddening ruminations.

He shifted his eyes toward her as they adjusted to the interior of the dark carriage. Burke couldn't quite make out Lady Sennett's expression. For a moment, he wondered if she feared her husband.

His mind conjured an image, unbidden, of himself in a heroic role, taking her from an abusive situation. But that was not the way of things. She did not fear the wrath of Lord Sennett. The lady did not want to upset the dear friend to whom she was married.

"He's your husband," Burkes stated. "He has a right to know you were attacked."

"Please, Lord Darington," she said, placing her

delicate hand on his sleeve. Had a woman ever before touched him without sensuous intentions? Her guileless entreaty was like the puppy, sweet, innocent, and rife with trouble.

"Ashton has been so very good to me. I don't want to cause him any distress."

"He should never have allowed you to come down here by yourself," Burke said.

Her fingers stiffened just before she withdrew her hand. Burke could rightly claim he witnessed her gain height as she harvested what little mass she had and tied it into a taut bundle. When she spoke, her voice flashed an unmistakable sharpness as her statement pruned his remark.

"Ashton is my husband, not my owner. I'll thank you to keep your directives to yourself."

Burke smiled in the dark. No man should tolerate such impertinence from a woman. In no situation should he even find it amusing. Burke found himself not just indulging both, but also enjoying her bold show of mettle, immensely.

"Are they not one in the same?" he asked. His sole purpose to elicit a response.

"No, Lord Darington, they are not," Lady Sennett answered, with definite emphasis on the last three words. "At least they are not in our marriage."

Her seething demeanor, at odds with the sweet woman he'd seen in the courtyard hugging children moments before, and the perfect hostess at last night's soiree, added yet another tier to this fascinating woman.

Her distinct spirit flew on forbidden wings and she would not see them clipped. He wondered if the lady was aware of her distance from the norms of society.

Yes, of course she understood the way of things. She knew how to behave amongst the upper classes. Her public comportment showed nowise a flaw. Beneath her polished propriety, though, beneath the manners and decorum, beat the heart of a peppery woman.

His man's mind envisioned her passion unleashed, emblazoned, golden hair free of her straw bonnet, of her pins, body liberated from gown and shift and stockings, warm and naked, spread across the mussed sheets of his bed. His body reacted as if all the desires the image raised had the ability to make it real by the power of want.

"Lord Sennett treats me as an equal," she stated.

The images in his mind did not instantly fade, but rather drained from his pores in tortuous wonder like a phantom siren, departing with a final, taunting caress. Eventually, her outlandish statement came into focus.

Burke repositioned himself before saying in a roughened voice, "I've never heard of such."

"My husband is a very…unique man. There is none better."

"I meant no insult," Burke said. He no longer wanted to see her riled. In the aftermath of his minds imaginings, he sought now her softer side, marveling, though, at the whole of her. "It is only natural for a husband to be concerned for his wife's safety."

"True," she said, in a more conciliatory tone. "The fact is, when I visit the foundling home without Ashton, I always take Big Bart with me. He was unavailable and the day was too lovely to miss. There is no taking back what happened today. Telling Ashton would serve naught but to upset him."

If she were his wife, he would want to know of the

attack. If she were his wife…Burke saw her again, not in a seedy alley, or the courtyard of a decaying building, or even tucked away within the confines of his bedchamber, but in sunlight.

With utter clarity, he pictured her on a picnic blanket beside the crystalline pond on the property of his country estate, children frolicking about the summer trees. The scene, wondrous enough to be the fruit of a peaceful slumber, ripe with love and place, humming of absolute rightness. It was as if the vision was too wholehearted, too anxious, and too keen to wait until he closed his eyes this night and drifted into sleep.

They hit a rut and the carriage jolted to the left, shaking loose the sublime image to which he yearned to cling. Lady Sennett kept her eyes on him, beseeching through the dark, her heart worried for the feelings of another.

"I'll hold my silence, on one condition," Burke said. He didn't have to intuit the lady would do as she pleased, but his sanity compelled him to demand this one stipulation. "Give me your word you will never again travel to the foundling home without proper protection."

She paused, only a beat or two before saying, "I promise. Thank you, Lord Darington." She reached for him again, this time placing her hand upon his. "You truly are a good man."

Burke drew in a quick breath. No one had ever said such a thing to him before. He grew up hearing his father speak of him as tainted beyond redemption. On rare occasions, when his mother bothered to spare him a tick, she would offer some small measure of defense. Her weak-hearted efforts only left him craving more.

The fact that defending him at all required effort was itself a parental statement of his lacking.

From Lady Sennett, however, her simple, unbidden words nourished a soul he believed starved beyond resurrection.

Burke turned his hand over and squeezed, careful of her bones, small and fragile in his large hand. When he would have released her, should have released her, he kept a firm hold. She made no effort to pull away. In fact, her fingers curled around his hand, returning his affection.

A covetous wish to possess this woman, this mix of purity and passion, of the unexplored and untainted, leapt over his walls and affixed itself between his desire and his good sense. Before he knew what he was about, Burke bent until his lips brushed against hers.

Her small gasp of shock quelled a bit of the folly that had overcome him. Burke held himself still and paused before he would have backed away, would have offered a humble apology. Before he could do either, however, she stretched up and touched her lips to his.

Her kiss was unsure and awkward. Had she never even experienced a kiss? After drawing in a breath full of her sweetness, he touched his tongue to her lower lip, and the question was lost in her taste.

Burke slid a hand to cup her neck, his fingers inching up her downy nape, beneath her bonnet and into the silk of her golden hair until her head cradled in his palm. At the tentative touch of her tongue to his, at her innocent bid for more, his breath turned ragged.

With his thumb, he tugged on her chin. She opened for him without hesitation, met him, curious, receptive, and responsive. Shifting his body over hers, he drew her closer, until his chest pressed against the firm rise of her breasts. A sharp catch of her breath told him the penetrating sensation affected her as much as it did him.

A sound at his mouth, a small whimper, an expression of her growing desire, inflamed his passion, and he strained to keep from crushing her against him.

Dragging his hand down the slope of her narrow waist, over the rounded curve of her hip, Burke gathered handfuls of her skirts, lifting them inch by inch.

Nothing in this world had ever beckoned him so as this maddening need to touch her. In that instant, he would swear it was the only reason his lungs drew in air and his heart pounded out another beat. Before he could lay hand to skin, though, the carriage came to an abrupt stop.

The fact that they were no longer moving, that his coachman was at the very moment setting the break, after which he would climb down from his perch and open the door, occurred to him before it did her.

"Rose," he breathed against her sweet lips, their unsated desires quivering between them. "We're here."

Her eyes fluttered open and for a moment, Burke would swear she was unaware of her place and position. Her long-lashed lids blinked several times before a blush bright enough to see in the dim light rushed up her face. She jumped back as if he had scalded her, which, ironically, is much how he felt. His advantage was experience. Not that it made frustration easier to bear, just easier to understand.

Burke leaned back and gave her a moment to collect herself. He found himself in dire need of the same.

By the time his coachman opened the door, Rose was brushing down her skirts with shaking hands and tucking errant strands of hair back into her crooked hat. He affected her. He'd awoken in her passions to which she had been completely unaware. That pleased him beyond understanding, though it helped naught with relief.

Burke stepped from the carriage before helping her to alight.

"Good night, Lord Darington," she said, flicking her eyes no higher than his chin.

The lady rifled through her chaotic state in search of her perfect demeanor. Her breath was unsteady. Her hands fluttered, straightening and patting and brushing at her skirts, her bonnet, at nothing at all. He had aroused her senses and offended her sensibility. Burke might find that more amusing if she'd not had the same effect on him.

Her husband's outlandish request that not twenty-four hours ago had him shaking his head now tempted him beyond reasonable sanity.

"Good night, Lady Sennett." He reached for her then and she gasped. "My coat," he said, taking it from her shoulders, grinning at her flustered condition, bemused at his own.

His eyes stayed on her as she carried herself with all the dignity she could muster, up the stone walkway toward the front door of her home. She was almost to the porch steps when she stopped. Her head and shoulders rotated until she faced where he stood.

Burke speculated as to whether or not enough moonlight fell from the sky for her to see his face. Some mischievous, adolescent aspect, to which he'd never before granted access, inspired him to set his most wolfish grin on her.

From his place beside the carriage, Burke heard Lady Sennett's quick intake of breath. He wondered if she heard his low chuckle.

****

Having slipped unnoticed past Ashton and Lewis as they sat sipping brandy in the drawing room, Rose tiptoed up the stairs with quiet intention. She needed to change her mussed clothing. She needed to set herself to rights. And, she needed a few minutes to sort her head before facing the two gentlemen with whom she lived.

In her lovely, spacious room of cream and coral, Rose removed her straw bonnet and dropped it on her dressing table before lighting some candles. Her trembling legs carried her across the fine Aubusson carpet where she flopped, face down, across her bed. The counterpane absorbed her disconcerted sigh.

After rolling onto her back, Rose let her hand drift up until her fingertips touched her lower lip.

The earl had kissed her! And he did so in a very intimate fashion. What's more, she'd allowed it, encouraged it even. Embarrassment summoned her hands to cover her face. Never in her life had she behaved in such a shameful manner! The palms of her hands muffled her groan, a low, pitiful sound.

What shocked her most about those moments alone with Lord Darington in his carriage was she'd enjoyed it, just as Ashton had told her she would.

Since they'd married, her husband had urged her to seek her pleasures. She wasn't exactly sure what that meant and was too embarrassed to ask. All she knew of men's ways was what Piers had shown her. Repulsive, all of it, and she'd never been able to imagine it any better.

The night Ashton had taken her in, the night she fled the baron's home with nothing but an amber pig and a hatful of trouble and she and Ashton made their bargain, he'd made it clear he would not be sharing her bed. She could not have been more pleased.

Her husband was a dear man, kind, considerate, generous. Since she had no want whatsoever to feel the touch of a man, for her, it was the perfect marriage. For Ashton, too. They both had what they wanted, what they needed. If her husband was telling the truth, and she believed he was, his life was as happy as hers.

Except when Ashton was trying to convince her of all she was missing, Rose didn't give the issue of intimacies even the tiniest of considerations. At least, she hadn't until tonight.

Could she really partake in an affair? When Lord Darington caressed her, when he kissed her, what she experienced was far from revulsion. It was haunting, this sensation, foreign, exotic…desirous. How much more was there for a woman to feel? Could it be even more intense? Based on the sensations still roiling through her body, she had to assume so. Her curiosity climbed another degree.

She didn't need to scour her memories to recall where the earl had touched her, for the warmth of his large hand against her back, the firm press of his lips to hers, their hearts beating against each other, still resonated. The smell of him, soap and musk and man, stayed with her, too. Yet this unearthing of newness did not fill a void, but rather, created one.

A peculiar rift for which she had no knowledge gaped vacant through the center of her mind's ruminations. What else transpired between a man and a woman? How far was she willing to travel into that mysterious abyss?

Her curiosity piqued with the same strange force of her yearning to feel once again Lord Darington's touch. Maybe Ashton was right. Perhaps she was denying herself a wonderful facet of life.

For the longest time she lay in perfect stillness on her back and stared at the intertwined vines of ivy in the white, plaster ceiling moulding.

Chapter 5

Rose enjoyed a long gander at the evening's bustling scene outside the carriage window, before returning her attention to Ashton and Lewis.

Both men were dressed for tonight's event in navy breeches and crisp white shirts with ruffled cravats. Lewis's tailcoat was also navy. Ashton's blue tailcoat carried the same hue, though several shades lighter and was the exact same color as Rose's soft cotton gown with a fine, batiste overlay, and matching wrap. Her dear, attentive husband saw to it her slippers were dyed to match.

Cora had styled her hair up with curled tendrils hanging loose from her temples. At her throat hung a round-cut ruby on a shiny, gold chain, a gift from her generous husband.

"It appears as if everyone in town is attending the opera tonight," she said to the men. Her fingertips tapped an excited tempo upon her thighs. She swiveled toward the window, eager for another look at the throng of enthusiasm.

Coachmen could scarce negotiate the street for all the well-garbed people crossing and milling about. A woman's trill of laughter preceded the guffaws of several men on the other side of the street. Rose caught glimpses of them through the fluid crowd as the small group bantered beneath the yellow glow of a streetlamp. Most, however, scuttled toward the entrance to get inside and take their seats. She was not alone in her excitement for the evening.

They'd taken her to the opera twice since she and Ashton had wed, but neither time had such excitement teemed through the event. Anticipation of the night's performance was visceral.

"Sophia De LaGrange is singing tonight, my dear. She's all the rage across Paris," Lewis told her as the carriage slow-rolled to a stop in front of the theater.

They'd taken the landau this evening, but due to the chilly night, Ashton had ordered the top to remain closed. The low-reaching windows on the sides, however, still allowed for greater viewing. It appeared all the aristocracy wanted to attend tonight's performance. And they'd arrived in their best attire. Lords and ladies, dandies and fops, all moods high, eager for the night's special event.

"Yes," Ashton said. "We were lucky to get tickets. This evening's show sold out weeks ago. You're in for a real treat this night, Rose."

As the footman assisted them in their exit from the coach, an elated cacophony of sight and sound surrounded them. Carriage wheels on cobblestones, chatter and laughter, excitement for both the social gathering and the anticipated entertainment to come, filled the walkway in front of the theater. The trio conversed with a few friends and acquaintances, stopping several times in the short distance to the theater doors.

As Ashton concluded a conversation with a business associate, Rose happened to glance about at precisely the wrong time. It was too late to pretend she didn't see them. They already saw her. The pair strolled up the sidewalk straight toward her, her sister Edwina and her sister's husband, Piers.

The couple wove through the crowd and stopped before her. Edwina took in Rose's fancy new gown and matching wrap before giving her a smile too tight to hold so much as a crumb of cordiality. No words of greeting or interest could fit through, either.

Rose offered a smile of her own. Perhaps something so simple could open a door, maybe even begin to mend what was broken. Since Rose no longer resided in the house, it was possible her sister might now see her in a different light, a friendlier light. But no. The notion was too imprudent to be anything above wistful.

Instead of even a flicker of warmth, Edwina's eyes narrowed with the gravity of a sentried gate. Whatever shreds of hope Rose had for family salvation shriveled in her sister's clear message of rejection.

Piers' gaze lingered on the ruby necklace she wore. Her brother-in-law let his leer drop to her very moderate display of cleavage before raising his small eyes to meet hers.

"We were just out for an evening stroll," Piers said, his smile as genuine as Edwina's paste earbobs.

Piers was better dressed than his wife. Eddy wore the same drab coat and sturdy shoes she'd had for years. Her brother-in-law, however, sported a new, brocade pique coat and a new cambric shirt. The spoils of his settlement with Ashton, no doubt. It appeared all that went to Eddy was new pair of red gloves.

"How fortunate we ran into you, Rose," Piers said. "It's been far too long. You appear well, my dear."

Ashton had his arm around her as soon as he heard the man's voice. Then Lewis positioned himself on her other side. Their obvious displays of support reminded her how very much she loved these two men, and how grateful she was to have them.

Rose spared Piers a mere half glance before shifting her attention back to her sister. "How are you, Eddy?"

"I'm quite well," answered Edwina.

The loose form of her words belied them, as did her appearance. Her cheekbones protruded. The drag of liquor gave weight to her eyes. She leaned on Piers, but this was no show of affection. Eddy used her husband to keep her balance.

"If you'll excuse us," Ashton said, managing politeness without warmth. "The performance is due to begin soon."

"Of course. How very fortunate you are to have tickets." Piers said. He focused again on Rose, smiling as if that terrible night in her bedchamber had never happened, and said, "You should come by the house for afternoon tea, dear. Your sister and I would love a visit."

Again, Rose set her attention on her sister, hoping for an invitation from her, even a simple nod of agreement would suffice. Eddy raised her drooping head. No sisterly warmth calmed the chill of her gaze. Naught but loathing lurked in the shallows of her sister's glassy eyes. It forced Rose to accept her sister's true feelings had always been there, and were not likely to ever change.

Edwina had just turned twelve when Rose was born into their family, siphoning their parent's attention with an infant's needs. By Rose's eighth birthday, Edwina was married to the baron, a man for whom she held little affection, a man who had perpetrated a gross mislead regarding his finances. Rose suspected now that Piers had overestimated the wealth of her family. The inheritance they'd received after her parents' death was less than her sister's dowry.

Edwina once accused Rose of possessing more than her fair share of luck. She said, in a statement rife with bitterness, the best of life's offerings always went to Rose. Even now, Edwina appeared as if she would like nothing better than to spit on Rose's lovely gown.

"Perhaps," Rose said in answer to her brother-in-law's invitation, the response so quiet as to be almost inaudible. She said only that much out of civility, for Rose would never set foot inside the Rutherford house again. It stung, but not as bad as she would have guessed. Maybe a part of her had been prepared, and it was just as well.

Once through the doors of the theater, Rose excused herself to the ladies retiring room. She removed her reticule from her wrist, and set it on a table beside a pitcher and bowl. She then dampened a cloth with cool water and kept it pressed it to her face.

"Are you unwell?"

She lowered the cloth to see Lady Prudence Hortence at her side. Her lemon yellow, low-cut gown was a fine compliment to her dark hair, piled high atop her head with a yellow, beaded ribbon running through it. Her stiff up and down inspection of Rose laid a crust of churlish curiosity over her concerned expression.

"I'm fine. Lady Hortence, isn't it?"

"That's right," the woman said, tipping her head.

For a moment, her high hairstyle appeared at risk of a fall. "We were introduced at your soiree last week."

"Yes, of course."

"We barely had a chance to converse, but Burke, um, I mean, Lord Darington," Lady Hortence said through a twist of a smile. "Lord Darington has spoken of you."

"He has?" said Rose, surprised to hear such. She worried, then. Had Lord Darington boasted of their indiscretion in his carriage? Certainly, no gentleman would. Of course, he'd not behaved so gentlemanly the night he'd taken her home. Nor had she behaved the lady.

"Yes. You made quite an impression on him." The woman's almond shaped eyes ran an inspection over her again, slower this time, with overt interest dry of any alarm for her well-being.

"I had no idea," Rose said. She dropped the cloth in the basket and retrieved her reticule, anxious to be away. The woman's voice carried a snide tone reminiscent of Edwina, and for a reason she couldn't begin to guess, Rose had the impression Lady Hortence was aggravated with her.

"Yes, apparently you are a paragon of women." Her voice took on a distracted tone then, as if her mind had drifted off. "I've never actually heard him quite so effusive." She caught herself, reined in and rushed to add with great enthusiasm, "Except, that is, when he plies me with flattery."

"I'm afraid I don't know him well enough to say if he's talkative or not." Lady Hortence's expression said she didn't quite believe that.

"Of course," the woman said in a hushed voice.

She then stepped close for a private exchange even though they were alone. "Lord Darington doesn't dally with married women. You should know that before you make a fool of yourself, my dear. Speaking of, I must go." She laughed then, an artificial sound through a fabricated smile.

Lady Hortence's voice returned to normal as she spun away and glided toward the door. "He gets so impatient when I'm out of his reach. Enjoy the show."

What was that all about? The woman sounded as if she were jealous.

The evening had barely begun, yet the rough scraping of animosity already dulled the shine. She, Ashton and Lewis had so been looking forward to this. No, she would not allow family or acquaintance to ruin the night. She squared her shoulders, patted her hair, and stepped through the door.

Rose met her two gentlemen who waited with all patience in the noisy vestibule. They wound their way through the chattering crowd, up the stairs, and to their private box.

Though Rose refused to allow Lady Hortence and her snide treatment to spoil the evening for her, the woman's words continued to make passes through her head. Had Lord Darington truly spoken of her in such lofty terms? Though it was silly and pointless, and she couldn't say why, but Rose liked knowing she was in his thoughts, even if Lady Hortence did not.

Once settled, Rose took a cursory scan of the crowd of people finding their seats below, as well as the boxes across the theater. She didn't see Lord Darington. He would be easy to spot, as he was taller than most, not to mention the bright yellow of his companion's gown.

Then Ashton was explaining the opera, as it would be performed in Italian. Lewis offered some interesting insights, and before long the musicians were playing, and the burgundy curtains opened with a grand, sweeping flourish.

Although she spoke not a word of Italian, the splendor of the music, the passion of the singers, told with great clarity the story of the trials and treasures of realizing true love. Before long, the story had her immersed in the character's plight. Sophia De LaGrange was indeed a talent. Her voice flowed deep into one's heart, and when it flowed out again, left it with longing.

During a slow, moving ballad by one of the male performers, Rose let her gaze drift across the theater. On the other side, in a private box that had been empty when they'd entered theirs, Lord Darington sat with Lady Hortence.

He was staring straight at her.

Rose refused to hang her head in shame, though the memory of her behavior in his carriage urged her to do just that. After her wanton conduct, she hated to think what his opinion of her must be, regardless of what Lady Hortence had said. Of course, it was possible his idea of a paragon was a woman of minimal moralities. In which case Lady Hortence had not only been unkind, but correct.

Warmth flooded Rose's face, yet she did not look away. On the contrary, she lifted her chin and stared back, defiant. She cared not a whit if her impudence angered him. She'd surpassed the time in her life when she would allow a man to intimidate her.

At her audacious response, the one that should have piqued his vexation at her utter lack of humility, Lord Darington had the gall to grin.

Rose's jaw dropped a tad as she drew in a quiet gasp. The man was a cad, a rake, a scoundrel. Rose lifted her chin higher and swung her attention back to the stage. It required all the will she possessed not to look back.

****

Burke escorted Lady Prudence Hortence out the front doors and through the mad crush of people, all waiting for their carriages to collect them from the front of the theater. The performance had been excellent. At least, so Pru told him. His mind, as well as his attention, kept drifting across the theater to where Lady Rose Sennett sat in harmonious fashion with her two male companions.

Even now, with Pru whispering indecent enticements into his ear, his gaze traveled the throng, seeking out Lady Sennett as if such a thing was natural for him. Indeed, it was not. Had he ever cared whether or not a specific woman was in attendance to any event? No. Never. And to his chagrin, this particular woman wasn't even close to his usual taste in women.

He admired the lady's mettle. Her mind challenged him. The situation in which she'd inserted herself to establish her safety was fascinating, to say the least, and roused his curiosity from its long dormant state. If he were to be frank, most everything about her roused him in one way or another.

All right, well, perhaps he did appreciate certain aspects of her. Though it stopped at any interest beyond her unconventionality. The women he chose to share sparse time with were not innocent, nor were they shy in expressing their amorous interests. These qualities made them a perfect, albeit temporary, match for him. Lady Sennett possessed neither of these qualities. So why was he searching the crowd for her?

Burke was on the verge of calling himself every kind of fool and taking what the voluptuous woman beside him offered, when he spotted her.

Deep in conversation with Lord Lewis Da Ville, Lady Sennett did not at first see him, but her husband did. Burke placed a hand between Pru's shoulder blades and guided her through the crowd and in their direction.

"Lord Darington," said Lord Sennett, a welcoming smile upon his youthful face at their approach.

"Lord Sennett, how are you this grand evening?"

"Quite well, and yourself?"

"Fine, just fine. I take it you and your companions enjoyed the performance."

"As did everyone fortunate enough to attend," Lord Sennett said. "Miss De LaGrange has a voice to cow the angels."

Burke tipped his head in agreement, and then motioned toward Pru. "Lady Prudence Hortense."

"A pleasure to see you again," Lord Sennett said. He took her offered hand and touched it with a quick kiss. "You did me the honor of gracing our soiree with your attendance. And this is Lord Lewis Da Ville. You may have met him, as he too attended our event."

"Lord Da Ville," Burke said.

After Da Ville acknowledged the lady and the men shook hands, Lord Sennett said, "You remember my wife."

"Of course. Lady Sennett," Burke said, taking her

hand and brushing a light kiss across her knuckles. "How could any man forget such a lovely creature?"

"Lord Darington," she said with a polite nod and a hint of discomfort. "How nice to see you again."

Before he let go of her hand, Burke gave her fingers a meaningful squeeze, accompanied by a fleeting but pointed and impish leer. The woman brought out a juvenile facet in him. Awareness of his folly prodded him to stop. He ignored it.

He surprised himself because it was not his habit to indulge in playful banter. He didn't tease, he didn't cajole, and he certainly didn't flirt. The women with whom he was intimate understood what he was about and vice versa. Invitations might be outright or implied. Either way, getting to where they both wanted to be required a minimum of words.

Once between the sheets, he thoroughly enjoyed taking his time pleasuring a woman, and taking his pleasure with her. Some things in life deserved one's full attention. Until that point, however, coy preambles held no appeal to him. Speaking with a woman was for the sole purpose of reaching a destination. Conversing itself offered no gratification.

At least, so it had always been in the past.

"Have you visited the foundling home lately?" Burke asked with deliberate directness. He kept his smile polite as the lady's cheeks reddened.

"I visited the children, briefly," Rose said.

Her words trailed off at the end as she cast a meaningful glance toward her husband. Her face bore an obvious beseech. She wanted to leave. Lord Sennett was either oblivious or set on further pursuit of his request. Burke would bet a purse full of coin on the latter.

"We were just going back to my home for a brandy," Burke said, though it was a complete lie, something else he never did. He saw what lies did to his parents, to his family. One lie led to another, and then another, until the hole was so deep there was no chance for ascension.

Yet, here he was, conjuring a story for the sole purpose of having a bit of time with her. What had come over him? No, this was different from what his parents had done. Nothing here was of any consequence. This was just for fun. *When in his life had he ever done anything just for fun?*

"Would the three of you care to join us?" Burke said.

Lady Prudence Hortence made a valiant attempt to hide her shock. Pru had never stepped so much as a toe over his threshold. Short of business, he rarely had visitors, and he never entertained. He kept his home a private sanctuary. All his sexual exploits, without exception, took place in the women's beds. He'd never invited even one of them to share his.

"Brandy sounds lovely," Lord Sennett said, answering for his trio, an unmistakable spark glinting in his eyes.

So, the man had not lost hope for this seduction for his wife. Lord Sennett must not have approached anyone else for the task. There was no reason for this to please Burke, yet it did.

Sennett placed his hand on the small of his wife's back. If the displeasure she was unable to hide was any indication, the man would get an earful on the ride to Burke's home. Burke struggled to keep the corners of his lips from rising.

"Yes, indeed," Lord Da Ville added with a smile. "Splendid idea."

Neither of the women were even close to happy with the change of plan. Beside him, Lady Hortence smashed the toe of her yellow slipper on top of his foot while her fingernails dug into his arm. Burke smiled through her quiet protestations, finding an inordinate amount of humor in the way Lady Sennett strained to mask her panic. Before she could summon a reason to cry off, though, the parties were all heading to their respective carriages. He hoped the lady would not invent an excuse to go home on the ride.

"We had plans for this evening," Prudence said as soon as the carriage door was closed. She'd not yet even settled into her plush seat across from him before her hard-edged complaint bore into his ears.

"Our plan was to attend the opera. We have done so."

Pru folded her arms across the ample display of her bosom. After but a few seconds, she pried open her tight lips to say, "I cannot for the life of me understand why you would want to spend time with them. Those men, there is something odd about the two of them. I can't quite put my finger on it. And his wife—"

Before Prudence could besmirch Lady Rose Sennett, which he had no doubt she about to do, Burke said, "If you do not feel up to socializing tonight, I will have my driver deliver you to your house."

Both her high-arched brows rose halfway up her forehead. Burke half hoped she would throw one of her fits and demand he take her home. After a moment he assumed she used for contemplation, weighing entrance to his house against sharing the evening with others, Prudence flattened her features and brooded in silence for the remainder of the ride.

Half an hour later, the five of them sat fireside in Burke's gold parlor, named so for the gilt draperies hanging at each of the three tall windows and the broad, matching trim of the oriental carpet centered in the spacious room. Gold brocade adorned the backs of two pearl-white sofas. Shimmering gold thread wove through the pearl and black fabric of the eight chairs spread about the parlor.

When they'd entered the foyer with the white marble floor and crystal chandelier, Timmons, Burke's trim, silver-haired butler collected their cloaks. After handing them to a maid, Timmons followed them into the gold parlor and saw to it each guest held a snifter of fine, French brandy, except for Rose who requested tea.

Rose sat on one of the sofas, flanked by Ashton and Lewis. Across the low, Chippendale table, on the other sofa, Burke sat with Prudence. They discussed the opera they'd just seen, followed with an exchange of some small pleasantries, during which they all consented to the use of their given names.

"So, tell me of the progress with the Foundling Project," Burke said to his guests, though his eyes were on Rose. He wasn't teasing her this time. He was in all truth curious, and caring more, now that he'd seen the condition of the ancient building the children called home.

"Rose, it turns out, is quite the business woman," Ashton said with a proud nod toward his wife. "She not only procured the parcel of land we wanted, but managed to bargain it down to a reasonable price. The final papers are being drawn up and will be signed in a few days."

"As I told you, Ashton," Rose said. "Lord Darington deserves much of the credit."

"Burke," he said, reminding her to use his name. He liked the sound of it from her lips. Soft lips, according to his clear memory. Soft, sweet, malleable beneath his.

Lewis said, "Yes, Rose, but it was still you who secured the deal."

"Here, here," Burke said, raising his crystal glass in a toast. "To a new home for the children. To the woman who made it all possible."

All but Rose sipped from their drinks. "You are all too kind," Rose said, before shifting her eyes toward Burke. "From the start there've been many parties involved in this endeavor. I merely put to use the information you passed on to me."

To Rose, Burke said, "What's impressive is the clever way you made use of the information, Rose." To Ashton he said, "Perhaps I should take your wife's counsel on my next business venture."

"If you are a wise man, you will," Ashton said without a trace of anything less than sincerity.

"Rather masculine, isn't it?" Prudence said from beside him. The point of her chin lifted above her stiff posture to the very verge of condescension. "Unseemly, even. A woman engaging in business matters? I've never heard of such a thing."

Burke slanted a hard glance her way before saying, "Not at all, Prudence, dear." He shifted his attention back to Rose, softer, intent. "I find it rather refreshing to see a woman make good use of her talents, rather than hide them for fear of appearing unfeminine."

Burke did not need to turn toward his companion for the evening to know Pru was furious. He also found he did not care.

"Prudence," Lewis said. "Have you noticed the sky on this clear night? The constellations are quite visible."

Ashton stood and offered his hand to Prudence. "Yes, let's see how many we can find, shall we?" At her hesitation, he added, "Nothing is as lovely as stargazing with a beautiful woman."

Prudence gave him her shy smile, the one Burke knew she reserved for people who did not know her better, and took Ashton's hand. The two of them followed Lewis to the tall windows on the far side of the room.

"I want to apologize," Burke said to Rose. The remark surprised him more than it did her, he was sure.

Burke couldn't remember the last time he made an apology. It wasn't in his nature. He made good decisions, he answered to no one, and in all frankness, it was rare he happened upon a reason or situation where an apology was required.

Not that he regretted kissing her, or touching her. He wanted to do so, her own husband had requested such, and there was no doubt the lady had enjoyed herself. She'd not protested, not with words or with actions. Rose hadn't shown a smidgeon of hesitation during their brief moment of passion. Quite the opposite. The moment she lifted her lips to his was a moment he would always keep treasured. What he didn't like was the idea of Rose carrying any guilt over their mild indiscretion.

"Yes, well, I too behaved in poor manner," Rose said on a quiet sigh. She flicked a backward glance to see the others engaged in conversation at the window. "Why don't we both just pretend it never happened, shall we?"

"I'm afraid such a thing would be impossible," Burke said.

She tipped her head, frowning a tad in a way he found utterly adorable. "I don't understand."

"A man doesn't forget the sweetest wine he ever tasted, the loveliest sunset he ever had the good fortune to behold, or enchanted kisses from the most tempting woman ever to cross his path."

Burke almost laughed at his own waxing. He'd never said such things to a woman before. Even if he could take it back, though, he would not. He meant every word.

Her pink-hued lips parted slightly, and even as he called his sanity into question, Burke longed to kiss her again.

She twisted her hands together once, twice, before shooting a glance over her shoulder to make sure none of the others listened in. "Lord Darington…"

"Burke."

"Burke. What happened between us, what we did in your carriage, well, it was a mistake."

Leaning in, elbows resting on his knees, his eyes boring into the blue depths of hers, Burke said, "Tell me you did not enjoy it."

The moment the last word left his mouth, an adorable blush claimed her face. She sputtered before taking a sip of her tea. She set the cup on the saucer with a mild clatter, and folded her hands in her lap.

"Tell me," he prompted.

"I...well...I..."

"The truth."

After letting out a breath, she leaned in, too. It was apparent in the sternness of her expression, the edge in her voice, and the flicker of displeasure in her eyes, agitation had absolved her shame.

"Fine, yes, I enjoyed it. And don't you dare grin. For a man with such an austere reputation, you certainly do grin a lot."

No, actually, I do not.

"I will not apologize," he said.

She grinned herself, then. "You just did."

"Not for kissing you."

"Then for what?"

"Because it left you feeling embarrassed about something as natural as life itself."

Her gaze widened, before growing thoughtful. For a moment they sat there peering into each other's eyes, thoughts churning, different, but only in accordance to the vast degrees of dissimilarity of their experience.

"Burke," Prudence said at her approach to the sofa. "I've grown quite weary and I believe it's time for me to retire."

Rose stood. "Yes. I believe I'm ready to go home now, too."

Burke summoned Timmons, who proceeded to dole out their coats. He helped Prudence into hers while Ashton did the same for Rose. At the street, where their carriages awaited, the group bid their farewells. Burke waited until his guests rolled away in their carriage before escorting Prudence toward his, where his coachman stood at attention.

She halted, tugging on his arm for him to wait. His feet stopped and he dragged his attention from his mind's wanderings and gave it to Prudence.

"You know, Burke, we don't have to leave. The night is yet young, and…" Pru finger-crawled up his arm and over his jaw. "I've never seen the inside of your bedchamber."

It was like having a strong spider creep about his body. He took her hand, anxious to be alone with his thoughts. "I don't share my bed. You've known that from the start, Pru," he said. He nodded to his coachman, who then opened the carriage door.

Wandering ruminations stunted what little conversation they shared on the ride to her house. Her aggravation honed a sharp edge to what few words she spoke. At her door, Burke wished her goodnight.

"You're not staying?"

"Not tonight, Pru. I'm tired."

She slipped her hand beneath his long, unbuttoned coat, her fingers pulsing down his chest and over his belly. "I believe I can revive you," she purred.

Burke took her wrist in a gentle but firm hold. "Another night, my dear." Following a bare, passionless kiss on her cheek, he pivoted and strode down the paving stones.

As he walked back to the street where his coach awaited, Pru's front door slammed, the message resounding in the otherwise quiet night. She was finished with him. That was fine. They'd run their course and they both knew it was time. He had no doubt Pru would have him replaced with a new lover in a fortnight, if not sooner. And he cared not a wit.

"I'll be walking home tonight," Burke told his

coachman as he passed.

The coachman sputtered at this odd turn. "Do you want...sir, should I follow you?"

"No," Burke answered, his pace never slowing.

Chapter 6

The rain had slowed to a light drizzle and thick rays of late-day sunlight succeeded at breaking through the cloud cover to chase off morning's chill. An eastward breeze still blew with some strength, though it, too, was losing might. The world appeared pointed toward positive progress.

As soon as the carriage door enclosed them within, Rose and Lewis could shed their detached decorum. They clasped each other's hands, laughing, before sharing a tight, congratulatory hug.

"The papers are signed; the deal is done. You did it, Rose!" Lewis said, as excited as she.

"We all did, all of the efforts of the committee, you, Ashton, Lord Darington. I really had very little to do with it."

"Nonsense. The deal closed on the way you pled our case. In fact, I think you left Lord Cavendish in a bit of a quandary."

"Whatever do you mean, Lewis?"

"I believe at this very moment the man is all in a lather trying to decide what to do first, dance with the bank draft we left him, or run about town bragging of his charitable generosity."

Rose gave into full laughter, as did Lewis. When they calmed, Rose said, "There is so much to be done now. We still have enough to begin construction, but we'll need to raise more money to finish the building."

"You've a small committee to help. Now that we have secured the land, or rather, you have, I believe we can count on the *ton* to jump aboard whole-heartedly."

"Oh, Lewis, do you think they will?"

"Undoubtedly! A charity ball is most favored. Extravagance and debauchery for a good cause, it's catnip beneath their twitching whiskers."

Rose laughed again, and threw another hug around her dear friend who returned her heartfelt affection in kind.

When they settled back, Lewis made an abrupt turn in the conversation. "So, you and Lord Darington seem to get on well."

Rose blushed again, thinking of that kiss, that wonderful, shameless kiss. "Yes, he seems a fine man."

"Very attractive, too."

Rose cocked a brow at him. "Both you and Ashton certainly do sing his praises."

"Well, if you don't object to me speaking my mind…"

"Lewis, of course I don't. You must know you are as dear to me as Ashton."

He laid his hands atop hers.

"Ashton and I love you with all our hearts, and we both want nothing more than to see you happy. Life is so short, Rose, and positively overrun with trials."

Rose touched a gentle finger to the scar on his forehead hidden by a fall of his soft, ginger hair. She and Lewis had both left their homes under such horrible conditions, and knew all too well the awful way their lives could have gone. They were both ever grateful at where fate had deposited them.

"I know," she said.

Lewis took her hands in his and squeezed, pumping them once to stress his words. "Take your pleasures where you can, love. You know you have Ashton's blessing."

"Oh, Lewis, I wouldn't even know where to begin."

"So, you're considering it?"

A blush warmed her face as she sat back, folding her hands in her lap.

"Good," Lewis said with encouraging emphasis at her unspoken answer. "All you must do, Rose, dear, is tell Lord Darington. He will take care of the rest."

"I couldn't!" Rose said at a near shout. "I wouldn't know what to say. And even if I did, it all seems so sordid, so improper."

"I used to feel the same way about my...myself. Ashton taught me propriety is a mere matter of perspective. In the end, as long as you're not causing harm to another, there is no harm.

"You make it sound so simple."

Lewis sighed. "Life struggles for simplicity. However, the whole of it can be quite wondrous. All one must do, is open oneself up to the possibilities.

"Like you and Ashton. Your views are much like my husband's. Both of you keep such a liberal outlook. Is...is that how you and Ashton stay so happy?"

At the very mention of Ashton's name, Lewis's entire face lifted in joy. It then sagged a little at his recounting.

"When I first met Ashton," Lewis said. "My family had turned their back on me. From a very early age, I believe, it was clear to them I would never live up to their expectations. I had money and a home, but my heart was desolate and they would never understand why."

Lewis quieted. He swallowed, gave a slight shake of his head, and then continued.

"They put every effort into 'correcting' me. Women were presented to me like sweet cakes at a tea party, prettied and ready for courtship, almost on a daily basis. I did make an effort to please my family. It was torture, trying to be what I wasn't. I thought I would live alone with my shame for the rest of my life."

"Ashton has spoken to me of his loneliness before he met you. He says you saved him from a life of emotional isolation."

Love's joy misted Lewis's eyes. "And here I am quite sure Ashton is the one who saved me. And you, dear, are a hero to us both."

Taken aback, Rose said, "You two had already found each other. Perhaps I helped ease the living situation a bit, but hero is much an overstatement."

"Not at all, dear. The way matters are now, I'm more than happy and my life is better than I ever dared to dream. Ashton would say the same. Your presence in the house, as his wife, has made it all much easier for both of us. Ashton never gave up hope we'd find a way to live together. Though your path to us was treacherous, and I'd not wish such a thing on anyone, we are ever grateful it led you to us. You came to our rescue, Rose."

"I suppose we all rescued each other."

"I suppose we have. So, in answer to your original question, yes, being open to possibilities allowed them a way in."

The carriage slowed and then stopped in front of their home. The pair stepped out of the carriage and into the warming day, the wind, now little more than a stiff breeze. Small puddles remained on the ground, but they were already shrinking as they dried in the broadening sunlight.

The front door opened and Ashton made haste getting to the street. He must have been waiting for them at the window. The image brought a smile to Rose. Their home, filled with love and acceptance, was indeed a dream come true.

"It's done, Ashton," Rose said, throwing her arms around him. "The papers are signed. The land is ours!"

Ashton gave her a broad smile and another hug, cheering as he lifted her and spun her around before setting her back on her feet. Just as they parted, the loud report of a pistol rent the air. Rose's scream followed the deadly blast.

Chapter 7

Burke sat back in his tufted, wine-colored chair at one of the gaming tables of White's Gentleman's Club. As he waited for the dealer to shuffle the cards, he tapped a long finger on one of the half dozen stacks of chips before him.

To his right at the horseshoe table sat his one true friend, Lord Andrew Worthington, Drew to his friends. Drew had several respectable towers of his own chips. An earnest opponent in cards, as well as in the boxing ropes, as they were of equal size, and close to equal in skill. They both enjoyed getting their exercise testing each other's pugilistic abilities. And, Drew was one of the very few people Burke trusted.

Lord Foxboro, a lean man with a seemly face and ears protruding beyond his thinning, mud-colored hair, sat on the other side of Drew, glaring at the one short stack of chips remaining in front of him. The man possessed no skill at all in the realm of gambling. To his detriment, Foxboro believed he did.

As the dealer sent cards sliding across the baize table, Foxboro grabbed for his as if they were driftwood, and he was drowning in a turbulent sea.

Lord Snively, a portly baron in the habit of dressing in the most foppish of fashions, approached the table as the first cards of the new hand were dealt, and wiggled himself into the seat to Burke's left.

Today, as he so often did, Lord Snively appeared quite the peacock with an orange jacket over a yellow waistcoat and pea-green breeches. Burke gave him a brief nod before returning his attention to the game.

"Quite the news going about town," Lord Snively said, taking in the three other men at the table.

His plump fingers danced upon the baize, while his wide stare bounced about the room in a forged, nonchalant manner. A quick poke of his tongue wet his lips. The dealer paused to see if Lord Snively would join the game by making a bet, but Snively ignored him. The dealer continued his distribution of cards.

Knowing the man as he did, Burke would have bet every stack of chips before him Lord Snively had not come in to play cards, or any other game of chance or skill, but to partake in his preferred entertainment. The man had entered the establishment with gossip he was anxious to share.

"Haven't you heard?" Snively asked when no one took his bait.

Burke glanced at his friend.

"Don't look at me," Drew said. He shifted sideways in a casual lean. "I've been in this gilded pit all day. It could be raining elephants, for all I know."

Burke grinned at the truth of his friend's humor. If Drew wasn't gambling, drinking, or chasing skirts, he was making those around him laugh. What most didn't know about Drew, was beneath the abundance of wayward behavior and indulgences, beat the heart of a good man. Burke hoped Drew would calm his ways before they landed him in trouble too big to traverse.

"What's happened?" Lord Foxboro asked in a distracted tone as he awaited his next card. Perspiration glistened along his hairline and over his lip. "None of us have heard a thing."

"Truly, none of you have heard?" Snively asked.

"Oh, good god, man. Enough with the dramatic preamble," Drew said. "Out with it."

Snively huffed, feigned his leave with a shift of his soft shoulders. When no one begged his news, he gave in and told them what he'd come in to say.

"There's been a shooting," Snively said, wide eyes full of histrionics. The men at the table gave him their attention, but it flitted away when offered no details to support the dire account. So, he added, "Quite a bloody mess, too, from what I've heard."

After a quick, disgusted peek at what the dealer had given him, Lord Foxboro flipped his cards face down on the table and said, "And just who was shot?"

"I don't precisely know. But it happened right in the Sennett's dooryard, so I assume it's the lord or lady of the house."

Burke swung his head around with a glare so fierce Lord Snively cringed. The earl was on his feet in an instant, his cards fluttering the short distance before landing about his stack of chips.

Chapter 8

The butler forbade him entrance.

Burke didn't give a damn what the priggish, over-starched man deemed to allow or not allow. He'd only made the polite request to see Lord or Lady Sennett out of civility. Two words into the butler's second refusal, Burke barged through the front door.

Upon striding in to the Sennett's front parlor from whence came murmured voices, the first thing Burke saw was a bucket of bloody bandages. Sick dread bloomed in his stomach. In a quick assessment, he took in the rest of the scene.

Wearing a bloodstained shirt, Ashton paced before the sofa where the doctor sat wrapping Lewis's arm in a stark white bandage. Rose sat on Lewis's other side, holding his hand. Burke scrutinized her head to shoe, twice, before her apparent state of wellness permitted him a full breath.

Lewis, on the other hand, was pale much beyond his normal fairness. The man sweated to dampen his white shirt, with the left sleeve cut off, against his body. Rose had a cloth in her free hand and used it to dab at his brow. She spared Burke a bare glance, as all her attention was on Lewis. The fear and worry in her eyes made Burke want to kill whoever had inflicted such pain into this home.

"My lord," the butler said in a huff as he stomped

into the room. "I informed this, this man it was not the proper time for a visit. He shoved his way in."

"Burke," Ashton said upon seeing him. "It's all right, Stefon. Thank you. You may go."

The butler lifted his chin, blew air through his nose, spun away, and marched from the room.

Burke crossed the floor. "Who did this?"

"None of us saw," Ashton said, his voice tight with the same raw emotions haunting Rose's eyes. "The three of us were standing outside. I can't even say from which direction the shot came. There are abundant shrubs in which the scoundrel could have hidden. The sound echoed all around us, and then Rose was screaming, Lewis was on the ground, bleeding." The man closed his eyes, as if seeing the horror again.

Burke glanced at Lewis, slumped back on the sofa, appearing on the verge of a faint, Rose speaking to him in a calm voice. Her composed demeanor belied the terror and the tears she held back in valiant form.

To Ashton, Burke said, "Have you received any threats?"

"No," Ashton answered before flicking his head, signaling Burke to follow him to the far side of the room. In a low voice, he said, "There are some people who...have suspicions of what they consider impropriety."

The man did not lower his eyes in shame, but rather, held Burke's gaze in a hard one of his own, as if itching for an excuse to use his fists on someone.

"Make a list of anyone you even suspect," Burke said. "I'll take it to Bow Street myself."

For a moment, Ashton's expression did not change. Burke waited through the next half minute or so as the man absorbed everything encompassed in the statement; the acceptance, the kindness, the utter lack of condemnation.

The doctor closed his black bag with a snap, clasped it, and stood. "Well, my work here is done," he said.

Gray hair hung limp an inch or so over his bushy, gray brows. His rumpled clothing gave him an overall disheveled appearance. His blue eyes, however, showed every bit of his sharp intelligence.

"Will he be all right?" Ashton asked as he approached the man. His concern flickered to Lewis, and then back to the doctor.

"The ball passed clean through his arm and missed the bone. Barring any complications, Lord Da Ville should recover quite nicely. See he gets plenty of rest and hearty, vegetable broth. I've left laudanum for the pain and instructions with Lady Sennett on how to use it. Tomorrow I'll return to check on him."

Rose walked the doctor to the door and Ashton took her place on the sofa beside Lewis. Their butler glided into the room and said, "I've turned down the bed and laid out a fresh sleeping gown."

"Thank you, Stefon," Ashton said. "Come now, Lewis. You must rest."

Before Burke could cross the room and assist, the butler brushed passed him to help Lewis up to bed. Burke stood alone for no more than a moment or two before Rose returned.

The raspberry color of her gown helped mask the sight of blood, but the stains still drew her eyes until she dragged them away. Only Rose could manage to look both strong and fragile at the same time. He took a step toward her, but she paced to the sideboard, wiping her eyes as she did.

"May I offer you a cup of tea, or would you prefer a brandy?" she said.

"No, but I think you should have one, a brandy, that is."

With a slight shake of her head, Rose said, "I've never had a drink in my life."

"Never? Not even so much as a glass of wine?"

"No. My...I've seen what overindulgence can do to a person. And I prefer keeping my wits about me." Staring past him toward the window, beyond which dusk was darkening into night, she said, "I could do with some fresh air, though. I believe a walk is in order."

"No," Burke said with all finality.

Rose shot him a hard glance. For the first time since he walked through the door, Burke had her full attention. "I was not asking your permission," she said.

Burke almost laughed through his irritation at her insolence. Perhaps it was the trauma of the day, but at the moment, the woman had more backbone than sense.

"It's not a good idea," Burke told her. "The shooter is still out there."

Her eyes shifted from him to the window, and then back to him again. "But they were after Lewis," she said.

"Perhaps."

"He was the one shot." She glanced at the bloodstains on her bodice before raising her eyes back to Burke. "We were all three out there."

"Were you all standing close together?"

"Yes."

"There was enough wind this afternoon to affect the ball's trajectory. Or, the shooter's aim could have been poor. Perhaps one of you moved at just the right time. The fact is, Rose, any one of you may have been the target. Do you know someone who might want to harm any of the three of you?"

She cast her eyes downward before shaking her head. Maybe he saw denial. Or it could have been deceit.

"No," Rose said in a quiet voice, still looking at the floor. "I…don't know anyone who would have done such a thing."

Burke saw the lie, heard it in her halted response. There was no mistaking it. Why wouldn't she want the killer caught? Was she protecting someone? That she might have had a hand in the shooting seemed unlikely. Or was it? He wondered as his thoughts turned dark.

His mother could lie through an innocent smile or false tears and be quite convincing. Burke bought every lie she sold until their ruthless pounding quashed the trust of his childhood. His father pretended belief until his third or fourth drink, when rage wielded its brawn and held his face to the truth. Burke had been a fool for having ever trusted in either one of his parents.

He directed a contemplative eye to Rose.

Desperation can be a driving force, capable of the highest deceit. Rose's fretting might well be a facade. Examining her circumstance from a particular perspective, one could even say she had motive.

If the gunman had killed her husband, she would inherit everything. She wouldn't be the first person to arrange a spouse's murder. Rose had fled an untenable situation and married Ashton for protection, when in fact all she required was his money.

Burke's eyes followed her as she paced before the low-burning hearth. Occasionally she slowed for a long glance out the window where night was quick to descend. Her hand drifted to the demure neckline of her gown, fingertips giving a subtle tug. Was she afraid for her life, for the lives of her companions? Or was she imagining the hangman's noose tightening around her slender throat?

Burke shoved at the darkness. He was too much the cynic, too ready to believe the worst in people. That he was often right in thinking so didn't suit this time. Rose was not a killer.

She nearly killed her brother-in-law.

The lecher got what he deserved. She defended herself with admirable resolve.

"Change your gown and get your wrap," Burke told her. "I know a place where we can walk without concern."

****

"Where are we going?" Rose asked once they'd settled into the lush cushions of Burke's carriage.

"My gardens."

At his words, Rose clasped her hands in her lap and stared out the window, seeing nothing but a looming scandal. This was beyond improper. Then again, if Society knew the truth of her life, well, it was all a looming scandal. Lewis's words ran through her head. If she is causing no harm, then there is no harm. It was just a walk, after all.

A walk alone with a man she found exceedingly attractive, and had already shared a brief indiscretion.

Burke Darington was also the man with whom her

husband had encouraged her to have an affair. After much hinting around, Ashton had said so straight out upon leaving the Darington estate the night of the opera. Rose almost laughed at the grand degree of impropriety in her life.

Such close proximity to Burke, to his exuding masculinity, drew her mind to the night of her first kiss, the taste of passion she'd experienced with the man sitting beside her.

And here she was again, alone in a carriage with him.

On their way to his home.

"Lewis's injury will heal in quick time," Burke said. "Fret not. You will all be hosting parties again before you know it."

Relieved he thought her quiet contemplations were for the day's horrid event, and not what this evening might yet hold, Rose responded to what he said, instead of what she was thinking. "I'm concerned for Lewis, of course. But I don't much care for parties."

"No? It's been my experience most women adore social gatherings, soirees, balls, even a costume."

"I gravitate toward more tranquil endeavors. Reading, afternoon tea with loved ones, walks out of doors. I adore walking outside. I enjoy doing so in all of the seasons. Ashton and Lewis have been very accommodating, strolling with me in all manner of weather. I find it quite pleasant."

"More so than donning an expensive gown and dancing through the night?"

"Yes, very much so. All I want from life at this point is to be left in peace."

Burke kept a thoughtful gaze on her for a long time

before shifting to stare out the window.

The carriage made a right turn into a curving, torch-lit drive. As the house came into view, Rose caught her breath at the stateliness. The last time she was here, she'd been engrossed in her efforts to convince Ashton to make theirs a short visit, and had not so much as peeked out the window of their carriage. She took it all in now.

Lord Darington's home had to be three times the size of the house she shared with Ashton and Lewis, and she considered their home grand. Three floors of white stone, a center-gabled roof, and each end capped with corbelled corner turrets with pointed tops.

Light burned a glowing welcome from each of several tall, arched windows along the ground floor. Between those windows, box hedges, waist-high and thick as the length of a tub, lined the wall of the house. Marble pillars supported a grand porte-cochere of pale gray stone on the right side of the mansion. The driver pulled to a stop underneath.

After exiting the carriage, Burke escorted Rose to the gardens by going around the house, rather than through it. Relief eased her mind a bit. The thought of being alone with him inside his home had her already unsettled nerves frayed. With that concern removed, Rose could better take in her surroundings.

The full moon was a great lamp hung centered in the sky, casting a mystical, soothing light. Their feet sounded on the paving stones as they passed through a vine-covered archway broad enough to accommodate them both side by side.

Hedgerows made solid walls for about the first ten or fifteen feet. After which, chest-high shrubbery cut into a neat triangle split the path in two directions. Burke guided her to the right where rows of red and yellow tulips a dozen deep lined both sides of the walking path.

"Is this where you grew up?" she asked.

"It is," he said, taking a scan of the moonlit gardens.

Rose followed his line of sight.

The foliage stretched farther than she could see, even with the generous light of the moon. She tried picturing him as a little boy, romping about with a stick as a sword, playing pirate or soldier or knight in battle armor. It was difficult to imagine him ever being so lighthearted. Aside from a couple of inappropriate grins, his manner, his bearing, even his countenance, almost always bore a staid veil.

"This must have been a wonderful place to be a child," Rose said, urging him to talk, as she'd become curious about his past.

A few more steps carried them through a pause quiet of all but their shoes on the paving stones. When Burke finally spoke, he did not respond to her comment.

"Does Lord Da Ville share a residence with you and your husband?"

Rose cast a small but wry smile his way. "You're not up on the more faint of rumors, are you?"

"I'm not up on any rumors, if I can help it," he said with a touch of disdain. Then his tone turned candid. "I'm not passing judgment, Rose. I only want to find who is responsible for shooting Lewis."

As they passed a long line of topiary carved in curves and waves, intermingled with perfectly round balls of designed growth in varying sizes, Rose slanted him a long glance.

She'd never told a soul of the arrangement in which she lived. If Burke was telling the truth, however, and she sensed he was, trusting him might well serve the greater good. Besides, she was sure he already knew, and had asked the question as a fit opening.

"We are all three very careful. Before I came along, Ashton and Lewis were cautious in every way. Ashton keeps a minimal household staff. Those who work for us are loyal and well paid to keep their tongues behind their teeth. It's the reason no one outside our home can speak ill of us with any certainty."

She paused then, to see what Burke might say. Until she spoke again, nothing but the easy pace of their footsteps and the garden crickets sounded in the night.

"When it comes to the two of them," Rose continued. "It's merely whispered gossip and spoken only amongst the most salacious rumormongers lest someone call them out, or worse, put their word at risk of coming into question. Lewis maintains a townhouse not far from us. On occasion, he entertains there to keep appearances. But yes, we all live together in the same home."

She stopped walking then and faced him. Crickets played their music without the accompaniment of their footfalls as she awaited his reaction to what she'd told him.

Tilting his head downward to meet her gaze, Burke said, "The gossips will get no confirmation from me."

It had been so long since she'd spoken with such

openness to anyone outside her home. None of the small handful of friends she'd made in her work on the Foundling Project knew her marriage was so far from conventional. Before she said more, though, she needed to know how much Burke knew about her.

"Do you know how I came to Ashton's house?"

"He told me," Burke said. His face then hinted at a smile. "Did you really smash your sister's husband in the head with a pig?"

Rose hoped the moonlight was not bright enough for him to see her flush of embarrassment. If he knew about what she'd done to Piers, he must think her the worst kind of harridan. She wouldn't lie, though, or even soften her deed. If he turned from her now it was just as well.

Rose held his gaze and said, "I did."

"Good."

To her astonishment, Burke gave her a full smile then, along with a nod of approval. It was the same expression Ashton had shown when she told him what she had done.

Most men would have seen her punished for such an offense against her own guardian, not praised. It seems Lord Darington shared certain unusual traits with her husband. She wondered if he shared others, or if he differed in his carnal interests.

"I envisioned it." The words pounced from her mouth without her permission, as if she and Lord Darington were old friends, as if he was a confidant and she was free to speak her thoughts. At first, Rose wanted to take back her words and put a halt to the conversation while it was still amicable, and before it went too far, but then she didn't.

Burke tipped his head to the side a bit, his sea-green eyes ever focused on hers. "Is that so?"

"Yes," Rose said. "Every time Piers put a hand on me I thought about what it would be like if I not only had the rights of self-sovereignty, but the physical strength to overpower him."

"It sounds to me as if you did quite well with what you had."

His approval shouldn't have mattered, but for a reason she could not identify, it did. Perhaps it was the day's fright, knowing a killer was still out there wanting to see either she or one of her two closest friends dead. Or maybe Lewis's words, combined with Ashton's encouragements, emboldened her. Whatever the reason, she held tight to her courage before it slipped away and she escaped into cowardice.

Rose lifted her chin and said, "Of late, my mind's wanderings have been about you. About..."

It was as far as she could speak. She simply did not know how to pursue this any further. She wasn't even certain what 'further' entailed. Her sister had never spoken to her about matters of intimacy. Ashton would explain it all to her, she had no doubt. But she was too embarrassed to ask. Besides, up until quite recently, she hadn't been all that curious. As far as she was concerned, Piers had shown her more than enough to know such intimacies held no interest to her.

Or so she'd thought.

For a moment, Burke stood as still as the moon nailed to the sky, and Rose was sure she'd been too audacious. The man must think her far too bold for a lady and without due shame.

Slow and focused, he stepped toward her then,

making her think of a lion stalking his prey. He didn't stop until he stood so close to her she could swear the heat from his body warmed hers. His hand crossed the short distance between them, unhurried, dreamlike. The brush of his fingers along her jaw tingled. A slight pressure tipped her face upward. He bent, slow, not stopping until his lips were but a breath from hers.

"About," he said in a low rumble, with a brush of his lips against hers. When he lifted his head, he was still close enough to warm her nose with his breath. "…This?"

"Yes," she whispered back. And he again lowered his head.

The kiss was barely there, a mere touch, a tantalizing taste of this man. Rose strained upward, wanting more.

"And this?" he asked, touching his tongue to her lower lip. When she opened for him, he withdrew, just a little.

"Yes," she said, tugging on his lapels.

His other hand was on her back, drawing her closer. Rose went willingly. At her eagerness, his passions enflamed. His kisses grew wild as he held firm her head in the clasp of his strong hand, keeping her in place. Not that it mattered. She didn't want to leave.

The hand on her back slid downward, lower, and lower still, until he was cupping her, drawing her against him in an intimate manner ripe with sin. Rose's breath became elusive while her heart pounded a mad beat against her ribs.

His other hand left her neck and slid around to her throat, gliding down, never lifting from her body. Then, in a move bold enough to shock, he caressed her breast.

A thunderbolt of sensation shook her senses, leaving her dazed and unsteady. Rose made a sound. She knew she did. It was foreign, breathy, and distant, from a faraway world beckoning her with exotic promise.

Suddenly, everything tilted and Rose could swear she was floating. It took her a moment to realize Burke had lifted her into his arms. Then he was walking.

She wrapped her arms around his neck and every few steps he stopped to feed her more kisses. The cool night air, the crickets, the moon, all disappeared, along with the sound of his footfalls. He no longer walked on paving stones, but on a wood floor, then a carpet that absorbed the sound. They were inside his house.

Flashes of portraits and candlelight caught the edge of her vision as Burke carried her through his home.

He kissed her again, long and thorough, before carrying her up a wide, winding staircase. She could put a stop to this now. She should. However, if there existed a good reason for her to demand he set her back on her feet and take her home, it hadn't the strength to tame her wants.

He carried her down a long corridor. Light ebbed and flowed on the fringe of her vision from the flames of interspersed wall sconces. The pulse of light and dim accentuated the excited strangeness of the moment.

And then he stopped. They were before a grand set of double doors Rose could only assume led to his bedchamber.

"If you want to leave, say so now," Burke said, gazing down on her, his hooded eyes teeming with passion, his entire face expressive of his desire. A husky pitch thickened his already deep voice. "Once I carry you through this door, Rose, there's no going back."

Rose knew a moment of trepidation. He was giving her a chance to leave and if she didn't, this night would change her forever.

Her life was content now, the way things were. But then she remembered the words of her companions. Life is unpredictable and could end at any moment. Lewis's almost ended this very day. It could have been her, and maybe tomorrow it would. She did not want to live her life without knowing this part of womanhood.

Just tell him, Lewis had said. And he will take care of the rest.

Rose gazed up at his handsome face, at her desire reflected in the darkened depths of his eyes. Yes, she wanted him, too, wanted to know about these pleasures of which Ashton had spoken. She wanted more than the mere brush with intimacy Burke had shown her in his carriage.

"I don't want to leave," she told him, certain of that truth.

Burke shoved the door open with his foot and carried her over the threshold.

Inside, he backed against the door until it clicked shut. He set her on her feet, but he did not let go. For that, Rose was grateful. For her full blend of feelings, excitement, longing, even a bit of fear, left her balance a tremulous thing.

A small fire burned behind the grate. The flickering orange glow was the only light in the huge room. A variety of thick rugs softened the parquet floor. She caught sight of dark, masculine furnishings, a bed big enough for four among them.

Burke bent to her, taking her earlobe into his

mouth for a small, but ever-sensual kiss. When he stood upright, her cloak dropped to the floor.

Before Rose had time to think about that, about what might come next, his lips were on hers. This was not like the frenzied kiss they'd shared in the garden. He took his time, exploring her mouth, inviting her into his. She calmed so at the unhurried pace, she hadn't realized he'd unbuttoned her gown until it fell loose around her shoulders. It dropped to the floor in a soft rustle of fabric, soon followed by her petticoat.

Burke led her to step out of the garments before trailing his mouth down her throat, nibbling light kisses at the sensitive skin just over the top of her thin chemise.

He lowered himself then, his lips dragging more kisses across the fine lawn, not stopping until his mouth closed over the delicate fabric covering her breast. He opened his mouth farther and dragged his tongue across her tautening bud. Rose gasped, leaning against him as if she had no choice.

Burke drew back, blowing soft breezes on the dampened fabric. Her lips parted as she sucked in a full breath. Rose clutched his head, intending to thrust him away, as the sensation threatened to overwhelm her. All she did was hold onto him. Burke brought his lips to her again and kissed his way downward, over her stomach, upon her most intimate places.

She would have stepped back, thought to, for such could not be at all proper. But he held firm to her thighs, having what he wanted. Rose let him. She wanted it, too.

His fingers slid unhurried down the backs of her stocking-clad legs. At the end of the journey, he slipped one shoe from her foot and tossed it aside, then the other. Beneath her chemise, his warm hands glided back up her legs, searing a trail and drawing a gasp from her.

Burke looped his fingers in her garters before sliding them off. One by one, he removed her stockings, slow and methodical, his fingers sampling every inch of skin he laid bare.

Burke stood, taking her chemise with him, lifting it over her head, and dropping it on the floor with the rest of her garments. She stood before him, naked, suffused in a sudden vulnerability exposed to him this way. He must have sensed her apprehension, for when his hand crossed the short distance between them, he touched only her hands.

"I want to look at you, Rose."

While she could not quite meet his eyes, she did not cower. He continued to keep a firm hold on her hands. A small string of pops sounded from the grate, and then the room was quiet again, and still, but for the travel of his gaze over her body.

What was he thinking? Was he disappointed?

Burke came to her again, close. He slid the pins from her hair and dropped them to the floor. Once her locks were free, he combed them with his fingers, and swept it all behind her shoulders where the ends brushed against her lower back. He retreated then, and continued his visual pursuit.

Rose grew uncomfortable under his scrutiny. She considered grabbing her clothes to cover herself and leaving, when he finally spoke.

"You have nothing to be embarrassed about, Rose. You are by far the most beautiful woman I have ever seen."

A question popped into her head, making her forget her state of undress. She set aside for a moment all thoughts about the path upon which she was embarking. Rose met his eyes now.

"Just how many unclothed women have you seen?" she asked.

Burke chuckled as he drew her close. "Rose, as of this moment, I can say in all honesty I can't remember a single one of them."

She smiled into their kiss, and soon thoughts of the others who'd come before her were no more than ashes beneath the fire. He lifted her again, this time, laying her upon the soft mattress. As he removed his shoes, shed his jacket, and yanked off his cravat, Rose gathered the counterpane so she could cover herself.

"Don't, Rose. Don't deny me this vision."

She granted his want, though it was difficult. However, as Burke removed his shirt, she found herself forgetting her own nudity.

Never before had she seen a man bared so. Could they all be this magnificent? Arms of sculpted muscle boasted his strength. The broadness of his chest did not diminish without his clothing, sprinkled with dark hairs marking a trail into his trousers.

He stopped what he was doing. Burke was watching her watch him. Her face must have colored because he smiled the way he always did when something embarrassed her.

"It's all right to look, Rose. Do I please you?"

She raised her head, allowing her vision a slow climb up his half-clothed body until her eyes met his. "Yes. I like the way you look. I like it very much."

"Good," he said through a grin before bending to kiss her.

He drew back to stand again, but she wanted more kisses. To her good fortune, Burke was happy to oblige.

He lay with her, kissing, touching, their passions rising. She grabbed his shoulders, hard muscle beneath heated skin. The feel of such utter masculinity further elevated her whetted senses.

He trailed kisses from her lips to her breast. This time, no fabric served as a barrier. Rose sucked in a breath as he drew her farther into his mouth. He shifted to her other breast, taking his time, building an inexplicable tension inside her.

Burke then kissed his way back to her mouth, tasting her bottom lip, and then her top, before delving in for a string of heated kisses. His hands roved, exploring where his lips had been, gliding down, farther down. At the power of his intimate caress, Rose cried out his name.

He whispered in her ear, calming words, though she couldn't say what they were. She thought to take his hand away, as the sensations were too potent to bear. But then he stopped, and she found she didn't want that either.

What was he doing? But then she knew. He was removing his trousers. The reservations of propriety and fear of the unknown slipped in to cool her passions. When Burke gazed at her again, he must have seen. It amazed her how attuned this man was to her feelings.

"It's not too late to stop this," he said, offering her egress even though it went against his earlier statement about no going back. His gentle fingers brushed the hair away from her forehead. "All you have to do is say so."

She considered it. She truly did. Her life had been fine. These last months had given her naught about which to complain. Well, almost. She would never have a child. The sacrifice was huge, but peace always comes at a price. If she took this night for herself, for nothing other than selfish reasons, who was she harming? No one. No one at all.

"I'm not changing my mind," Rose said. "Are you?"

He gave an airy chuckle, low and rough. "Not for all the fortunes yet to be mined."

He kissed her then, moving as he did. His knee between hers, nudging her thighs so he could shift his body atop hers with intimate pressure. His breath grew harsh as his body began a gentle pulse, pressing against her, backing away, pressing against her again. Soon, Rose's breath was as ragged as his was. She raised her hips to meet him, but, to her frustration, Burke took himself back.

"Tell me you want me," he said on a hard breath. His eyes stayed on hers, the entirety of his body rigid. The pressure of his weight was both frightening and exquisite. "Tell me, Rose."

"I want you, Burke. I do."

Rose cried out at the sudden and unexpected pain. She struggled to get away from him, but he held her still with the strength and mass of his body.

"Be still, love," he whispered into her ear. "It will pass. I promise. Just be still for a moment."

Rose did as he said, but she didn't believe him. It was all a lie. Everything Ashton had told her about pleasures was all a lie. This wasn't good. This wasn't enjoyable. It only hurt.

He continued to whisper comforts until time proved him right. The pain passed, just as he said it would. A yearning she couldn't explain or understand took its place.

Rose opened her eyes. Burke gazed down at her, serious, concerned, his temples damp from his restraint. Still, he didn't move. Using his thumb, he brushed away a tear.

"Please don't cry, love," he said, touching his lips to her brow. "It will be better soon. I promise." He kissed her again, stroked her face with the backs of his fingers, and smoothed back her hair. After another minute or so of his tending, he said, "Rose, are you all right?"

"I…I think so. Are we done now?"

The smile he gave her was sweet, brimming with affection. "Only with the bad part."

With his gentle motions, an inner heat built, coiling, searching, wanting. As if the same urgency charged through him, so too became his movements. And then, in a sudden rush, the world erupted.

Rose flew to the stars on mighty wings, becoming part of the mystery and magic of life. She was free of all restraints, no longer grounded to this earth. Her body soared. Her mind, uncomprehending. Intensity of pleasure so overtook her, she could not have uttered her own name.

****

Rose awoke to a dreamy haze and waning night, the promise of full dawn not far off. For a moment, she didn't know where she was. Nothing of her surroundings were familiar, not the room, or its furnishings. She didn't even feel familiar. That was a strange thought, however accurate.

With a slow, quiet motion, she turned her head. Sound asleep on his back beside her lay Burke. The sheet draped just below the firm muscle of his bare chest. She knew he was bare beneath the sheet, too. She was just as naked.

It shouldn't have surprised her, but for an instant, it did. She'd made love with him last night in this very bed, more than once. The wonders of it played in her head. Never could she have guessed such pleasures existed. Yes, she was different now. She had a secret and her secret made her smile.

While she had no regrets, quite the opposite, Rose did not want to feed the rumor mill. Discretion was of particular importance, considering her living situation. His servants would be up soon, readying for the day, moving about the house. She had to be gone before anyone saw her.

She considered waking Burke. No, she'd better not. He might want her to stay. As much as she'd like to, to remain in this house even a minute more was too risky. A glance at the window showed her morning's first light peeking above the horizon. She needed to go, now.

As quiet as possible, she slipped from the bed and dressed. Once, when she dropped a shoe and it made a light thud on the rug, Burke stirred. She froze in place. She didn't even breathe. If he woke, even if he didn't want her to stay, he would insist on seeing her home. All it would take was the two of them being seen by one pair of eyes and her whole world could be destroyed, as well as the carefully crafted world for Ashton and Lewis.

She had to crawl on the floor to find all of her hair

pins in the meager light. As best she could without a mirror, she twisted her hair into a knot at the back of her head and stuffed in the pins.

Burke sighed once, adorable in his sleep, before shifting to his side and facing away from her. Seconds later, Rose crept from the room.

Leaving through the front door was far too risky. So, once at the bottom of the broad, winding staircase, Rose wound through the halls making her way toward the back of the still quiet house. As she passed a doorway, the glass panes in the room beyond showed the light of early dawn. It showed something else, too. The room was Burke's study.

The last thing she should be doing is lingering in this house. Every passing minute inched her closer to scandal. The temptation to know more of this man, however, overruled her good sense. With little more than a quick glance around, Rose slipped into the room.

Fully stocked bookshelves covered an entire wall, save for a narrow set of French doors framing a perfect view of a colorful rose garden. On one side of the room, two wingback chairs covered in sage green fabric sat on opposite sides of a low, round table. The other side of the room hosted an impressive, mahogany pedestal desk. Rose circled the desk, dragging her hand across the top of the sage, tall-back chair behind it.

She caught his scent there, clean, masculine, unique to Burke, she was sure. Rose wondered if anyone else could detect it, or if that was something exclusive to lovers.

A smile touched her lips as her attention went to his desktop. It was busy, but orderly. Three varying sized stacks of papers lay in a neat row across the middle. A crystal pen and ink set sat on the right side. On the left, a small pile of notes.

A noise from above drew her attention. Was Burke awake? A better assumption was the servants going about their morning routines and getting ready for the day. Perhaps Burke's valet was already in the master's suite tending to him. Would Burke come looking for her once he saw she had left? Enough of this. It was past time for her to be gone.

Rose walked toward the edge of the desk and was halfway through her next step when she spotted something familiar, very familiar. It was a leaf and stem design done in three shades of green. She'd helped Ashton and Lewis choose those colors, as well as the design. After a quick glance at the door, she tugged the heavy foolscap from the stack.

It was the invitation to their soiree. Rose barely gave it a glance when a thud sounded just above her head, causing her to jump and drop the card to the floor. She scooped it up, intending to tuck it back into the pile where she found it and be gone from this house posthaste. Until the writing on the back caught her eye. Ashton's handwriting.

Rose read the note. She couldn't help it. She knew of no personalized messages on any of the invitations they'd sent. And then she read it a second time, forcing aside her denial at the implication. Ashton had a special, very personal matter to discuss with Burke? In an instant, Rose found herself at the edge of a storm-darkened sea, where a colossal wave rolled over her.

No. Oh, no. It couldn't be. Ashton would not have orchestrated what she and Burke had shared last night. But he had. All she need do is think on recent events, and the truth was as clear as the coming day.

It all made sense now. Her husband had left her at the table the night of their soiree, alone with a man she didn't know, something he normally would not have done. Then there was Burke's invitation to have them join him at his home after the theatre. Everyone knew Burke Darington *never* entertained. Ashton and Lewis had drawn Lady Hortence away from them, again leaving her and Burke to converse in private. The men had arranged it all.

Her humiliation and fury joined forces and raged an uncontainable tempest. The invitation crumpled within her constricting fist before she hurled the ball of foolscap across the room. Rose found the back door and strode home, her anger mounting with every stomp of her foot.

Chapter 9

"How could you, Ashton?" Rose all but shouted after storming into the breakfast room.

She stood across the table where Ashton and Lewis sat in the early morning light, both attired in varying shades of plum with dark neckcloths and crisp, white shirts. A sling supported Lewis's arm. His color was good and his nearly empty plate attested the return of his appetite.

Rose noticed, and was thankful for, these things only at the very furthest edge of her turbulent emotions. The vibrancy of her wrath diminished everything outside the awareness of what her husband had done.

"Tell me," Rose raged on. "Did the two of you make a bet on the day and time I would lose my virginity?"

Ashton set his fork down beside his half-eaten meal and stood. When Lewis scooted his chair back to do the same, Ashton placed a hand on his shoulder to keep him in his seat. Her husband then returned his attention to her. He had the gall to look not the least bit sorry. His lack of contrition only made Rose angrier.

"First of all," Ashton said. "No, Lewis and I did not make any bets in regards to your relationship with Burke. You should know we'd never do anything so vulgar. Second, I spoke with Burke because I could not allow you to live your life a virtual spinster. Third—"

Rose's hand slapped over her heart. "*My* life. It's *my* life, Ashton, for *me* to decide. We had a bargain. You had no right!"

Lewis folded his hands and lowered them to his lap. "Rose, dear, Ashton only made the request to Lord Darington out of concern for your happiness. His intentions were all for the good, I assure you."

"How can you defend this, Lewis? I am utterly humiliated!"

"Rose," said Ashton. "You're viewing this from a skewed perspective. Besides, it's all irrelevant anyway. The fact of the matter is, Lord Darington—"

"Irrelevant?" Rose said, too angry to listen to his excuses. Nothing he said would justify what they'd done to her. She paced the length of the table in short, crisp steps. "Tell me, Ashton. Am I truly so hideous you must beg for lovers as a vagrant begs for alms?"

"Now Rose, that's not at all the way of things. Do not even think it. I apologize from my depths if my efforts caused you distress. My intentions were only to see to your happiness."

Stefon strode into the fray before Ashton could say anything more. The normally unruffled servant had a vexed appearance about him, forehead wrinkled, jaw stiff. He stopped just inside the doorway and addressed Ashton.

"Lord Darington is in the front parlor," Stefon said. He shot a brief but sharp glance toward Rose. "He's come to see her ladyship."

"Good," Rose said with a curt nod. She spun toward the door. "I can settle things with all you arrogant, high-handed men in one morning."

Rose marched into the parlor, and wilted a tad

when she faced Burke. Well, maybe a bit more than a tad.

He swung around as soon as her footsteps sounded on the parquet floor. The anger flashing in his eyes, the harsh set of his focus, and the taut refrain of his stance, stole from her mind the words she'd composed on her walk from the breakfast room.

"Well I see you made it home safely," he said.

From his surly tone, she wasn't at all sure if he meant that as something good. The fury radiating from him had her rethinking her stealth exit this morning. Perhaps she should have awakened him, or at least left a note. Thoughts of a note, however, reminded her of the invitation. It reminded her this man had seduced her by way of her husband's request. Suddenly, Rose's anger equaled his.

"Yes," she said, clipping her voice. "It wasn't too far and I didn't want to wake you."

In two long strides, he stood before her. Burke's powerful hands gripped her upper arms. His expression managed to become even more furious than a moment before.

"You will *never* sneak away from me again."

"Let go of me," Rose said. She fought to jerk away from him, but he only tightened his grip. "Stop this, you're hurting me."

The second the words passed her lips, he released her. Burke stepped back and ran his hands through his hair. He did not look any calmer. In fact, the man had the fervid appearance of a boxer ready to leap into the ropes and pummel his opponent to mush.

He swung a fierce glare on her. Rose refused to cower beneath his intimidation. Instead, she raised her chin.

"I only meant to be gone before your servants were about." She'd grant him an explanation, but not an apology, not after what she'd learned this morning. "I'm accustomed to guarding against gossip."

"I can handle my servants," he shot back. "You need not worry about them." After but a moment's pause, he said, "And why are *you* so angry?"

Rose did her best to keep the wrath prominent in her voice, but feared some of the hurt streamed through. At this point, however, it almost didn't matter. What they'd had was over. Yet, Rose could not stop herself from asking, "Was any of it true, Lord Darington?"

"Lord Darington?"

"Or was it all a script Ashton helped you compose to charm me into your bed, perhaps with some help from Lewis."

Her humiliation pried into her heart, splitting it in two. She shouldn't care this much. It wasn't as though he'd been courting her, as if the future held anything more for them than a secret liaison. Still, the pain was real. More so than his attraction to her had been. All she meant to him was a favor done for a friend. He blurred in the tears filling her eyes before she managed to blink them away. She would not let him see her mortification.

In a gentled tone, Burke said, "Rose, what are you talking about?"

"While I was trying to find my way out a back door this morning, I wandered into your study." She jammed her hands on her hips and shot him a scathing glare. "I saw the note."

"What note?"

"You are far too smart to play the fool, Lord

Darington. I saw the note Ashton wrote to you on the back of the invitation."

Understanding smoothed his face and he nodded before saying, "You searched through my desk?"

"I wasn't searching." Rose huffed out a breath. "I know very little about you. I was curious. The invitation was sitting right there on top. Well, almost on top. Oh, don't change the subject."

"Rose, I declined Ashton's request."

"You...How can you say that? Have you forgotten last night?"

His grin was immediate. "If I live to be a thousand, I will never forget last night." He became serious then. "Rose, what happened between the two of us was because of us, not because of some ridiculous request."

She longed to believe him. It stunned her how much she wanted to feel confident he was telling her the truth. Now that they'd both expelled some of their anger, Rose had an almost desperate need to trust the sincerity projected in his steady gaze.

"You might have told me about the note last night," she said.

"You might have given me the chance this morning."

His point was valid. They both could have better handled the situation. She believed the worst without giving him a chance to explain. From the moment she read Ashton's blasted note on the back of the invitation, she'd assumed their affair contrived.

If he was telling the truth, such was not at all the way of things. What happened between them was all of their own doing. And if Burke would believe she'd truly left this morning to avoid gossip, and not him, they could leave behind the day's awful beginning.

At the softening of their expressions, an unspoken truce passed between them. Then, Burke's countenance changed to concern and he eyed her with critical scrutiny.

"How do you..." He paused and blinked before finishing his sentence in a lowered voice, speaking to her in an intimate fashion. "Are you all right, today?"

She dipped her head a bit and nodded. "I'm fine."

"When I awoke and found you'd sneaked off—"

"I did not sneak off." At his stern look, she had to concede. After all, he was correct in his assessment of her exit this morning. In his place, she would have felt the same. Maybe he was right about the other, too. Perhaps what happened between them was indeed genuine. Her heart lightened at the possibility.

"All right," she said. "Maybe I did sneak off. I assure you, it was not my intention to upset you."

"I would say the same. Next time—"

"Next time?"

His gaze intensified, became seductive to the point of heating her. "Oh yes, Rose, there will be a next time. And I might just tie you to the bed to guarantee you'll be there when I awake."

Her shock tugged his lips into a smile. Rose could but stare at the man. Was he joking? In all truth, she couldn't tell.

"Don't look so appalled," Burke said, before leaning down to whisper in her ear. "You might like it."

Rose gasped before muttering, "Insufferable men."

Burke chuckled and the last of the tension dissipated.

"Do you have plans for later today?" he asked.

Ashton entered the room just then and said, "We're meeting the builder at the property about the new foundling home." His eyes shifted between Burke and Rose. "Is it safe?"

"I don't know," Burke said with a slight grin. "Where's that pig of hers?"

The two men chuckled.

Rose's eyes widened. Her mouth opened a moment before she found her words. "That isn't the least bit funny."

Their mirth exploded into full-blown laughter. Crossing her arms, Rose rolled her eyes. The men simmered down to chuckles when Stefon strode into the room.

"Your carriage is ready, milord."

"Thank you, Stefon," Ashton said.

Rose gave a regal nod to the men. "I will bid you both a good day, gentlemen."

"My Warrior Lady," Ashton said, giving her a full bow.

"And let's not forget Soldier of Indignation," Burke said, doing the same.

On her way out, Rose shook her head and muttered, "I should shoot the both of you."

Stefon gasped, and from the corner of her eye, Rose caught his appalled expression. Burke and her husband, however, belted out laughter loud enough to shake the very floor on which they stood.

Chapter 10

Burke stepped from his solicitor's office and into the yellow slant of late afternoon sun. He tugged on the gold chain fob looping out of his waistcoat pocket, flipped the lid of his gilt and shell watch, and scowled at the time.

He'd hoped to conclude his business much sooner so he, too, might meet Ashton and Rose at the site of the new foundling home. He had some idea's he thought to contribute. It was half past four. Chances are, they were already back home. He ordered his driver to take him to the Sennett house. There he would find out what they'd learned from the builder.

And he would see Rose.

His feelings for her both invigorated and disconcerted him. During his meetings of the past few hours, he regularly had to brush back images of her so he could concentrate on the matters at hand. Frederick Ames, his solicitor, had to repeat himself at least twice. The man must have thought him half-drunk, so unusual was his state of distraction.

After settling back against the squabs, Burke huffed and shook his head, as if he could dislodge the prepossession disrupting his life. It should have upset him more than it did. Truth told, having Rose occupy his thoughts pleased him more than it troubled him. He couldn't help but chuckle at his peculiar state of disarray.

Pride in his stalwart deportment had always been a given. From an early age, his emotions functioned under his guarded control. He was comfortable in his solitude. Life, his life, tolerated nothing that might trifle with his peace and order. He'd been happy, hadn't he?

At the very least, he'd been content. He had everything a man could want, wealth, title, a solid knowledge of his life's path. When his baser needs required attention, those too were sated. So why, since meeting Rose, did the notion of 'more' keep tugging at his concentration?

He couldn't say. For the moment, he cared not a whit for the why of it. He only cared to spend time with her. Perhaps, well, more like as not, what they had would run its course and in time they would both go back to their settled lives. To his consternation, the thought saddened him. So, he banished it. Until their feelings dwindled back to their rightful place, he would enjoy every moment of his time with her. And see to her pleasures, as well.

The coachman made a righthand turn and Burke stared out the window at the fine homes rolling by, not quite fast enough to please him. In another minute or so he would arrive at their house, and he would see Rose.

As his carriage rolled up to the Sennett home, a bolt of fear shot through him. A Bow Street Runner dashed from the house, hand holding the brim of his tall hat to keep it from flying off. A glimpse of the man's red waistcoat flashed beneath his jacket. He was no sooner out the door, when another Runner scurried across the lawn and into the house. Both men bore grave expressions.

Burke leapt from the carriage before his coachman even climbed down from his seat. The front door of the house stood wide open. He hurried through. Stefon, their butler, was nowhere in sight. Burke followed the sound of weeping into the parlor.

He recognized Constable Arness. The man stood in the center of the room speaking in a low voice to the runner Burke had seen rushing into the house. Lewis sat bent on the same sofa where the day before he had his arm bandaged, crying into a handkerchief. His sling hung empty at his side. Blood soaked one large splotch across his white shirt, as well as several smaller smears. After a quick sweep of the room, Burke's heart picked up speed. Rose was not there.

In an instant, he was beside Lewis. "Lewis, what's happened? Where's Rose?"

"Ashton. It's Ashton." Lewis gulped air before saying, "Ashton is dead."

"What?"

"Rose killed him. I wouldn't believe it if I hadn't seen it with my own eyes."

"You saw her? Are you sure?" *No. It couldn't be true.*

"Yes. I saw her," Lewis said. "She shot him. Rose wanted the money, wanted her independence. It's the only explanation. She fooled us. She murdered my Ashton."

His last words were difficult to understand, as he had fallen into hysterics.

Burke placed a hand on Lewis's shoulder, but grief had too firm a hold on the man for any comfort to seep through. Burke's head swiveled in slow rotation toward the Constable. Arness, a trim man in his mid-thirties with fair hair and a neat beard to match, stared back at him.

"What happened?" Burke asked as he approached the man, his feet mired in dread. The edges of the room distorted in a haze of disbelief.

Rose wouldn't have done such a thing as to commit murder.

She almost killed her brother-in-law. No, that was different.

Arness dismissed the runner and nodded toward Lewis. "Apparently, when Lord Lewis Da Ville arrived at the vacant property on Vant Street, Lord Ashton Sennett was on the ground, shot once through the heart."

Burke swallowed through a dry throat. "Lord Da Ville told me he witnessed the murder."

Arness gave affirmation with a stiff nod. "Lord Da Ville heard the shot just before his curricle rounded the corner of the property. Lady Sennett was leaning over her husband's body, checking to make sure the job was good and done, no doubt."

"Just because she was there doesn't mean—"

"The pistol in her hand still smoked. Nobody else was there. Da Ville had a good view of the area and confirmed it. Lady Sennett killed him, all right. Apparently, she hired someone to do the deed yesterday, but the assassin shot Da Ville in the arm by mistake. Took care of the matter herself this time, she did."

To his ears, the recounting of what Rose had done questioned his judgement, as if a faraway voice castigated him from the realm of a nightmare.

"Perhaps…"

"It was her pistol," the constable continued. "Da Ville said her husband had given it to her for protection."

She'd told him about the pistol she carried in her reticule the night she was accosted at the foundling home.

"There's more damning evidence, too," the constable said.

Burke's heart rebelled. His mind took immediate note from every angle in hopes of finding a mistake. But his brain could not dispute the proof. Lewis cared for Rose. He wouldn't damn her so if it were not true. Besides, Lewis would want whoever murdered Ashton to pay for the crime.

"What other evidence?" Burke asked in a half-hearted voice. His mind still searched for a reasonable answer. But there was a witness to the killing. Lewis knew her quite well and would not mistake her for someone else.

"The Sennett butler, Stefon, heard this very day Lady Sennett threaten to shoot her husband."

She'd threatened to shoot them both this morning.

But it was only a jest, wasn't it?

She'd already proven herself capable of violence. Perhaps her brother-in-law was but another innocent victim, a means to get Ashton to propose their marriage. Her sweet face, the sugar-dusted wholesomeness streaming from her, had even him believing she was guileless. All the while her machinations had been at work.

Perhaps her next step was to elevate her status to an earl's wife. Someone of her plotting mind could well see herself as a countess. If Lewis hadn't come along when he did, she might have gotten away with murdering her husband. Claimed another had committed the deed, and then disappeared into the surrounding woods. With a few tears, she'd be quite convincing. Yes, like the rest of them, he'd been duped.

Anger set a slow boil in the sick twist of his stomach. He'd given her more trust than he'd given any woman since his mother. Both times had been monstrous mistakes. At least with his mother he had a good excuse. He'd been but a child. He was a grown man now, and Rose had managed to make a fool of him.

"Where is Lady Sennett now?" Burke asked, already knowing what the man would say, and glad for it.

Arness sent him a hard look. "Where she belongs. Newgate."

Chapter 11

Rose huddled on the bare, straw mattress upon the floor, her back pressing into the rough, stone wall. The narrow bed took up almost a third of her windowless cell. A dented chamber pot sat in the corner.

She wrapped her arms around her knees in an effort to keep warm. It was useless. Even if one of the gray walls hosted a hearth fully afire, the cold engulfing her ran too deep, and the chill temperature of the cell could only take partial blame.

Her husband was dead. Ashton, her sweet savior, her dearest friend who had gone to outrageous lengths to secure her happiness, murdered.

And she sat imprisoned for the crime.

Fresh tears rolled down her face. Their warmth a sharp contrast to her cold skin. The first tears she'd shed had fallen onto Ashton's body, the salty drops instantly lost in the mass of blood spreading across the white of his shirtfront. And then Lewis was screaming at her, accusing her. How could he think she would do such a horrible thing?

Nobody believed her. The way things looked, nobody ever would. She was going to spend the rest of her life in this filthy, dank cell, and worse, whoever had killed Ashton would get away with murder.

Rose had another worry, too. The foundling home. With this horrendous scandal, the contributors would run. The project would wither and the children would grow to adulthood in that crumbling mess. Whoever pulled that trigger condemned many innocent lives.

Had Burke yet heard what had happened? She wondered. Would he use his status and influence to help her? Or would he believe the worst? He'd known her in the most intimate of fashions. He must know she was not capable of such a horrendous act. Of course, Lewis knew her well. They'd shared a home for months. They were *friends*. Yet, Lewis had damned her for the murder upon first sight.

From a cell somewhere down the dim corridor, a woman's long and mournful wail echoed like a heartbroken ghost imprisoned in this wretched place for all eternity. The woman had been sobbing straight for an hour or two. Her cries grew louder these past minutes.

So pitiful the sound, Rose wanted to go to her, to offer some bit of comfort. But even if she could, even if iron and stone did not separate them, what encouragements could she dredge to offer? Hope shunned all locked in this fetid gaol.

Rose stared through the bars. Across and to the right of her cell, a torch in the wall gave her a bit of orange light. Some small, long-tailed critter scurried across the pocked floor just outside the bars. She drew her feet in closer and tucked her gown, still stained with her husband's blood, under her feet. She then wrapped the grimy blanket that had been in the cell when she arrived, around her, too.

The sobbing woman cried out two more times in long, weeping howls. Following her wails was the sound of heavy boot-steps and the jingle of keys ever dangling from the guard's belt. Rose couldn't see him, but his voice carried down the dim corridor to her cell.

"Shut yer yap, before I come in there and shut you up."

The woman quieted, and the guard walked away. Then she cried out again. This time, her voice was muffled, as if she screamed into her blanket. The guard's footsteps ceased, and Rose willed the woman to quiet herself before she took a slap to the face.

The heavy boot steps picked up once more, growing louder. He passed the point where the woman's cell would be, and kept walking. Rose threw herself down on the mattress and pretended to sleep. The trick had worked before. Her heart pounded as she tried not to react to the foul reek of the mattress, and hoped the guard would pass her by. He didn't pass, though.

His heavy footfalls stopped outside the bars of her cell.

"Ye are a pretty one, aren't ye?"

Rose held herself still, eyes closed, saying nothing.

The jangle of keys at the guard's belt, she was sure, was him fumbling for the one needed to open her cell door. Her heart almost stopped at the sound of one of them sliding into the lock.

"Freddy!" a man's voice called from the other end of the corridor. "Freddy, we need some help up here, now!

The guard spat a round of curses before yanking out the key and trotting away.

Rose turned her face into the rough, filthy blanket, and she wept.

Chapter 12

Burke paced the floor before the hearth in his bedchamber. The solid thud of his boots pounded a harsh contrast to the fire's soft crackle.

As he passed his bed, his eyes flickered toward it. His jaw tightened and his hands clenched into fists as he remembered the feeling of abandonment when he awakened to find Rose had snuck away. He'd gone directly to her house, like an ignorant, besotted boy who'd experienced his first taste of passion. She'd made an utter fool of him, of all of them during her violent, social ascension.

He'd cared for her. He'd believed her guise, even after his mother had taught him better by her abhorrent example. Worst of all, what kept eating at him, was a part of him still yearned to believe Rose innocent.

She was not innocent, though. The sweet Rose they all knew was a well-crafted façade, a fraud of the worst sort, a cold-hearted murderess.

There was a witness. Her own friend, Lewis, had seen her kill her husband. Burke had believed Rose to be above other women, women who set out to get what they wanted, without regard of the cost to others. She was worse. Her deceptions more refined, her goals substantial, and her ruthlessness knew no limits.

Her disguise was good, very good. Her behavior at the foundling home, pretending to be unselfish, drew him in like she had Lewis, and poor Ashton. But Burke's life experience should have given him the advantage. He should have known better. He was not a man easily taken in. Yet Rose duped him as if he was dull as a mooncalf.

Snatching his glass of whisky from the table, Burke drained it in one hasty swallow. He then hurled the fine crystal into the fire where it shattered and flashed a violent blue.

The clock downstairs chimed midnight. If he had any sense at all, he'd go to bed and forget he ever heard her name, forget Ashton Sennett's ridiculous request and everything after.

What Burke could not forget, however, was the way Rose had responded to his kisses, to his every touch. In that, at least, his mind held no doubt she'd been sincere. Her innocence had been intact and she had not the experience to affect such a deception.

Nor could he forget the way his body responded to hers.

Never had he experienced such a union with a woman. When their bodies joined, the ecstasy enveloping him transcended primal sex. At her climax, her heart beat in perfect rhythm with his. And in that moment when his body tensed and flowed into hers, the beats linked not in tandem, but as one.

Cursing himself six ways a fool, Burke stomped down the stairs, grabbed his coat, and stormed out the door.

****

Burke followed the skinny, slovenly guard he'd overpaid to let him into the prison at this late hour. The watchman wore clothes at least a size too big. Neither he nor his garments had seen the inside of a washtub in some time. Once they'd descended the stone steps, the man's stink mingled with the other foul odors embedded within the dismal walls.

The stench of sweat, unwashed bodies, and human waste permeated the air. Burke had been inside but a few minutes, and already he longed for a breath of fresh air.

Rose was somewhere in this horrid place.

The guard led him down a long, dingy corridor consisting of a pitted floor, a damp, stone wall on one side, and small cells on the other. Flaming torches in brackets on the wall lighted the miserable place at intervals.

They passed by the cells of a dozen or so women in all manner of disarray. Some were curled up and sobbing upon their thin mattresses. Others paced. It was quite clear a couple of them were crazed. One was having a whispering argument with herself. Another woman stood in the center of her cell, in full nudity. She danced in a provocative manner when he glanced her way.

A fat roach scurried across the floor. One of the women wailed as they passed by her cell, her cry muffling into her blanket before they had moved on. Two vacant cells in a row came next. A bloodstained bonnet lay upright on the floor of one. On they walked through the ghastly prison. It took no imagination whatsoever to hear a spectral dirge leach from the very walls.

At last, the guard stopped at a cell and shouted as he slid in a key.

"Wake up, gel! You got yerself a fine, fancy

visitor."

The door creaked open and the guard motioned for Burke to enter. As he did, the guard sent him a leering wink and said, "Ye take yer time. Just make sure the cell door is locked when ye leave and you bring the key back."

Burke ignored him and stepped into the cell.

"Oh, Burke," Rose cried, springing up from her curled position on the mattress. A moment later, her arms were around his middle, squeezing him, her head pressed against his chest. "You came."

He didn't put his arms around her, though it killed him not to do so. He wanted to believe it was all a mistake so he could take her out of this putrid hellhole. But she wasn't innocent. She was a deceiver, a liar, and a killer.

At his rigid stance, she stepped back and looked up at him. "Burke?"

"I just want to know why, Rose. Why did you do it?"

"Oh, Burke," she whispered, shrinking before his very eyes. "How could you think I would kill Ashton? There was no one dearer to me."

"Spare me your denials. There was a witness. Or have you forgotten one of your own friends happened by at the precise moment you murdered your husband? He *saw* you."

"Lewis is mistaken, or lying, though I don't know why he would lie. Everything was so wonderful." She shook her head then, perhaps to emphasis her denial. "I would never hurt Ashton. Why would I? He saved me. He gave me everything."

"Perhaps if he'd been one of those husbands who

left his wife in a country estate while he lived in London, he'd be alive today. Isn't that what you wanted, Rose, to simply be left in peace?"

"My life with Ashton and Lewis has always been peaceful."

"Has it? You had to be his wife at every ball, every party, at every social event. You must have found the Season intolerable. You said yourself you hate such activities. As a widow in mourning, you could spend the rest of your life alone with your walks and your books."

"I never wanted to be alone!"

Tears filled her eyes, and a tremor passed through Burke's heart. *Ignore it. Don't let her make a fool of you again.*

"Why did you come here?" Rose asked.

For a moment, Burke stood silent. He couldn't answer the question even to himself. She was so convincing, still, with all the evidence against her. A man with less sense would find it difficult not to be susceptible to her fashioned ploy.

Finally, he said, "To make sure you are where you belong." He then gave a quick once over to her dank, filthy cell before saying, "You are."

Giving her his back, he was out of the cell in two strides. He slammed the bars behind him with a loud, ringing clank, then he turned the lock and took the key. After a step or two, he swung back around. He couldn't help it. It was as if an unseen force spun him back to her one last time.

She stood in the center of the putrid cell. Her chin was to her chest and she gulped air. In that instant, Burke also found it hard to draw a breath. His foot slid an inch or two over the gritty floor before he stopped himself.

No, he would not go back and comfort her. He shouldn't have come here in the first place. Yet, he did not leave right away.

Rose sank down to her small mattress. She reminded him of an autumn leaf in an early winter frost, letting go, conceding to her fate, simultaneously falling and dying.

Burke forced himself to wheel away from the sight before he gave into his irrational wants. After making a brief stop at the keeper's house, he walked away from the prison in long, brisk strides. With each step putting distance between him and Rose, he was able to let his anger, and the irrefutable truth, fold over the piercing ache in his heart.

Chapter 13

Viscount Andrew Worthington set his glass of brandy on the polished, teakwood table between him and Burke, his poor, stinking drunk friend. Drew had taken little more than a sip of this, his second drink. It was clear from early on one of them was going to have to stay within close sight of sober. That someone would not be Burke.

Burke could not quite keep his posture right. Focus evaded his usual sharp attention. His sight drifted here, there, nowhere in particular. He spoke too loud and said too much, at least for a public place. All of it unlike him.

As good fortune would have it, Drew had managed to get them seated near a corner with Burke's back to the room. The salon he'd chosen in White's, their preferred club, was not much populated this time of day. The day, however, was rolling into evening. Others were sure to stream in soon. As of yet, their presence had not snagged anyone's attention. Such luck would not hold.

Drew let his casual glance wander, waiting for a clear path to escort Darington from the club. He'd not allow the gossips to feed on Burke. A few had already linked the man's name with Lady Rose Sennett, though so far only by way of a vague association. If the brandy should loosen Burke's tongue any more than it already had, by this time tomorrow his name would be deep in the chatter.

Drew had never seen his friend in such a state. Nothing got to Burke, certainly not a female. Of course, Burke had never before cared so for a woman. Truth told, Drew had never seen the man care over much for any woman. Burke didn't even keep a mistress, though he could well afford to.

Drew thanked his good sense he'd taken a personal vow to keep him from ever landing in such a sad state. A glance at his friend had him reaffirming the promise he'd long ago made to himself. He would *never* allow any woman to so upend his life.

Elwin, part of the ever-diligent wait staff at White's, approached their table in his pressed, black breeches and tailcoat, white neckcloth against his white shirt, shoes shined to a gloss. The man had been employed at White's since the full chalk of his hair was not more than speckles in deep brown. Drew liked him. Elwin didn't spread gossip and he knew how to take a signal.

Elwin carried fresh drinks for them on a shiny, silver tray. Drew flicked an eye roll to the side with an ever-so slight tip of his head, signaling the man to leave before Burke caught sight of him. The last thing his friend needed tonight was another brandy. Quiet as a breath, Elwin responded with a small nod, pivoted, and left the room.

Burke spoke, his speech more mumble than words. All Drew could understand with certain clarity was Rose's name, and a tone managing to be both angry and heartbreaking. His friend fell silent, then. Burke shifted a questioning gaze to Drew, as if Drew held the blessed answer for which he searched.

"You're certain there is no doubt to her guilt," Drew said with little more than a hint of a question. They'd already give the matter a thorough discussion, and there wasn't much left to be said. His primary goal now was to keep Burke awake enough so the man could walk out of the club with little to no assistance.

Drew glanced past his friend and about the room again. Only two other men occupied the wood-paneled salon at present. The elderly gentlemen sitting at a table near the fireplace had completed their game of draughts, and had no more than a sip or so left of their drinks. If they were on the verge of leaving, and if no one else entered, he and Burke could soon make a discreet exit.

"Lord Da Ville witnessed the murder," Burke said. He could have been speaking to anyone, or no one, for all his drifting, glassy gaze showed. He then repeated the sentence.

Burke's words were a bit clearer the second time, but were still quite soft at the edges. It was appalling to see him so. Drew wiped the concern aside for the moment and pictured the scene. Perhaps he could spot something missed.

The chances this woman had not committed the murder were slender, at best. The evidence against her was strong. Yet, when so much is at stake, he would be remiss if he did not help his friend explore every avenue before condemning her in full. Besides, the more he thought about what Burke had told him before the brandy had so muddled his head, the more one particular point bothered him.

"You said Da Ville heard the shot just before his

carriage rounded the corner," Drew said.

"So? Burke said, sounding as if this meant nothing. He picked up his glass, saw it was empty, and set it back on the table.

Drew leaned forward, his elbows resting on his knees. "Lord Da Ville could not have actually seen her pull the trigger."

Burke raised his heavy gaze from his glass that had no more brandy to offer. He blinked, one slow movement, and then blinked again and furrowed his brow, appearing to make a fine attempt to form clear thoughts with an unclear head. "Lewis heard the shot. He did not in fact *see* her shoot the pistol."

"No," Drew said. "According to his own accounting, he did not. He missed the actual shooting by a mere moment or two."

Burke squeezed his eyes shut and shook his head. "She held the pistol in her hand. Arness told me the barrel still smoked."

"She could have picked it up after. If someone else committed the murder, that person may have dropped their weapon in their haste to escape."

A wisp of hope flickered across his face, and then died. "The pistol belongs to Rose. She always carried it in her reticule. She told me so herself."

Drew thought about this for a moment. "It wouldn't be the first time an item was stolen from a lady's reticule. Now that I think on it, leaving her pistol there, if another is the killer, was clever in its condemnation of Rose."

Drew tapped a finger on his chin before continuing. "And if I remember correctly, much of that parcel of land is heavily wooded. It may well have been more than a mere moment between the time Da Ville heard the shot and he actually saw Lady Sennett. And, the dense grounds offer quick cover for an assassin to escape without being seen. What is her version of the events?"

"...I don't know. With the evidence against her so strong, I didn't...I don't know if anybody..."

"If anybody what?"

Burke rubbed his temple. Perhaps trying to regain his wits, struggling to make sense of his own thoughts. "I never asked her to tell me what happened."

"You told me you went to the prison to question her. I'd assumed it was to get her side of the story."

Burke gave a slow shake of his head, tortured by his soggy contemplations, if his pained expression was any indication. "No," he whispered.

"What was it, then? What did you ask her?"

Burke blinked, slow and hard. He blinked again once more before saying, "I asked her why she did it."

He'd gone to her with more accusation than question. "What was her response?" Drew asked.

"She said she was happy with her life with them. She denied killing him. But of course, she would."

The vacillating emphasis of his comment ill-supported the man's skepticism. Burke was doubting. "You spent some time with the three of them," Drew said. "And your instincts have always been good. What did you think? Did she seem happy with her life?"

Burke halted his words before his mouth formed the first, and he fell quiet and still. His gaze shifted one direction, then a beat later, to another. A frown indented the space between his dark brows. Drew said nothing. His friend needed extra time to turn the possibilities around in his brandy-soaked brain. Burke stared at nothing. This time, Drew saw less refutation than an attempt to form lucid thoughts.

A minute or so passed without a response and Drew accepted his friend was too far in his cups for thorough thinking. That is, until Burke said, "Why didn't she kill Lewis?"

"What's that, you say?"

Burke shook his head, making a grand attempt, Drew guessed, to shake off the fog. "She'd already committed murder. Why would she not kill Lewis and be rid of the only witness?"

"Hmm, interesting. Such a pragmatic act had not occurred to me. Why indeed? While Da Ville was in hysterics over Sennett's body, she could have packed her small pistol with another ball and shot him, too. Or for that matter, smashed him over the head with one of those large rocks laying around the property. If she'd already committed a murder, what was one more? Especially if it meant saving her from doom. With both men dead, she could concoct any number of viable stories and there would be no one to say different."

"...I need some air," Burke said, shoving up from his chair.

Almost as soon as he gained his feet, he almost lost them. Drew caught his friend's arm and draped it over his shoulder. Burke shook him off.

"I can walk."

"My apologies," Drew said.

The two other men in the room had begun another game of draughts. Fortunately, they were too absorbed in their competition to notice anyone else. To his credit, Burke did manage the distance between his seat in the club and his carriage parked just outside without stumbling to the floor. It cost him much effort, though.

Drew climbed in the carriage after him. By the time the coachman had driven them halfway down the block, Burke was slumped against the red squabs, out cold. Drew sighed at the pathetic sight. Even though they were about the same height and weight, he was going to have a devil of a time getting his foxed friend up to his bedchamber.

Chapter 14

Rose lay on her side, as still as the cold, stone walls around her. Perhaps the guard would leave if he believed her asleep. Her hope in this trick waned. She still used it, though. It was all she had. She dared to open her eyes, just a tiny bit. The repulsive man was still there.

The same guard, Freddy, who had plagued her since the beginning of her imprisonment, stood outside the bars of her cell. Every so often, he let his fingers jangle the keys, maybe trying to wake her, maybe letting her know he could come in any time he wanted. The man relished the power he held.

So far, his duties had kept him otherwise occupied. Tonight though, the prison was relatively quiet. Except for the pounding of her own heart, Rose heard barely a sound from the other guards or inmates.

"Yer awake, aren't ye, gel."

Rose kept still, with her eyes opened to no more than slits, hoping in the dimness he couldn't tell. The guard slid a key into the lock. Hinges squealed at the opening. Rose closed her eyes as he walked over and knelt beside her mattress. He leaned close. She knew this because his foul breath skimmed across her face in a revolting, damp caress. And then he forced a blunt finger into her mouth.

Rose slapped at his hand, jumped to a sitting

position and scooted as far back against the wall as she could.

"Leave me alone!" she shouted.

Maybe one of the other guards would hear her. Maybe they would care enough to stop this man. As soon as the hope entered her head, the facts smashed it to bits. It had been no more than a week or so since her incarceration began, but she already knew the way of things. No one cared enough about her to come to her aid. The one single person in her life who ever had was Ashton, and he was dead.

The guards shout of triumph bubbled down into laughter. "Ah, I knew ye had some spirit in ye!"

"Freddy," another guard said from behind him. Rose hadn't heard the man approach. Maybe her hopes were not as foolish as she'd believed.

"You can't touch her," the other man said. "I told you, a man paid the garnish."

Rose couldn't see the guard at the door. Freddy blocked her view. She'd heard him with all clarity, though. Someone paid the price to see she remained untouched. Who would do such a thing for her?

Perhaps Lewis had regained his sanity and realized she'd never harm Ashton. No, if that were the case, he would have told the authorities and she'd be free. It couldn't have been Burke. He believed the worst, despised her. No. If anything, Burke would have paid the magistrate to hurry the case along so he could see her hang. Maybe her sister had come to her aid and paid the garnish. Beneath her outward disdain, Eddy cared. Yes, it must have been her sister.

"Come on, Freddy, let's go," the other guard said. "You can't have this one. She's protected."

"I don't care," said the lewd man before her.

"Freddy," the man hissed.

"I said I don't care!"

Boot steps scraped the floor. Freddy sprung to his feet and whipped around, hands raised to his waist and curled into fists.

"You'd better care," Burke said in a voice ringing loud and strong in the cell's harsh confinement.

In the dim torchlight, Burke's large frame towered over the guard. Lord Darington hunched in a threatening manner and his voice conveyed the same.

"Remember what I say," Burke told Freddy. No one could misinterpret the threat in his low tone. "If you value the use of your hands, you will *never* lay them upon this woman."

The silence following his ominous warning loomed as foreboding as the prison itself. Then, with enough wisdom to accept defeat in the face of such a formidable opponent, Freddy rounded Burke and followed the other guard. His unintelligible mutterings dissipated down the corridor.

Rose found her feet and stood before Burke, her heart and soul burdened with the combination of gratitude, anger, and uncertainty.

"Why have you come back," Rose asked, though she could guess. He wasn't yet finished tormenting her. He believed she'd deceived everyone, that she was a killer and he wanted her to suffer as much as possible.

"Tell me what happened at the property."

Rose spun around and spoke over her shoulder without looking at him. She did not want to see his skepticism and condemnation. Besides, her own fear and frustration churned into something harder.

"I already told you. I didn't kill my husband. I have nothing more to say to you, so you might as well leave now." She wanted him gone before he could hurt her again.

He took her arm in a firm grip and spun her around before clasping her other arm, too.

"Tell me what happened."

For a moment, she said nothing. Hate fought for its rightful place. But she didn't hate him, not really. She had to, though. For if she gave in to her heart's lure to crumble, what resolve she had left to survive this ordeal would flee through the bars that caged her.

The state of her emotions made seeing things from Burke's perspective, the way Lewis's story must have sounded to his ears, close to impossible. And she shouldn't have to. As with Lewis, Burke should have believed in her from the start.

He released her and took a step back. Orange light flickered behind him from the torch in front of the cell next to hers. It gave Rose the image of the man standing between her and the sunlight.

"Please, Rose."

In those two words, Rose heard the voice of the man she knew before her world fell apart. She heard something else, too, desperation. It drew from her what he wanted.

"Very well," she said. Then she took a deep, steadying breath before continuing.

"Ashton and I walked about the property discussing how to make the best use of the land when setting up the foundling home, what sections would work best on what part of the land and so forth. At one point, we wandered off in different directions. I was in a wooded area when I heard the shot. I ran out, toward the street where I'd last seen him. Ashton was on the ground, on his back. I dropped beside him, but he…"

She would never forget that horrible moment, Ashton's eyes staring, vacant of his vivaciousness, of his love, of his very life, and blood, so much blood. "He was already dead."

Her breath hitched, but she managed to continue. "At first, I didn't even cry. I know that sounds awful, but it just didn't seem real. Only a minute before we were discussing sleeping quarters and kitchen gardens. How could so much change in the mere blink of an eye? I saw my own small pistol on the ground beside him. *My* pistol. It made no sense. How could my pistol be there when I always carried it in my reticule? I picked it up. That's when Lewis arrived."

What torchlight made its way into her cell was at Burke's back and she couldn't see his expression. His words from the last time he stood with her in this cell stirred with her warranted imaginings. Rose braced herself for his censure, all the while wondering why he bothered sullying himself in this prison just to listen to her story.

"Where was your reticule that day?"

Rose didn't answer right away. Was his belief turning her way? It sounded so. If she misspoke, phrased something not quite right, would he pour doubt upon her tiny spark of optimism, extinguish her hope, and break her heart yet again? She didn't know, and when boiled down to the plain facts, it didn't matter. All she could do is tell the truth.

"It hung on my wrist, as usual," she said. "I thought I still carried the pistol with me. The sight of it on the ground only added to the implausible sensation of the moment. Up until that very instant, I would have sworn I had possession of it. I've no idea when it went missing. I'm aware that sounds like an excuse not well formed, but it's the truth. All of it is."

She raised her chin then, to Hades with whatever ugliness he might now spew at her. She would throw it back at him. She was innocent, and if he didn't believe she spoke the truth, he wasn't worth her broken heart. Looking him straight in the eye, she said, "So, say what you will and be gone. I'm weary of your questions."

Burke took a step toward her and she responded by taking a step back. Would he try to enact a physical punishment himself? Before the myriad of terrible possibilities could present themselves, his arms were around her, crushing her against the hard mass of his chest. One of his hands cupped her head and his rough voice rumbled soft in her ear.

"I'm sorry. Oh, Rose, I'm so sorry for the awful things I said to you before."

She resisted, at first. Then the entirety of the ordeal stripped her of her defiance, and she sunk against him and wept. After the torrents of tears she'd shed these past days, Rose didn't think she had any more left. But they flowed, sudden and profuse, propelled by fresh emotion.

"You believe me."

"Yes, I believe you. I should have from the start. In my heart, I knew you could not commit such a heinous act. But my stubborn cynicism got the better of me. When Lewis said he saw you…"

"To Lewis it must have looked as if I'd pulled the trigger. I suppose I shouldn't blame him. But I do. He should know I would never harm Ashton."

"I should have known, too," Burke said.

He laid his face atop her head while his strong hands massaged the tension from her shoulders. Rose could have melted from the comforting bliss of it.

"I let my suspicious nature and the words of an hysterical witness taint my instincts," Burke said. "That will never happen again. You have my word. I can't even beg for your forgiveness, Rose. I don't deserve it. But I *will* earn it."

He leaned back then, thumbing away her tears. "I'm going to see my solicitor now. We'll have you released into my custody by the end of the day."

"You can do that?"

"I can and I will."

"But they think I murdered Ashton."

"As soon as I secure your freedom, I'll hire every thief-taker in town and I will find the real killer." The meaning in his eyes flared fierce enough to see even in the dim light of the cell. "I promise you, Rose."

He wrapped her in his arms again, tight enough to squeeze the air from her lungs. She relished the consolation, while at the same time, resisting the draw.

"Before I leave, I'll reaffirm my threat to the guards, and double the garnish to make sure you'll be left alone until I return with the proper papers to gain your release. Don't be afraid, love. This will be over soon."

Chapter 15

Rose let her fingers skim across the top of the steamy, lavender scented bathwater before sinking down in the tub until her chin dipped into the water.

Humidity filled the bathing chamber, hanging a warm, soothing mist in the air. Three branches of candles set about the room provided ample light. The chamber's high window would allow the morning sun to brighten the room. Rose looked forward to it.

When she first emerged from the prison, the sudden light blinded her after the days and nights she'd spent in such bleak darkness. And it had already been close to dusk. She vowed to never again take daylight for granted.

When they'd pulled up at Burke's home, Rose didn't hide her surprise. She'd assumed he would take her back to the house she'd shared with Ashton and Lewis. Lewis was most certainly back in his townhouse, as spending time in the Sennett home now would raise all manner of gossip. But Burke told her he was concerned for her safety, and he could better protect her as his guest. He made no mention of the gossip this arrangement could stir.

Cora had laid a clean night rail across the chair in the corner of the bathing chamber. Burke ordered her maid to burn the gown she'd worn during her stay at Newgate. Rose was glad for it. She never wanted to see that retched gown again. No matter how many washings it took, she was convinced the stench would remain. Besides, it would always be the dress she wore the day Ashton was murdered.

Her lady's maid, as well as several trunks filled with her belongings arrived just moments after she and Burke entered his home. The next thirty minutes were a flurry of activity. Most of which Rose only heard through the door as Cora was as anxious to get her bathed as she was to wash away the filth and the foul reek of the prison.

Through the door connecting the bathing chamber to the generous room where she would sleep came the sounds of drawers and cupboard doors opening and closing as Cora put away her things. After her maid helped her wash her hair, Rose requested some time alone to soak in the hot water. And to think.

Burke had installed her into a suite of rooms consisting of a spacious sleeping quarters, and her own private bathing chamber. The broad spaces, the soft peach and blue colors, all gave an even grander presentation after her days locked in that horrid cell.

She could be in that cell again. No matter Burke's promise, in the eyes of the law, as well as Society, she was the most likely culprit. If the real killer escaped the avenues of Burke's perusals, all eyes would again be on her.

"My lady?" Cora said from the doorway.

Rose shifted her head toward her maid. Cora had begun fretting over her the moment she'd seen her in the foyer. Burke and Cora worked with what seemed every servant in the house to arrange for her care and comfort, and then Rose was sinking into the most welcome bath she'd ever taken.

"His lordship has had a meal sent up for you," Cora said. "I'll keep everything covered until you're ready, which should be soon. My, that water must be going tepid by now."

Cora bustled over to the tub, the ruffles of her mobcap bobbing, and dipped in a finger. "Oh, yes. You must get out now before you catch a chill."

The maid bid her to stand and Rose stepped into the plush towel Cora held out for her. Once properly dressed in her soft night rail and wrapper, Cora had her sit in the chair while she brushed out her hair. The women then walked into the bedchamber, well-lit with candles. A moment later, Rose was laughing.

Silver domes buried the table before the roaring hearth. Two more covered plates sat upon another small table. In the mix, Rose also spotted a cloth-covered breadbasket, a teapot, and a decanter of wine.

Cora chuckled. "I guess Lord Darington wanted to make sure you didn't go to bed hungry."

"The entire household could be sated on this feast."

Rose took great pleasure filling her empty stomach with sliced mushrooms and roasted apples, plump strawberries and blueberry tarts. A crock held a stew of potatoes, onions, and kidney beans. The bread was warm and the fruit jam was sweet. After subsisting on meager portions of gruel these past few days, she savored every last bite of the succulent meal.

While she ate, Cora took her time turning down the bed and fluffing the pillows. She bustled over to the table to pour more tea for Rose and to spoon more stew onto her plate.

"I tried to come and see you," Cora said, a quaver

in her voice. She returned the small ladle to the crock and stepped back, wringing her hands as she surveyed the table.

Rose set down her second tart and gaped at her maid. "You did? You went to the prison?"

"The keeper wouldn't let me in unless I paid three pounds. I would have paid it if I had it," Cora said, raising her gaze to Rose's. "I surely would."

The last of Cora's words hitched on emotion and her eyes filled. Rose popped from her chair and wrapped her arms around her maid.

"I've been so worried about you," Cora said.

"Oh, Cora," Rose said, hugging her back, fighting her own tears. After a minute or so, she stepped away. "I'm much better now, at least for the time being. But if we don't find who murdered my husband, I'll be right back where I was."

Cora shook her head, sending the ruffles of her mobcap into a swish. She tugged a cloth from her pocket and dabbed at her eyes. "That won't happen. The earl's hired all kinds of men to find the real killer."

"Already? He must have been working every minute since he came to see me."

"Sit," Cora said, ushering Rose back to her chair. "You've lost weight these past days. Eat some more, now."

Rose smiled at the kindness and wiped her own eyes with a white, linen napkin. Cora stood only a couple of feet away, arms folded in front of her, and gave a sharp nod to the plate.

Rose smiled again and spread a heaping spoonful of blueberry preserves over a thick slice of bread. She was already full, but this evening she would gorge herself on the bounty. For whether or not this freedom would last, regardless of Burke's efforts, she did not know.

"Cora, has the earl really hired so many men?"

"Oh, yes. He's been taking meetings since you came up here. Why, I've never seen so many men in such a—"

A brief knock interrupted their conversation. Cora opened the door. There was a short, mumbled conversation before her maid turned back into the room and spoke.

"It's Lord Darington, my lady. He'd like to speak with you."

"Do let him in." Rose stood and cinched the tie of her wrapper. "You may go now. And Cora…Thank you."

Cora hesitated at leaving. After a moment, she said, "I'll come back and check on you later." And then she did as her mistress bid.

Burke stepped into the room, handsome in his fawn-colored breeches, shining black boots, and russet shirt. The smile he gave her bore a fair amount of caution. Then his eyes shifted toward the table, and he frowned.

"You haven't eaten much. I'm in the process of hiring a new cook, as my last one had to take a permanent leave. The one I have now is temporary. I've not yet tried much of his fare. If none of this is to your liking, I'll have him prepare something else right away. All you need do is tell me what you want."

"All of it is to my liking. You sent up enough food for a dozen people." Patting her stomach, she said, "I ate enough for three."

They shared a smile, but Rose's faded soon and she let her gaze rest upon the colorful, Persian carpet. Holding his face in her view could be a dangerous thing, because she feared at any moment his anger and accusation would return. He believed her now. But what if his money and efforts do not produce the real killer? Would he believe her guilty again? Would his rage increase tenfold for what he would perceive as a further deception?

His voice dragged her from her mind's dark wanderings.

"Rose, can you tell me how someone might have gotten the pistol from your bag?"

"That question has run through my mind a thousand times," she told him. "I just don't know. It's not as if I leave my reticule lying about town. When I'm not holding it, the bag sits in my private chambers."

"You left it in the carriage that night at the foundling home."

"I didn't carry it in to play with the children. But Horace was with the carriage the whole time."

"Asleep on the bench."

"If my pistol was stolen in that neighborhood, it would have been sold, or used in a robbery, not carted all the way across town, used to kill Ashton, and then left to implicate me."

With a nod of his head, Burke said, "Yes, you're right. That scenario is a far stretch. What about your maid?"

"Cora?" Rose could still feel her maid's strong arms around her when she'd entered the house, and then again just moments ago. She sprung to the woman's defense. "Cora is a dear woman, and ever-loyal to me.

She knew how happy I was with my life. She'd have no reason whatsoever to hurt any of the three of us."

Burke paced a moment, hands clasped behind his back. He stopped, pivoted toward her, and said, "Let's look at this from another angle, then. Who hated Ashton enough to want him dead?"

"No one," she answered without hesitation. "Ashton was a sweet man. He never caused harm to anyone, not in business, and not in his personal life."

Burke nodded. Ashton Sennett never struck him as the devious type. He was charitable, and considerate. His work for the foundling home was proof enough of his nature. Even his outlandish request had been for the happiness of another.

"Rose," Burke started, but paused a moment before continuing. "When Lewis was shot, I asked you if you knew anyone who might do such a thing." He hesitated before finishing. "You looked guilty."

After releasing a heavy breath, she said, "I felt guilty."

"Why?"

She tugged on the cloth belt and brushed her hands down her wrapper. "Because I thought of my sister."

"You think she could have shot Lewis, killed Ashton? Why would she do such a thing? I need to know the truth."

"Eddy is an angry, bitter woman. Her life has not turned out as she had wished. Years of overindulgence in spirits have worsened her outlook. When you asked if I knew anyone who might have wanted to harm any of the three of us, for a moment, I thought perhaps jealousy and alcohol had driven my sister to delinquency."

Rose rubbed her hands up and down her crossed arms before finishing. "I was ashamed at having thought such a thing."

"You don't believe it now?"

"No. Eddy has turned cold. Disdainful of me, even, but I don't believe my sister would go so far as to commit murder."

"What of her husband?"

"Piers?"

"He attacked you, did he not?"

"Yes. Piers is a miscreant with a severe deficiency in morals, but I can't see him risking his life for a vengeance that would gain him naught."

"Still, I plan to speak with the two of them myself."

"When you do, Burke, please be kind to my sister. Even though she's been…harsh with me, I do still love her."

"I will. But Rose, if she is guilty of these crimes…"

"I know. I'm sure it wasn't her, though. That's why I felt guilty when I thought of her."

Burke nodded, but curved his glance away as soon as he did. He was not so sure of Edwina's innocence. Doubt shaded his eyes, and perhaps his opinion. Or, maybe, an unearned trust shaded hers. Could her sister have done such a horrible thing? *Please don't let it be Eddy.*

Wanting to change the subject, Rose said, "Cora told me Ashton's funeral is tomorrow. I want to go."

"Not a good idea," Burke said with a shake of his head. "People still believe you murdered him. You'd be exposing yourself to all manner of insult."

"He was my husband, and my friend, my dearest friend. If it hadn't been for Ashton, I don't know what would have happened to me. I have to go to his funeral."

Burke sighed, and gave a pause before conceding. "We'll attend the burial."

Chapter 16

Rain patted atop the black umbrella Burke held over both their heads. Not a hard rain, but steady, and chilled. It rolled off and dropped into the cool, white mist floating about their feet, the fog lingering like ghosts crawled from the surrounding graves. Today Rose was glad for the fog and the rain. It made their discretion feel less contrived.

She and Burke stood away from the crowd. At Burke's insistence, they'd arrived a bit late so the other mourners would have their backs to them. Their dark clothing was lost in the copse of leafy, black poplars. Rose kept silent, holding a fistful of lilacs in her ebony gloved hands. Burke kept an arm around her shoulders, giving her much-needed comfort.

As the preacher said his final words, Burke bent to her ear. "The service is almost over. We should go now."

"I want to leave these flowers on his casket," she answered in the same low voice. "Ashton adored lilacs. He had them planted all around the house. Couldn't we remain until they've gone? They'll all go left toward the road when they leave and I doubt anyone will notice us back here."

"We can come back later, cover his grave in a pile of lilacs, if you wish. We should leave, Rose."

She almost argued with him, but he was right.

People still believed her a murderer. The last thing she wanted to do was cause a scene at Ashton's funeral. She could only imagine what they were all saying now that she was out of prison, and had taken up residency in Burke's home. It was fortunate she had no covetous hopes of Society ever welcoming her back into the fold.

Rose nodded, clutched the delicate flowers against her chest and the two of them stepped out of the trees to walk away from the closing service.

"There she is! I knew she'd come looking for sympathy. As if she deserved it! Utterly shameless, she is."

Though she had not seen her sister in the gathering, Rose recognized Eddy's voice. Almost as one, the black-clothed mourners rotated until they all saw her, a storm within the drizzle, ready to bear down on her. Their sorrow hardened in an instant by a condemning belief already taken root. On some faces, like her dear, sweet Lewis, outright hatred stabbed fresh wounds into her already fractured heart.

Edwina stepped from the crowd, out from the protection of the umbrella held by Piers. Raindrops spattered her face, but she appeared unaware, or unconcerned. A twisted smirk emerged through her wrath.

"You've got quite the cheek, haven't you?" Edwina sneered in a voice loud enough to carry over the tapping of raindrops.

Her speech was clear and sober. Her eyes blazed, not with anger, but with power. The preacher had stopped speaking. Nobody so much as whispered. The mourners were all listening to her sister's every word, believing what she said because now she was the good girl.

"Eddy, please don't do this," Rose begged. "Not here, not now."

Ignoring her desperate plea, Edwina altered her expression to one of anguish before wheeling around to face the crowd. "Spoiled she was, her whole life. And it was never enough. Nothing was ever enough, not what our parents gave her, not what we gave her. She only wanted more, more, more. She nearly killed my husband during one of her violent tantrums, left the poor man bleeding on the floor."

A unified gasp arose from the crowd, followed by a wave of murmurs. The flow of it swelled. Soon, though, everyone quieted again. They were waiting to see what was said next.

Ashton had paid Piers and Edwina a small fortune to secure a promise they would never speak to anyone of that night, the night Piers tried to rape her and she'd struck him in the head with her amber pig. Rose supposed since Ashton was no longer here to hold them to the bargain, Eddy believed there was no more bargain to keep. And her sister and brother-in-law could tell the story of what happened that horrible night any way they pleased.

Rose didn't bother with a defense. No one would believe her, and whatever she said would be twisted to suit.

"Her husband not even in his grave and she's taken up residence in the home of another man!" Eddy finished with a dramatic flourish.

Another gasp. The gossips were going to crucify her.

"That's enough!" Burke said, loud. Not a shout, but

a booming statement which demanded attention. Quiet fell again as every stunned face, including Rose's, turned to Burke.

"Lady Sennett is a guest in my home, invited to stay with me and my Aunt Eloise, as they are old friends. My aunt was quite concerned for Lady Sennett after she was *wrongly* accused. If not for the weather, she would be here at this service today. The dampness does not agree with my aunt, so I insisted she remain at home."

With his false explanation, Burke elevated the status of her residence from something below a mistress, to an attended guest. He also managed to speak her innocence, pouring doubt onto what Eddy had planted. What Burke had told them would go a long way in saving her name. Tongues would still wag after this scene in the cemetery. However, tomorrow would hold discussions, rather than a mass persecution.

Her sister's face reddened, nettled by the drawback of amending attitudes. The tide was shifting. Without the support of the crowd, Eddy might be considered sour, or even cruel. Before her rage at not being the object of sympathy could spew from her rigid lips, Piers took hold of his wife and dragged her back to blend into the gathering.

Rose stared at her sister's retreat. Her own anger, fresh, or perhaps enlivened from dormancy after so many years of forced restraint, bloomed hot in her belly.

Eddy had no right or reason to treat her so. And as for herself, she was tired of turning the other cheek, of hoping and waiting for a caring sister who wasn't coming, who, in all actuality, never even existed.

Ashton had given her the beautiful,. true knowledge of what it meant when another person cared for her. She couldn't go back to expecting less from someone she cared about. She wouldn't.

A part of her would always feel sorry for Eddy, and she wished her sister no ill. However, Rose was finished with her childish, naïve dreams of a loving sister. She couldn't have what didn't exist.

Murmurs rumbled behind them as she and Burke made their way out of the cemetery, the deliberations already begun. After but a few steps, Rose stopped sudden. She spun away from Burke's protective hold. Then, she hurried back, skirting the other mourners without taking in their surprised faces, until she reached Ashton's casket. There she stopped, and held still for a moment while raindrops patted on her black bonnet.

The casket was constructed of knot-free pine. The breast plate on top was engraved with Ashton's full name, and the date of his death. Angels in flight were engraved on either side of the script. Lewis must have arranged all of it with a funeral furnisher. Even after his horrid accusations, Rose's heart twisted with the image of him handling all this alone.

With the reverence of gifting royalty, she lay her lilacs upon his casket and fussed with the arrangement until she was satisfied. Rose whispered to Ashton. One last thank you for all he had done for her. One last promise to always keep him in her heart. Then, before she would break down and be called a false crier, she made haste getting back to Burke.

A minute or two later, the carriage rolled away from the cemetery, away from Eddy and Piers, from the questioning eyes of the attendees, away from Ashton's grave. Rain tapped on the roof and the wheels cut a watery trail through sporadic puddles. Some were big enough to splash muddy water against the side of the carriage.

"Your Aunt Eloise?" Rose said after they exited the cemetery.

"She'll be arriving in a few days or so. A common cold has delayed her, but I received a note this morning saying she's well on the mend. I should have told you, but in all honesty, with everything else happening, I forgot."

"Thank you for inviting her, and for placing doubt on my guilt. What you said back there, I want you to know I understand the risk to your standing if word got out your aunt has not yet arrived."

Burke accepted her appreciation in quietude before saying, "Your sister. She's hell-bent on destroying you."

"That may be a bit strong."

At his raised eyebrow, Rose said, "Eddy is so unhappy with her life. I think she's mad at me because she can't be angry at herself for making a poor choice in husbands, or because she's ruining herself with drink. To blame herself would only make it worse. I'm an easy target for her. Still, Burke, as awful as Eddy can be, I still can't believe she would murder Ashton just to hurt me."

Burke held her gaze for a moment, saying nothing. His doubts about her sister's innocence were wearing on her. *Maybe because they're your doubts, too.*

"So," Rose said, needing to change the course of this discussion. "Tell me about your Aunt Eloise. I should know about my old, dear friend."

****

Rose flipped from her left side to her right, snuggling into the soft mattress, the fine linen sheets, and the warm counterpane. Except for the low crackle from the hearth, not a single sound disturbed the comfortable room. Yet sleep would not come. Her head rang with Edwina's hatred, and her ugly words. No matter her defense of Eddy, the fear her sister may have been the one who murdered Ashton festered inside her.

Rolling on her back, Rose stared at the play of firelight on the ceiling. She tugged the soft counterpane up around her shoulders. The physical comforts did not soothe her to sleep. In fact, her mind could not have been more awake. Perhaps some fresh air would help.

Abandoning her hopes of drifting off, she flung away the covers, sat up, and swung her legs over the edge of the bed. After sliding her arms into her wrapper and cinching it, Rose padded barefoot down the stairs, through to the back of the dark house, out the back door and into the gardens.

The moon, at about half, granted sufficient illumination for a walk. Her feet chilled on the paving stones. She scarce noticed. The freshness of the cool night air soothed her almost as soon as she stepped outside. She breathed in deep through her nose all the floral and greened scents of the outdoors. Yes, this is what she needed.

Taking a different direction than when she'd walked with Burke, Rose took little more than a vague note of the rows of fragrant crab apple trees. Her mind's scattered worries about her future, about what her sister might have done, about her feelings for Burke, hindered any real focus beyond the serenity of being outdoors.

She should have thought of this earlier. The night air always helped her to sleep. She missed her evening walks with Ashton and Lewis. Or, sometimes just one of them, if the other had business to attend.

Well, she could walk alone. Especially here in these gardens, lovely even with nothing more than the partial moon to light them. She needed to organize her thoughts and contend with them one at a time. Out here in the fresh air, she could do so.

Burke believed her innocent, for the time being. Might that change? No matter how much she wanted to deny the existence of such a possibility as him reverting to his belief she was guilty, she could not. If he and the men he hired fail to unearth the real killer, if someone puts forth another piece of damning evidence against her, Burke might well reconsider his position. After all, he'd had no doubt whatsoever about her guilt before.

She wanted to forget that day in the prison, when he lashed out at her with such hatred his words struck like fists. Would it come to the same ugliness again?

He risked his good name to free you from the prison, and again when he defended you at Ashton's funeral. The man is making every effort to prove your innocence. He knows you are not a killer.

And if all Burke's efforts do indeed catch the real killer, what happens then? She'd shared his bed while married to another man. At best, all she would ever be in his eyes is a trifle, an immoral woman to serve as a distraction from his regular routine. Then, a thought slithered into her head, so ugly it weakened her knees and she had to sit on a nearby marble bench.

Perhaps Burke's belief in her was not sincere.

Maybe he took her from the prison to enjoy her company in his bed for a while before sending her back to her doom.

Rose shook her head. No, a person couldn't be so cruel. Then her sister came to mind, the hatred, and the bitterness. And Edwina was her flesh and blood. Rose wasn't a child, and she was able to face reality. Yes, a man she hardly knew could without doubt be that cruel.

Yet, Burke had made no advances toward her. He'd been a gentleman in all respects. And today at the funeral, he'd told a bold lie, knowing it would spread through town. If anyone suspected his aunt had not yet arrived, he would lose all credibility. No small matter for a man of his stature.

Heaps of thoughts, many of them opposing, tumbled through her head on a caustic gale. The pitiless blizzard was enough to cost her sleep for many a night to come.

Rose drew in a deep breath of the cool, night air, in hopes of cleansing her mind's distractions. She caught a sweet whiff of some floral scent and thought to come out here in the daylight so she could better see the gardens around Burke's grand estate. For now, though, she needed to get some sleep so tomorrow she might think with a clear head.

A rustling just beyond the nearby hedgerow drew her attention from her scattered contemplations. She rose from the bench, spun in a circle, and scanned the area. It was no doubt too late and too dark for the gardeners to be working. Perhaps Burke also had trouble sleeping and was walking in his gardens.

"Burke? Hello? Is somebody there?"

All was quiet, but for a few sporadic cricket chirps.

Chances were, what she'd heard was some small critter not yet settled down. Rose shivered as the night's chill bore into her. Funny, she hadn't been bothered by the temperature until just now.

She rubbed her hands over the thin fabric covering her arms. Her feet were cold and her head ached. It was time for her to go inside. Pivoting toward the house, she stopped sudden to listen. Did she hear something again? She was about to scold her imagination when another sound drew her attention.

It came from behind her.

Her heart sped and her scalp tightened. Whatever made the noise was too big to be a squirrel or some such critter. Before she could turn around to see what it was, something hard struck the side of her head, and the world went black.

Chapter 17

Burke flung back the counterpane and sprung from his bed. From a nearby chair, he snatched up his dressing gown and stuffed in his arms. He was pacing before he even finished tying the roped belt.

He'd spent the last several hours laying there, failing to settle his mind and fall asleep. Granted, the investigation into Ashton's murder had only just begun, but Rose's freedom, her very life, depended on his ability to find who had murdered her husband.

He'd hired every available thief-taker in London, offering a hefty wage as well as a reward so generous, the men were falling over each other to get to work. He would find the assassin, Burke vowed. He *had* to.

Other thoughts also kept him from sleep, far less honorable thoughts.

Rose slept but a few rooms away, soft and warm in her bed. Every moment of their one night together played in his head; her unique, woman's scent, the feminine sounds he drew from her, the way his entire body, his every sense, reacted to hers. Having Rose in his bed had been like imbibing a heady intoxicant, floating him to an earthbound heaven.

He desired her again. No, not again, still. For his want of her had never ceased. His hunger for Rose encompassed him whole. It gripped him from the top of his brain to the soles of his restless feet. The memory of her curious hand upon his skin set him a quiver, as if his body could relive that night for sheer want of it.

If he went to her now, would she welcome him? No. How could she? She'd accepted his apology. It was better than he had a right to expect. Yet, he wanted more. He wanted what he'd been too obstinate to accept. He wanted the trust she'd once given freely.

Remembering how he'd spoken to her that night in her prison cell, he doubted she would ever give him her trust again.

In her place, he would *never* forgive such a betrayal.

Burke paced his dark chamber in agitation, as that last was the most disturbing thought so far. What he had thrown away in his hasty belief of the worst, what he had treated with unheeded callousness, was the most precious thing he had ever experienced. It killed him to know he would never again see the unspoiled trust in her eyes when she looked at him.

What had he done?

Rose was so full of passion, so open with her feelings, giving herself to him as she had no other man. Yes, he'd yearned for her then, and yes, he yearned for her still. For Rose had lodged herself not just in his head, but also well within the protective folds of his heart.

In a rush so sudden he almost tripped, revelations assailed Burke like hurled bricks. All he believed he did not want he wanted with raw desperation, a wife, a house full of children, heirs to carry on his name and title. His vengeance against his parents to let the earldom die with him hurt no one but himself. They weren't here to care.

He was here, though. Rose was here.

He could make the choice to live alone with his bitterness, or with the enrichments of a true family. It was possible. Enough good existed in this world to make it so. Because of Rose, he understood all this now.

But was it too late?

Her nature was better than his was. Perhaps the scope of her forgiveness was also superior.

Burke's eyes shifted toward the double doors of his bedchamber. Perhaps Rose was also awake. Dare he hope she thought of him, too?

Burke crossed the room and his hand gripped the silver doorknob before he stopped himself. He dragged the flat of both hands against the door in an outward spread, resting his forehead between them against the cool wood.

He had no right to go to her now, not at this late hour. Besides, she needed to sleep. Rose hadn't had a proper night's rest since her husband was killed. She'd lost weight, telling smudges lay dark beneath her eyes, and the events of these past days, the murder, her incarceration, had diminished her light. And even if all was well with Rose, he still had no right, not when he'd said such terrible things to her that day in her cell. After she'd given him her innocence.

Burke swung around, putting his back to the door before temptation overwhelmed what decency he had left. Still fighting her lure, he paced to the window where he stared into the night.

Movement below caught his eye. For a moment, he thought he saw a spirit floating about his gardens. Then he realized the figure in flowing white catching the moonlight was Rose. Apparently, she too could not sleep. He knew she enjoyed walking outdoors. Perhaps a late-night stroll was a good idea for him, too. More so since Rose was out there.

However, Burke did not move. He stayed before the pane of glass, apprehensive about tempting himself so, alone with her late at night, and mesmerized by the enchanting vision she presented.

Rose swiveled around, her white wrapper floating about her legs in an ethereal swirl. He caught a glimpse of elegant bare feet, slender ankles, and a quick flash of her well-shaped calf. The sight could make one believe her a fairy princess come to sprinkle magic in his garden. Then Burke's wistful smile tightened into a frown. The night was chilly. Her feet were bare, and the thin wrapper she wore was not enough for warmth.

He tossed aside his dressing gown and got into his trousers and a shirt, buttoning his shirt as he strode down the hall. At the bottom of the stairs, he grabbed his coat from the rack and carried it through the house and out the back door.

Burke made his way along the paving stones at a slow pace, as he did not want to startle her.

"Rose," he called out in a low voice to notify her of his approach. She did not answer.

He continued on the curved path, rounding a tall hedgerow.

He raised his voice a bit. "Rose?"

A heavy clatter echoed from somewhere down the walking path. Burke picked up his pace. Around a curved marked by a square-cut bush, something lay on the paving stones. When he got to it, he stopped, staring with curiosity. A shovel laid across the path.

His gardeners were meticulous in their care. They did not leave their tools lying about where someone might trip over them. Had Rose been using it? Many ladies enjoyed gardening, and she did have a fondness for the outdoors, but digging in the garden this time of night?

When he picked up the tool to set it aside lest someone fall over it, a wet shine on the shovelhead caught his eye. He touched it with a fingertip. Even in the low light of the moon, Burke could tell it was blood. Its crimson color sat warm upon his finger.

"Rose!" he shouted, dropping his coat and flinging the shovel aside as he ran down the path. "Rose!"

Burke found her lying motionless on the ground, blood running from her head. He scooped her up into his arms and ran inside the house. Timmons must have heard him shouting, because when Burke carried Rose through the hall, the sleepy-eyed butler was cinching his robe.

"Sir, what's happened?"

"Timmons, send for the doctor, now!"

Burke whisked her up the stairs, kicked open Rose's door and carried her to the bed. He no sooner laid her down when Cora bustled into the room. "What's going on here? What's happened to my lady?"

"She's been attacked. Get some water and clean cloths."

Within minutes, the maid had everything he needed on the night table beside several lit candles and Rose's amber pig. Burke dipped a cloth into the bowl of water and with a most gentle touch, cleansed the wound. Rose groaned, but did not open her eyes.

Cora stood beside him, wringing her hands. "Is she

going to be all right, milord?"

"I think so," Burke answered, with more hope than knowledge.

Cora made a quick inspection of Rose. The maid then dragged the covers over her and tucked them around her. "Who would *do* such a thing?" she said, fussing a bit more, the worry in her voice unmistakable.

"I don't know," answered Burke through an angry grimace. "But I have an idea. Cora, send a footman for the constable."

"At this hour?" At his sharp glare, she replied, "Yes, milord."

****

Rose opened her eyes for less than a second before squeezing them closed again. The soft light from the candles beside her bed shone inordinately bright. She heard a groan, and it sounded as if it came from her, but her head swam with pain and confusion so it was hard to tell.

"Easy, Rose. Don't try to move."

"Burke?"

"The doctor just left. You've taken a bad blow to the head, but you're going to be just fine."

She lifted a hand and felt the bandage wrapped around her head. The room around her tipped one way, and then the other, before settling at a reasonable plane. She then raised her eyelids enough to see Burke sitting in a chair beside her bed, with a smile not quite strong enough to hide his worry.

He held her hand in his and his fingers gave hers a little squeeze. Her eyes had to adjust again. When they did, she raised them to meet the sea green warmth of Burke's.

"I didn't fall," she told him. "Somebody struck me."

"I know, sweet. Did you see who it was?"

He believed her. Only now could she admit to herself her concern, that he might suspect this to be some sort of ploy in order to retain his sympathy.

"No," she said. "Whoever it was crept up on me from behind. Did you see anyone outside?"

"No. But I have my suspicions as to who might have done this."

"Who?" As the question passed her lips, Cora entered the room.

"Oh, milady, you're awake. Thank goodness. I've been so worried. How are you feeling?"

"I just have a bit of a headache. I'm going to be fine."

"Of course you are," Cora said. To Burke, the maid said, "Timmons asked me to tell you the constable is here, milord. He's waiting in your study."

"Thank you," Burke said. He gave Rose's hand another squeeze before rising. To Cora he said, "Stay with her."

Cora nodded, already taking the chair beside the bed.

"Burke?" Rose said. She had questions. She wanted to know who he suspected, and why. *Please don't be Eddy.*

"You rest, Rose," was the only answer he gave. "I'm going to speak with the constable, and then I'll be back to talk to you, if you're feeling up to it."

He was gone before she could protest.

Chapter 18

The constable, Thomas Arness, scratched the yellow hairs of his short-trimmed beard as Burke paced the parquet floor of his drawing room. Light flickered across the heavy flocked wallpaper of rich greens. A fire burning in the hearth and several branches of candles lit the room, as dawn was still a couple of hours away.

"Her sister, you say?" Arness shifted in his chair, leaning his elbow on the embroidered cloth-covered arm.

"It makes perfect sense," Burke answered, stopping before the constable to make his point. "She's always been jealous of Rose. Her feelings are obvious every time Edwina Rutherford speaks to or about Rose. Lord Sennett was quite disgusted with Edwina's behavior, told me so himself. The woman is miserable in her own life and sees her sister as the one granted all the world's privileges. Edwina also drinks to excess, making her perspective even more deluded."

"And," Arness said. "It would explain why that blow she took from the shovel didn't do more damage. Had the assailant been even an average sized man…"

"Rose might well be dead."

Burke paused to grip the black marble mantel while a tempest rage toyed with his balance. At the very moment he was enthralled with her angelic form in his garden, someone was slinking up on her, about to strike her with a shovel. What if he'd not frightened the culprit away when he'd called out? Instead of dropping the shovel and running, would the villain have been satisfied with doing injury, or would they have stayed to finish the job?

The constable leaned forward in his chair. "Did Edwina Rutherford have access to Rose's pistol?"

"At the theatre, Rose hugged her sister. I remember Lord Sennett mentioning it to me later. It stuck in my mind because he said Edwina did not return her sister's affection. I thought it rather cold." Burke resumed his pacing. "It would have been nothing for Edwina to slip her hand into Rose's reticule."

Arness sat back and clasped his hands over his lean belly, fingers tapping a slow rhythm against the backs of his hands.

"For that matter, Edwina's husband Piers may be our culprit," Arness said. "He certainly had motive, after she'd done him injury. If he discovered his wife had stolen Lady Sennett's pistol, he may have decided to take his revenge for the bashing his sister-in-law had given him. Perhaps he stumbled when swinging the shovel and lost his balance. Or, became distracted when he heard your voice, or your footfalls, causing his power to falter. I'll go over to the Rutherford residence first thing in the morning."

Pivoting at the end of the room, Burke said, "I told Rose I would speak with her sister and brother-in-law myself."

"The lady's safety would be better served were you to remain here with her."

After only a brief pause, Burke nodded. The

constable was right. There had been attacks on three people residing in the Sennett house, one of them killed. And Rose had suffered time in Newgate. Burke's insides contracted at the memory of her in that hellish pit, at the vicious words he spat at her. Then he'd brought her here to his home, where she'd been attacked on his own damned property, almost in front of his very eyes. He not only owed her justice, but his utmost protection.

"You're right," Burke said. "I'll remain here and see to her protection. I gave Lady Sennett my word I would be kind when speaking with her sister."

"I'll see to it your word is kept."

Burke nodded his appreciation. Seconds later, angle, opportunity, and motivation revolved about his mind.

"In the meantime," Arness said. "Lady Sennett should remain indoors."

"Of course. I'll make sure of it."

Arness glanced at the Ormolu-mounted, marble clock perched in the center of the mantel. "Fine, well, I'll be off then."

As the constable stood to leave, Timmons showed Drew into the drawing room."

"How is she?" Drew asked before both his feet had even crossed the threshold. Though he appeared quite awake, his clothing was slightly rumpled and he'd missed one button on his waistcoat. His light brown hair was pushed back from his face in a haphazard manner. A fat lock bulged behind his left ear.

"New travels fast," Burke said, close to a smile at his friend's appearance, certain he knew just how Drew had come to such a state.

"Especially anything attached to the murder of Lord Sennett. Even in the wee hours, the town salivates for fresh gossip. It flows first to those of us forsaking sleep for our pleasures." Drew scowled before adding, "Even if it means interrupting others in the very midst of their enjoyments."

Burke did grin then at his rakehell friend, and the poorly timed interruption. Drew was a good man, but his exploits were many and far from discreet. If he were not careful, one day they would come around to bite him.

The flash of humor, however, did not last more than a few beats of his heart. Rose could have died this night. And whoever had attacked her was still out there, maybe already preparing to try again.

"Rose is going to be all right," Burke said. "She'll be better when her assailant is locked away."

"Have you any idea who committed this offense?"

"I believe it was Rose's sister," Burke said. "She had reason, at least in her mind she did. And, it makes sense because the injury would have been much worse had the shovel been wielded with the strength of a man."

Drew shook his head. "A shovel? Damn, and her own flesh and blood. My little sister, Olivia, is a hellion, but even at her worst she's done naught but throw a rag doll at my back."

"If I remember right," Burke said. "You deserved it." A slight smile tugged at Burke's lips. Olivia was a feisty little thing. Someday, she'd give a man a good run for his money.

Drew chuckled. "I'm quite sure I did." He then noticed the constable.

After a quick introduction, Arness said, "Yes, it appears Edwina Rutherford is the most likely culprit."

Drew nodded before saying, "What about Da Ville?"

"Lord Da Ville?" the constable said, surprise raising his expression.

Burke furrowed his brow. "You think Lewis may have had something to do with this?"

"It churned about my mind on my way over," Drew said. "Your logic of strength, or rather, lack of, suits my theory as well. He is not a large man. And what might he does possess is at present hindered. His intention may have been to kill her, but with his injured arm, he lacked the power to swing the shovel hard enough."

"Yes, but Lord Da Ville suffered a pistol shot, too," Burke said. "Rose was standing right beside him at the time."

Arness said, "His injury was not serious. It would be easy enough to pay someone to wing him. We were under the assumption Rose had hired a gunman who missed his mark. Perhaps Da Ville wanted to make it look as if Rose was trying to kill both men, adding to her damnation."

Burke shook his head. "It makes no sense. Before the murder, he and Rose got along just fine. They all three did. Da Ville had no motive for killing Lord Sennett, nothing to gain."

"Possibly," Drew said, rubbing his chin. "Until Lord Sennett took Rose to wife, he and Lord da Ville were always touring about together. Perhaps he saw Rose as an interloper, taking Sennett away from the free and single life. The two men could have had arguments

Rose knew nothing about. In his anger, Da Ville might have decided to rid himself of both of them with one shot. Also, Lord Da Ville *is* the only witness other than Rose. If she's telling the truth-."

"She's telling the truth," Burke shot back.

Drew replied with a conceding nod. "We're going on Da Ville's word he saw no other at the scene. For all we know, he could have helped a paid assassin escape."

"And," Burke added, pieces coming together and fitting well. "Having been grazed in a shooting himself, Da Ville would be distanced from suspicion. Also, Lord Da Ville could have taken the pistol from Rose's reticule on any number of occasions."

"Good points all," the constable said. "I'll speak with Lord Da Ville, too."

"I'm taking Rose to my country estate," Burke said before calling for Timmons. "She'll be safer there. I'll hire plenty of guards to patrol the grounds. It will be easier to keep watch there as no one should be about the expanse of property but us."

"Splendid idea," the constable said.

The butler delivered their coats to the two men and they all left the drawing room. Burke dismissed Timmons. Drew, Arness, and Burke bid their farewells at the front door. The constable exited the house before he had both arms in his sleeves.

"You know, Burke," Drew said, his hands working at a slow pace slipping the buttons of his coat through their holes. Pre-dawn chill crept in through the open door on a faint mist. "There is always the chance one of the women you've been involved with became jealous."

Burke considered the possibility before rejecting it. "I doubt it's any of them. I've seen disappointment, every so often a flash of temper, but never fury."

Pru had been angry.

Of course, burnt toast made Prudence angry. But an indulgence or two always doused her flaring temper, and she was ever proficient in finding her indulgences. Besides, he'd caught word she was already involved with Lord Stanley. Pru was not one to brood over any man for too long.

"Sometimes a woman seethes beneath her smiles," Drew said.

"I'll give the possibility further consideration."

****

"Pack Rose's things," Burke said to Cora as he strode into Rose's chamber.

The maid, sitting in a chair beside Rose's bed, swiveled her head toward him. She returned her attention to her mistress for confirmation.

Rose was sitting up, resting back against fluffed pillows. "Where are we going?" she asked.

"To my country estate. You'll be safer away from the city until this matter is concluded. I'll have a number of guards patrolling the grounds on twenty-four-hour watch."

Burke stepped to the foot of her bed. He was relieved to see blood did not seep through the white bandage wrapped around her head. But her color had not fully returned, and he feared he was about to make it worse. For a moment, he considered keeping the truth from her. No. If he was going to establish a trust with her, he needed to tell her everything.

"Rose, I'm sorry, but we believe it was indeed your sister who murdered Ashton, and who attacked you in the garden."

Rose shook her head, but said nothing. He could see the fading denial. She knew Edwina was capable. But it was still a damned hard thing to accept one's own sister would do such terrible things. He cast an ordering nod to her maid.

"We'll leave at first light," Burke said.

Cora walked over to the wardrobe and opened the doors.

"You can pack my things, Cora," Rose said. "I'll be leaving, but not with Lord Darington."

"Where do you think you're going?" Burke asked.

"Home."

"Back to the home you shared with Lord Sennett?"

"Yes. It's where I should have gone straight away. I shouldn't be here, feeding the rumor mill."

Without taking his eyes from Rose, he said, "Cora, leave us."

As soon as the door closed behind her maid, Burke said to Rose, "They all believe my aunt is here. Besides, I don't give a damn what Society thinks."

"You will if my being here begins to affect your business dealings."

"My investments have made plenty of men plenty of money. When it comes to filling their coffers, men have no misgivings about setting gossip aside."

Her eyes darted to her left and then down at her hands, as if panic swelled swift like a new bruise, and would soon darken beyond concealment. "Maybe it was a footpad who attacked me tonight."

"Footpads await pedestrians on dark streets, not in my gardens. Besides, all you were wearing was a night rail and wrapper. Clearly you had nothing to steal."

He paused then, observing her with a more

scrupulous eye. A shallow crease marred the smooth skin between her brows. She had the sheet bundled at her waist, grasped so tight the skin of her hands all but matched the white of the linen.

Burke's attention returned to her face. "It's something else, isn't it?"

Rose nodded, her misery evident upon her pallid face.

After a moment, Burke said, "You don't trust me."

She lifted her sad eyes to his. "I'm grateful for your help and will always be in your debt, but my feelings for you... are not what they once were."

"You must try to see it from my perspective," Burke said. He couldn't let her stay in the London, alone and unprotected. Nor could he bear the thought of what his careless words and actions had changed, what he may have forever lost.

"With the evidence presented, you can hardly blame me for what I believed," he argued. Desperation intensified his words. She had to go with him. Her very life was in jeopardy.

And so was his heart.

"Given what we shared, I certainly *can* blame you for believing me guilty of such a horrific crime, for coming to the prison for the sole purpose of furthering my despair, for fearing you will turn against me once more should your investigation come to an end with nothing to show for it."

"That won't happen," he shot back.

Burke huffed out a breath. Her emotions were heightened, the attack having whittled a spearhead to every spike under which she'd suffered. She needed to be angry at him right now. For one, he deserved it. For another, he was the only one here at present onto whom she could unleash her turmoil and fears.

"We will discuss all this in the country," he said.

"No! Don't you understand?" Her eyes welled. "I'm so tired of people I should be able to trust turning on me. My sister, Lewis, you." He winced from the inside out at her lumping him in with the other two. "I won't have it any more. I won't!"

"I apologized, damn it, that's all I can do!"

He was losing control here, control of the situation, and control of his emotions. How he wished he could erase the ugly things he'd said to her. He needed her trust to see to her safety. And he needed it for reasons weaved into his very being, into every human being.

Pure selfishness was playing a part here. Fine. So be it. If he was going to forgo his former life's plan, he would also have to accept he wanted what it was normal to want. And he wanted Rose. Not for a night. Not for a few. He wanted her in his life, by his side, forever.

"I accept your apology, Burke, I do," Rose said. "And I apologize for the accusation. That wasn't fair. You've gone far beyond compensation with everything you've done for me since. But I'm not going anywhere with you. I don't want your sympathy, I don't want your efforts born of guilt, and I don't want…"

Tears ran down her face and dropped onto the linen. It tore him apart. He would go to her, hold her, and make this right. But first, he had to know. Circling to the side of her bed, he took a handkerchief from his pocket and tucked it into her hand.

"What don't you want, Rose?" he asked in a gentle voice.

She wiped the tears from her face before meeting his direct gaze with her own. "I don't want your touch."

She was lying. She had to be. To think otherwise knifed an ache to his chest sharp enough to impale every new emotion she had roused in him. He wanted to argue with her further, quarrel until she believed him. But she wasn't well, and she wasn't safe. He would do or say whatever he had to, make whatever solemn promise she required, to see to her protection.

"I'll not place as much as a finger on you, if such is your wish. But Rose, you must think with a clear head here. Someone wants to see you dead, or imprisoned. Tonight, this person almost succeeded in assuring your demise. Next time you may not be so fortunate." At her obstinate expression, he added, "Nor might I."

"You?"

He was sinking low here, but he had no choice. He *had* to protect her. If it meant taking advantage of her soft heart, then such was the depth to which he must descend.

"What better way to make you appear the murderess than to kill me, another man with whom you are involved."

Rose gaped at him. A moment later, she sunk back into the pillows, as acceptance lay heavy upon her.

Whether or not a threat to him existed, he could not say. What he did know was Rose would not risk the well-being of another. Of that, he was sure.

"I can keep us both safe out there."

"Then go."

"Not without you."

Her face expressed naught but misery, and the force of it struck him as the lowest miscreant. But he would not so much as consider any alternatives. She *would* go with him. He would see to it, no matter what it took.

"Rose, I give you my word," Burke said, taking a step back as if to display his intent. "Unless you say different, I'll not touch you. But you must leave London. There are far too many people about. You simply are not safe here."

Her eyes shifted to stare into the fire. After a minute passed without a response, he added, "As your...friend, neither am I."

Rose closed her eyes and tipped her chin down. She would accept this. For her, there would be no choice. Even anger would not allow her to endanger the life of another.

"Very well. I'll go."

Following a silent sigh of relief, Burke said, "If there is nothing else you need or want right now, I'll be going."

The shake of her head was slow and tight. He gave her a nod he was sure she didn't see, as her gaze was unfocused and in her lap, and he swiveled around to leave.

"Burke." When he faced her again, she said, "There is something I want. You mentioned you're in need of a new cook."

"Yes. My regular man has left to care for his ailing brother. He informed me he'll most likely spend his remaining days on their family farm. Why do you ask?"

"Cora's husband, Claude, is a wonderful cook. He worked for Ashton as long as she did. And, well, they're dear people. It would be nice if they could stay together."

Without hesitation, he said, "And so they shall. I'll see to it. Is there anything else you would like?"

"No," she said in a quiet voice. "Thank you."

Chapter 19

It was as if the trip to Burke's country estate was taking them halfway around the world, so long and tedious was the journey.

Initially, Rose was glad when he told her he would be riding outside the carriage, along with the guards he'd hired. But the solitary ride left her far too much time to think. After endless hours of sitting alone with nothing but her headache, her heartbreak, and retched possibilities, she feared the bleak and encompassing sense of isolation would crush her. One fear in particular roosted in the time she'd already spent alone in the carriage, as Burke's reason rang true.

She knew her sister hated her. She supposed a less aspiring part of her had always known. But Rose never believed Eddy would go so far as to murder a man, or her. Her careless naivete had cost. Poor Ashton. He'd taken her in, rescued her from a horrid circumstance, and she'd repaid him by causing his death.

And yet, with all the misery Eddy had caused, Rose could not bear the thought of her sister languishing in the prison she well knew was beyond foul. Were such thoughts a betrayal to Ashton, to Lewis?

Lewis. She wondered if he would still believe her guilty once the constable arrested Edwina. Even if he should accept his mistake, ask and receive forgiveness, their trust could never be regained in full. Even at best, their beautiful friendship was forever degraded to a lesser rank.

For a few glorious months, Rose knew peace and happiness. Nothing was right now. Ashton was dead. All of London hated her, someone enough to see her in her grave. And Burke, the one man she believed she'd fallen in love with, she could never fully trust. How could she ever look at him without fearing he would turn on her. Or anyone else, for that matter. Her life was never going be right again.

Rose stared out the window at the wooded scenery rolling by. Sunbeams teased with imageries of magic dust dancing in their golden shafts of slanted, late day light. For an occasional moment or two, she could picture a fairy tale land where all was well and safe and one could by all rights assume a blissful ending.

Then, in but a blink of her heavy eyes, all Rose could see was the vast darkness between the beams of light.

Miles had passed since she'd last seen even a modest cottage. She was grateful for the view, though. Until they were well out of the city, Burke would not allow her to open the small curtain covering the window, making her isolation complete. She didn't even have Cora, for he ordered the maid to follow later with Claude and the rest of her belongings.

A rabbit, frightened by their noisy passing, hopped deeper into the forest. His graceful leaps made her smile. For a while, she sought out another rabbit, or maybe a deer. The search was fruitless, but it helped pass the time.

She'd hoped to fall asleep. It should have been an easy thing, for she was exhausted. Before they left,

Burke had seen to it she had a thick blanket and hot coals in a warmer on the floor of the carriage. For a while, she lay down on the well-cushioned seat. But her mind was too active for sleep to welcome her. Perhaps if she just lay there to rest a while, she'd drift off.

A basket of food wrapped in cloths sat on the other seat, as Burke said they would make only brief stops to take care of personal needs. She glanced across at it. But she didn't think she could eat any more than she was able to fall asleep. Her stomach was as knotted at her thoughts.

The farther they traveled from the city, the rougher the road became. An especially deep rut tossed the carriage left, then right, before resuming an even ride, until the next batch of ruts. Her attempt at rest became absurd. She sat upright again, and resumed her visual search for woodland creatures. After a while, she laid her aching head against the squabs and stared at the trees going by.

Three men rode with Burke, two behind the carriage, one in front with him. Before they left, she'd overheard him talking with one of the men about hiring more once they arrived. The guards, along with the driver, were armed and ready for trouble. Rose had every confidence they would keep her body safe. Her emotions, however, lay raw and exposed.

The feelings she had for Burke were a passionate, volatile mix. One moment she recalled his touch, comforting, arousing, and the next, his glare of hatred and accusation the day he'd come to see her at the prison. And in her heart, a longing so powerful it left her shaken.

In a sudden strike, weariness sunk deep into her

bones. Rose wrapped herself in the warm blanket and curled up on the seat again. This time, sleep was kind enough to claim her. She dreamt of fairylands, of family and love, and of trust solid enough to hold her for life.

****

"Shh, go back to sleep, Rose."

She awoke to Burke's hands sliding beneath her and then the deep timbre of his voice.

"We're here, sweet. Since you're awake, let's get some food for you and then you can go to bed."

"I can walk," she said, when he went to lift her from the seat.

With barely a hesitation, he slipped his arms out, exited, and helped her step from the carriage.

Night had fallen. There was no moon, but the mad scattering of stars lit the sky and several men carried lamps about the grounds. Their meanderings had purpose. If anyone had the audacity to be hiding behind a tree or a bush on this property, they would be found.

A pleasant faced woman of middle years who introduced herself as Miranda greeted them just inside the door. The woman settled Rose into a lovely, pink and gold suite of rooms and saw to it she had a warm bowl of peas soup with some crusty bread. She even changed the bandage on Rose's head, tending to her healing wound. In less than an hour after their arrival, Rose was sound asleep in a comfortable bed.

****

Traces of early sunlight leached through white, lacy curtains. Rose and the morning, it appeared, awoke simultaneously. The warmth and comfort of her soft bed tempted her to stay put. But her mind came fully awake and she was curious to inspect her surroundings.

She began with her own chambers, taking comfort in the first thing she saw, her amber pig on the bedside table. Burke must have seen to it the pig was placed where she always kept it.

White curtains complemented the pink and gold colors of her assigned chambers, as did the round, white and yellow rug in the center of the spacious room. A ceramic pitcher and basin, white with painted pink swirls, sat on a simple stand in the corner near a privacy screen. There was a dressing table of polished rosewood. Atop it, an oval-shaped mirror in a rosewood frame.

Through a wide archway was a small sitting room with a gold, brocade divan, the back carved in an ornate, curved fashion. Two simple, low-back chairs accompanied the divan. The rectangular window behind the chairs was almost as long as the room.

After straightening out the bedcovers, Rose went to the white-painted wardrobe to retrieve a morning gown from the small selection she'd brought with her, as well as her other necessities. She lay everything out neat atop the bed.

She washed and dressed before sitting on the padded stool at the dressing table to unwrap her bandage. Last night, Miranda washed and redressed the wound and told her it appeared to be healing quite well. Rose wanted to see for herself. Angling before the mirror, she turned her head to try and see, as her assailant had struck her just above and a little behind her right ear.

Even leaning close to the mirror, it was difficult to get a good look. With a careful touch, she felt the wound with her fingers. There was a bit of a scab, but it did not feel as swollen as she feared. Rose used caution when she brushed out her hair and arranged it back into a simple chignon.

She had just come to her feet when Miranda poked her head into the room. Her large hazel eyes grew even bigger at the sight of Rose up and about.

"Good morning, milady," she said, bustling into the room. "I was just going to pop my head in to check on you. I didn't think you'd be up and about so soon. You should have called for me," she scolded. "I'm to tend to you until your maid arrives."

"Thank you, Miranda. I awoke very early this morning."

Except for the few months she'd lived with Ashton and Lewis, she'd always tended to herself. Piers never afforded even his wife a personal maid, much less his indigent sister-in-law. It never occurred to her Burke would assign a personal maid to her. But of course, he would. His station in life would insist on such a courtesy.

Miranda toddled into the room straight for her, concern focusing her expression. "Nonetheless, should have given the bell-pull a tug. I'd have been in here right prompt. Does your head give you much pain?" she said, leaning in for a critical look. "I could rewrap it for you."

"It's just a dull ache. I don't think I need to wear the bandage any longer. I am rather hungry, though."

"Of course, you are," Miranda said, clasping her hands together. You didn't eat enough to feed a field mouse last night. Would you like to have your meal here in your suite, or would you prefer going down to

229

the breakfast room?"

"The breakfast room, please. I barely moved a muscle yesterday. I'd very much like to take a walk today and do some exploring."

"Fine idea, milady. It's a grand old house. His lordship had special, large windows installed to take in the views all around. Oh, goodness," she said, and almost stumbled. Following a tsk, she said, "You even straightened out your own bed. Well, come on, let's get you something to eat."

Miranda led her down a winding staircase and along a wide corridor to a sunlit room of pale greens and yellows. The yellow reminded her of the breakfast room in the house she shared with Ashton and Lewis and for a moment, grief rusted her lungs.

"When I finish my meal," she said to Miranda as she sat down. "I'm going to take a walk outside, while the day is so sunny. Is there any particular direction you would say is more scenic than another?"

"Oh, my lady," Miranda said, shaking her head, her expression tightening with concern and accentuating the spray of wrinkles fanning out from her eyes. "Lord Darington left very strict orders, you are to remain indoors at all times."

"Indoors? Even during the day?"

"He says it's not safe for you, with someone out there who wants to cause you harm. He's instructed all of us to keep a close watch." The woman brightened a bit then. "His lordship has quite the full library. I'm sure you could find something there to your liking. He mentioned you enjoy books."

"Yes, I do," said Rose, keeping her disappointment to herself while she wondered how long it would be until she felt the sunshine on her face, or took in a fresh breath of air. "Thank you."

"I'll show you the way as soon as you've eaten."

"Don't bother. I'll find the library myself. I'm going exploring anyway."

"A fine idea. It'll be like a treasure hunt."

Before Miranda could leave, Rose said, "Do you know if Lord Darington is awake yet?"

"Oh, yes, milady. He was up before the sun. He's been making all sorts of plans with the guards."

"I see. Thank you, Miranda."

"You're welcome, milady. I'll go and see to your breakfast now."

Rose ate her morning meal alone. Afterward, she wandered through the house for a while. It wasn't as large as his mansion in London, but it was no less grand.

Finely made furniture, sturdy and elegant, adorned each room. All of the chairs were cushioned and none of the fabrics showed signs of wear. Every carpet and drapery, every inch of marble and wood floor, was tended to with meticulous care. What caught her eye the most, however, was the view from the oversized windows on every side of the house. What she saw only increased her want of the outdoors.

Planted gardens bloomed hearty, as did the fields colored by nature's paintbrush with a mix of wild bluebells, primrose, and a bright scattering of poppies. Willow trees, a dozen, at least, swayed in grace upon the slight breeze. Their lithe branches all but voiced an invitation to sit beneath them.

Beyond a small grove of apple trees, Rose spotted a pond, sparkling as sun glistened off its placid surface.

How she longed to stroll about the flowers and the foliage, smell their sweet scents, maybe sit on the soft grass beside the water for a while.

She considered slipping out for just a quick walk around the grounds near to the house. The day was lovely, with but a few puffy clouds lingering about, and she hated to miss it in its entirety. Her fingers drifted up to the source of her lingering headache, the damage done by a swung shovel. Perhaps it was best if she spent the day with a book. A few minutes later, she found the room she was looking for.

Miranda's description of a full library was more than accurate. Mahogany shelves covered three walls of the spacious room from floor to ceiling. Each wall had its own rolling ladder in order to make every book accessible. Fat-stuffed chairs and sofas offered comfortable seating about the room.

Rose spent almost a full joyous hour browsing the tomes before deciding which one to read. She finally settled on James Dutfield's, *English Moths and Butterflies*. She chose a cozy chair near one of the large windows, and settled in for a long read.

After her solitary midday meal and another stroll through the house, stopping at the front windows in hopes of seeing the carriage of Burke's Aunt Eloise roll up to the house. She never did. After a while, Rose returned to the library. An hour later, she laid the book in her lap while she stared out the window.

She glanced down to take note of the page she was on before closing the book and setting it on the piecrust table beside the chair. After peering out the window for several minutes, she then shut her eyes to imagine the scent of foliage, the feel of the breeze, the warmth of the afternoon sun on her skin. She opened her eyes for a longing gaze at the well-tended property, barred from her by a single piece of glass.

The view from this side of the house presented ivy-covered acres, interspersed with a generous amount of graceful ash trees, their oval leaflets full and rich. A couple of white, fluffy clouds did nothing to hinder the shine of daylight. The splendid sight drew Rose from her chair to stretch before the window. She no sooner let out her deep breath than Burke strode into her vision.

Two men accompanied him as they walked across the grounds. They must be some of the guards he'd hired. Burke kept a grim expression as he pointed to different areas of his property as well as the house. The men nodded. One responded by motioning a hand westward as he spoke. The other said something to the small group in response.

The other two men might have even been mere outlines, for all Rose saw of them. Her eyes, and battered heart were too full of Burke.

Burke carried himself with confidence and authority, and he was so handsome the sight of him made her spirit ache. He wore black trousers and black boots. A white shirt clung to his muscular form. Even from her place at the window, Rose could see the tautness in his stance, his jaw, his stern expression both when he spoke and when he listened.

The other two men walked away, their heads together in discussion. Burke stood then with his back to the house. His head rotated in a slow scan of the grounds, and then back again. He pivoted in the opposite direction the other men had walked, taking long strides until he was gone from her sight. After quite a few minutes had passed, Rose returned to her book.

She ate her dinner at a lengthy, white-cloth-covered dining table with a silver branch of candles at her end only, as she was once again having her meal alone. When she finished dining, she returned to the library. Though, her head was aching and she was unsure as to how much longer she might be able to read.

The servants had been in to light the candles and stoke the fire in the library, as nightfall had taken the sunlight. She crossed the room, lonelier now, with dim corners and the stillness of life at the end of her solitary day. Rose stared out the window. Stingy, as it was but a crescent, the sliver of moon produced almost no light. The pane of glass before which she stood might as well have been facing a wall, for all she could see.

The day had passed without she and Burke exchanging a single word. She hadn't even seen him, but for those few minutes from her place at the library window. She glanced around the room where she'd spent most of the day in solitude. Her book sat on the small table where she'd left it. Two steps toward it, she stopped, then pivoted away and exited the room.

Rose paced the house as servants lit the lamps, most of them finished with their duties for the day and ready to retire. More than one of them inquired as to whether or not she needed anything. All she had to do was ask for something, and she received it almost as soon as she requested it. Everyone here was so nice to her, polite, attentive, always aware of her. Everyone except for Burke.

He'd not so much as shared a meal with her this day, or even spoken a greeting. His absence should have pleased her. She'd made her feelings quite clear to him, and he'd accommodated her by keeping his distance. Still, a guest in one's home had a right to expect a bit of civility. Or perhaps she was being unreasonable. It was this isolation, this loneliness and worry, all augmented by her confinement. If she could only take a walk outdoors she could better collect herself. Circumstances and one hard edict forbade even that.

With her eyes tired from reading, and the aching in her head becoming a nuisance, Rose retired to her elegant suite of rooms. She remained there until the next morning's sun arose.

The day was much like the one before. She ate alone, she read, she gazed out the windows, she paced.

Cora arrived not long after Rose had finished her dinner. Her husband, Claude, was ever so happy to be installed in his new position. Several times, Cora thanked her for seeing to it her husband found employment in the same household so they could be together.

She and Cora spoke for a little while, which was wonderful. But the poor woman was exhausted, and she still had to settle herself in, so Rose bid her a good eve with a promise to talk on the morrow after Cora familiarized herself with her new settings. Then Rose once again wandered the house alone.

As was her routine, she often stopped for longing looks outside the windows. Which is what she was doing, gazing into the early night, when the sound of the front door opening grabbed her attention.

Perhaps Burke's Aunt Eloise had finally arrived. She'd been so looking forward to meeting the woman, and having someone to visit with. She might even learn a bit more about Burke. Her curiosity had grown in the days since he'd come with his official papers and had her released into his custody.

As if she were a wild animal cruelly caged, Rose whisked herself in the direction of the foyer. By the time she bounded onto the empress green, marble floor, she was at a near run.

"Are you all right?" Burke asked, rushing to her. His expression of concern instant. With a sharp glance behind her, he said, "Is someone in the house?"

Burke was already shoving her behind him and grabbing the pistol from his pocket when she said, "No, no everything is fine."

Apparently not convinced, he still gave the hall a thorough scan before pivoting his gaze back to meet hers. The alarm in his sea green eyes faded in slow increments.

"It's quite dark out there," she said. It was the wrong time to ask. The worry lingering in his countenance told her so. But she'd been inside, for the most part alone, for two days straight and she'd had about all the contained solitude she could take. "I'd like to take a walk outside. Surely I'm safe way out here."

"No," Burke said, the harsh word instant and final.

"No one will even see me, as the moon is almost nonexistent tonight. Besides, there are guards everywhere. I've seen them through the windows."

In a softer tone Burke said, "I have plenty of men out there at every hour of the day and night. But until the villain is caught, you're safer indoors."

"Just a few minutes, please," she said, placing a hand on his sleeve. I'll stay close to the house."

Burke's eyes shifted toward the door, his expression no less grim. He faced her then, and after a glance at her hand, he took a breath and let it out. He was about to say no again, and disappear to wherever it was he went. She could tell. More time alone with her thoughts and worries. If this solitary isolation went on much longer, she would go mad with it. But Burke surprised her.

"How about a game of whist?" he said.

Withdrawing her hand, she said, "Whist?"

"Do you play?"

"Well, yes. I used to play with Piers and Eddy when we had a guest. But there are only two of us. The game requires four players."

"Whist can be played with two," he said, his voice and expression softening. "Come on, I'll show you how."

Rose walked with him to a small parlor of blues and golds. She'd been in here several times during her wanderings. The parlor was set up to be a game room, with two tables, a small, Sabre-legged tea table with two chairs, and a larger, Sheraton card table with four.

Burke took a few steps toward the larger table, placed near the window. Then he paused as if to reconsider, closed the drapes, and seated her at the smaller table at the back of the room.

"Burke," Rose said, settling into her cushioned chair and smoothing her skirts. "When do you think your Aunt Eloise will be arriving?"

Burke withdrew a deck of cards from a drawer beneath the table and shuffled with expertise. "I sent word for her to stay home. This trip is too far for her to make, especially since she's just getting over a bad cold."

Rose nodded, hiding her disappointment. She'd been watching through the windows all day, waiting for the woman's carriage to roll up the drive, and anxious for the company.

He set the cards out for Rose to cut before dealing eight cards face down on the table in the shape of a rectangle. He dealt eight cards face up on top of the face down cards, then a hand of ten cards each.

"Now you go ahead and bid," Burke said.

She stared at her cards, shifting quick glances to the ones on the table, and considered before saying, "I bid high."

Burke smiled at her for the first time since this nightmare had begun, and Rose thought him the most dashing man she'd ever seen in her entire life.

"So, you're out to win tricks this evening," he said, his tone teasing, his smile devastating to her defenses.

After a moment, Rose caught hold of her breath and managed to smile back with a confirming nod. "I am."

She won the first hand, but he took the next two. When she suggested playing for stakes, he declared with a suppressed grin, he believed she was duping him.

"How can you say such a thing when you've won two of the three hands?"

"Precisely. You're luring me in, letting me think I'm a better player."

She sighed in dramatic fashion. "Ah, well, perhaps you're right. Perhaps your whist skills are not at all superior and betting with me would clean you out of house and home. If you continue to challenge me, the next sunrise might well find you a pauper."

Burke chuckled. "Fine then. What sort of wager did you have in mind?"

Rose lifted her view from the table, thinking to look him in the eye while she decided what they would bet. But her eyes stopped at his lips, and memories flooded her head of those lips against her own, then raining passionate kisses over her body.

The memory of that night set a momentary quiver to her insides, and the room grew overly warm. She had to force herself to look away, lest he see her wonton thoughts displayed across her face. When she shifted her gaze to meet his, however, the simmering heat in his eyes told her he knew.

They stared at each other across the table and Rose did not doubt he was at that moment sharing her memory of the one heavenly night they'd spent together. She half-melted at the detailed recollection. And then, it was on the tip of her hungry lips to wager a kiss. Could she be so bold?

Images of Burke, unclothed, heated, strong, trembling with desire for her, made her entire body weep with longing. And then in an instant, it all cracked and crumbled to bits under the memory of his icy anger in the prison that terrible day.

After everything they'd shared, Burke had no trouble whatsoever believing she'd committed such a heinous act. He'd believed it without question. He'd condemned her without doubt. She shouldn't have such desirous feelings for this man. She wouldn't.

He must have seen her heat cool, for his drained

from his gaze. Burke glanced away. Did she see regret? Did Burke have deeper emotions for her plaited within his lust? Were there more to have? What they'd shared in his bed had to be unique, unequalled. Surely not all beddings left one's heart so entangled.

But no, that was but a covetous wish.

What she'd glimpsed was merely his mind's effort to maintain civility, not inklings of tenderness, certainly not love. It was clear. For when Burke brought his attention back to her, his blank expression spoke neither tale.

"My temporary cook baked some apple tarts for dessert," Burke said, his voice rough. He cleared his throat. "When I passed through the kitchen earlier, they were cooling. They looked quite tasty. I've not had mine yet. Have you?"

"No," she said, placing her attention where it should be, on the game.

She would make the best of this situation until she could go back to her own home. Polite, friendly, though not friends. A true friend would not have turned on her so.

Lewis did.

Lewis was heartbroken, distraught over Ashton's death. His mind was not in the right place. Perhaps in time, he might come to the truth. Burke could make no such excuse.

"I must warn you, though," Rose said, forcing a light tone. "I do love apple tarts and if we are betting your dessert against mine, I will be at my most competitive."

He gave her another smile, this one lacking the enthusiasm of the last.

And so they played the game, forgetting for a time death's emissary lurked out there somewhere. Forgetting he'd once believed the worst of her. Forgetting they'd shared something more extraordinary than anything she ever imagined this world had to offer.

Rose won Burke's dessert, but when he had them delivered, she was benevolent enough to share. And he was gracious enough to thank her.

They both yawned at the same time, and then laughed at themselves.

"Have you had enough gambling for one night," Burke asked.

"Quite. I believe I'm ready to sleep now."

They climbed the stairs together. Burke joked he would suggest sweets as currency the next time he played at White's. She replied how he would always know which players tended to win large, as they would be, well, large. They chuckled, more out of tiredness than good humor. He opened her door for her. The fire in the hearth burned hearty and candles lit any potential dark corners.

"Shall I send for your maid?" Burke offered. He stood before her, both of them just outside her bedchamber door.

"No. I'm sure she's asleep by now. Poor Cora was worn out from the trip."

"Miranda?"

"No, thank you. I'm fine."

"Very well. Then I'll bid you a good night."

"Burke," she said when his back was already to her. He cast a glance back over his shoulder. "Thank you for helping me."

He faced her then, stepping closer, his expression

serious. "It's the very least I could do after…"

Anguish tore across his face and it gashed her heart. Was he truly so repentant? It would be easy to believe, looking at him now. She could imagine he regretted the harsh words and accusations he spewed at her that bleak day in the prison. His actions since proved it. She wanted to believe…in more.

"Burke?" she started, not knowing what to say next. "I…I…"

Burke almost kissed her then. He wanted her bad enough to hurl his honorable vow into the flames burning high within the hearth. Rose was lovely, and sweet and strong. And if he lived to be a thousand, he would never forget her rousing passion, the feel of her gift in his arms.

His lust and his integrity erupted into a ferocious battle. His honor grew murky in the dust. Burke bent to her, ever so slightly, a drought-stricken man to rhapsody's water.

Rose leaned toward him as his keen eyes darkened with desire. His silent entreaty lured her longings back to the surface. Her eyelids fluttered closed and she tipped her head upward, awaiting his kiss.

Burke lowered his head, just a little bit more.

He was closer now. His heat embraced her, even if his arms did not. His breath touched her lips when she stretched up to meet him. And for an eternity, that's how they stayed.

It was killing him.

The lips that had whispered his name in longing dreams were so close to his he could almost garner her sweet taste on his tongue. Burke felt her desire with the same certainty as he felt his own. Shallow breaths gave a provocative rhythm to the rise and fall of her perfect breasts. Her head tipped back, eyes closed, her tempting, peach-colored lips parted the slightest bit. Yes, desire was there.

Burke teetered on the rim of his honor. His own yearnings had power enough to shove him over the edge.

In an attempt to block the entrancing vision before him, Burke squeezed his eyes closed. He couldn't do this to her. He'd given his word. Whatever trust she afforded him was already a fragile affair. If he broke his pledge to Rose to not touch her unless she said different, he might lose her forever.

And he wanted her forever.

She occupied his every thought, his every plan. The future to which he'd given very little thought, other than ending the bloodline, had opened like a burst dam. Holidays with children, laughter, shared meals, shared experiences, growing old with her, it all flowed over the desert of his existence.

Before any of it, though, if he were to have it all, if it was even possible, he had to make things right with Rose. He had to earn back her trust. He had to keep his word. And if he didn't back away this instant, he'd have her sprawled on her bed within the next hard beat of his heart.

He jerked back.

"Good night," Burke said in a harsh whisper. He spun away from her enticement before what little restraint he'd held on to snapped, and he ruined everything.

Rose opened confused eyes to see Burke striding down the corridor, as if she was a poisonous snake about to strike. She stayed in place until he rounded a corner and was out of sight. Even then, it was still another minute or so before she could gather enough wits to carry herself into her chambers and close the door.

In the quietude of her room, Rose reminded herself of the pledge he'd made. He would not touch her unless she said so. Perhaps he had not fully comprehended her desire for him. She certainly had not. A minute ago, she would have given herself to him in every way. She wanted to. Was that not clear? Or, perhaps his promise not to touch her was a convenient excuse to keep himself from the snare of a disastrous involvement.

That made more sense than she cared to credit, but it was a reason she could not ignore.

Her reputation was shattered beyond repair. She stood accused of murdering her husband. Even after the capture of the real killer, little would change in regards to her standing. Her name would always be that of the woman who, days after the murder of her husband, ran off to the country to take up residence with another man.

Sooner or later, someone would find out she had never been friends with his aunt, and that the woman had never arrived at either of Burke's homes. Society would never accept her in full, if at all. No matter his claims of autonomy, Burke could not be associated in the long term with such an outcast.

When this was all over, she would go back to the house she'd once shared with Ashton and Lewis. Rose accepted she would spend the rest of her life alone, isolated. The memories of her life with Ashton, and of whatever pleasures she should find here with Burke, would have to sustain her through the rest of her days.

And so, Rose determined, as she slipped into her lonely bed, she would have as many memories as she could gather.

Chapter 20

Burke rode his property yet again, passing and speaking with several of the guards he'd hired. So far, no one had seen anything suspicious. He repeated his warning to the men to stay vigilant. He reminded himself the same, in regards to his unruly lust.

Last night, he'd come very close to breaking his word to Rose. He should never have spent so much time with her. She aroused him beyond his good senses. But she'd been so anxious to get outside, he was afraid she might do so no matter his order. A wry smile touched his lips. The woman did have a habit of doing what she wanted.

So, he'd spent time alone with her last night, something he'd succeeded in avoiding since they'd left London. He could not allow such an instance to happen again. Rose was too damned tempting.

Burke had no sooner made his pledge, when he rode around the corner of the house to find Rose leaning in an open doorway.

Her golden hair was tied in a simple knot at the back of her head. She wore a rather ordinary lavender gown, with long sleeves and a neckline topping her collarbone. Her appearance was modest by even the most stringent of standards. On Rose, the blasted gown was nothing short of pure enticement. Of course, the woman could make a grain sack look enticing. More so, since he well knew what luscious wonders lie beneath.

Then, the dangerous reality struck him with a protective blow. Burke pulled up on the reins and scowled at her. "I told you to stay inside."

"I am inside," Rose said, nodding down at her matching lavender slippers, planted just within the doorway. "Would you deny me even a breath of fresh air?"

Burke had his mouth open, ready to give his command, when he changed his mind. If he ordered her locked indoors much longer, Rose would undoubtedly decide to sneak outside for a walk without his permission, and without one of the guards at her side. It was best if he took her himself. At least, that's what he told himself.

Burke held his hand out. "Come on, I'll give you an abbreviated tour of the grounds."

She brightened like the sun fresh from a week of cloud cover. It made him wish he'd offered to take her out sooner. Rose wasn't one to linger too long indoors. She needed to be out in the sunshine and fresh air, like all of nature's other wonders.

Without hesitation, she dashed to his horse with small, speedy steps. He helped her mount and seated her before him, both cursing and relishing the feel of her woman's body against his. Burke forced from his mind all thoughts of the placement of her soft curves by reminding himself someone who wanted to harm her still roamed free, possibly even nearby. The reminder crushed his mind's errant wanderings under heel.

On their easy ride, Burke kept to the open areas. Much of the beauty on his property lay within and beyond the mass of woods. But he would not take her anyplace that didn't afford him a long, clear view.

They rode at a slow pace around the house so she could get a thorough look at her surroundings from atop his tall horse. Burke pointed out the hill where as a boy he sledded, and his favorite climbing tree from which he once fell and bloodied his head but good.

"I have a difficult time picturing you as a carefree child."

Burke did not tell her little of his childhood was carefree. The few untroubled times he had, though, he had here at his ancestral home.

For the first few days after he and his parents arrived here, his mother would brood. She missed London's activities as soon as they left the city. The ride here was always gloomy and tense. His mother unhappy, snapping a complaint at every opportunity. His father ever angry at her, at his miserable marriage, and at the child fate forced him to feign fatherhood to in order to maintain his dignity. Eventually, however, things would improve.

Maybe it was the country air. More likely, the distance from everything that took his mother's attention away from their small family. With his wife in sight, his father was calmer. After a few days, his mother's mood evened. Visitors would come to call, and his mother eased into a slower-paced life. Occasionally, happiness would grace them with a few precious dribs.

They once built a snowman, the three of them together. The uniqueness of the moment made remembrance of it quite clear. They worked as a team, rolling snow, patting it, stumbling over each other. Their laughter echoed in the great expanse of the snow-glistened land. It was his most cherished childhood memory.

By the time the snow started melting, his mother would grow restless, his father disgruntled at his wife's short-lived contentment.

Burke thought of those as the empty days. The days when the snow no longer beautified the land and spring had not yet come to replace it. The days when his father's drinking and aggravation escalated. The days when the boy he was, if fortunate, became invisible to the people who hated him for ruining their lives.

"Oh look! It's a blue holly," Rose shouted, drawing his attention from more bitter than sweet remembrances. They'd entered a vast field of wildflowers. Rose almost leapt from the horse before he managed to grab her.

"Hold on," he said, dismounting. "You'll break a leg if you jump from way up there."

He helped her down, his hands lingering too long on the feminine bow of her waist as he set her on her feet. Did she notice?

Her gaze shifted up to meet his. Yes, she noticed his grip, as well as his man's desire for her. But she did not back away, as he would have expected at this questionable borderline of his vow. Instead, Rose met his steady regard with one of her own, and something else.

Desire heated the meaningful gaze beneath her long lashes. The clear beckoning delved past his vision and wrenched his core, striving hard to rip him from his damned vow.

A flash of uncertainty flickered across her face.

Rose hadn't any experience in seduction. More than anything, Burke wanted to teach her, in slow, thorough lessons. He would not, though. Not unless she released him from his vow. An inner sigh rattled around his taut insides. It was just as well, this painful test of his honor. It was a long stride in his affirmation to prove he meant what he said.

Burke let go of her and stepped back. He almost smiled at the vexation that passed over her exquisite features before she pivoted away from him, for he too was quite vexed. Vexed, frustrated, and burning for Rose as he had no other woman before.

She knew not how to proceed further, and he, shackled by his word, could do naught but let it go. Burke set his attention on what had drawn Rose there to begin with. After a moment, she did the same.

Rose tiptoed toward the butterfly, careful not to frighten it away. She lowered herself to her knees a few feet from it. Delicate, blue wings with black trim fluttered in Burke's peripheral. It was Rose who brimmed his vision.

She looked adorable with her graceful hands clasped before her, a smile of fascinated admiration lighting her face all the way to her sapphire eyes. Sunlight caressed her candescent skin, touched her golden hair, envious, without doubt. The glowing effect encompassed all of her like a celestial corona.

It was an effort to wrench his gaze away. Only his deep concern for her safety made it possible.

"So, you're fond of butterflies," Burke said, standing off to the side, keeping a watch on her a bit less than their surroundings.

"Oh, yes. In fact, I'm reading a book from your

library about them right now."

"Dutfield?"

"Yes. You're aware you have that particular book in your library?" she asked, shooting him a quick glance.

"I am. I enjoyed that book very much. Why do you look so surprised?" he asked when she continued to gape at him. "A man can appreciate the beauty of nature's most dainty creatures."

Her eyes lingered on his face. "I'm glad to hear that," she said. He caught sight of an expression he couldn't quite name, contemplative, pleased, maybe, before she turned her attention.

"Butterflies are spectacular beings," Rose said, watching the delicate blue wings hinge as the butterfly settled upon the seed head of a dandelion. "They're graceful, they resonate with splendor, and they're completely free."

Like you. Burke took a few steps to see her better. He scanned the area from this different angle, though his eyes always curved back to Rose.

"It infuriates me when people want to capture them," she said, a hard wrinkle forming between her brows. "Once, when I was a child, I saw a boy confine a butterfly to a jar. It broke my heart. Some things are not meant to be possessed."

Yet possessing her, Burke mused, at some point had become his obsession. Last night, when his body at long last eased enough to fall asleep, it was only to dream of Rose. The morning found him more wanting, and more frustrated, than ever.

"I'll talk to my head gardener about installing more plants that attract butterflies," Burke told her.

Rose stood to face him. Her expression of joy and gratitude only made him want to please her further. But then her face fell somber.

"I won't be here that long," she said.

"Perhaps I've learned a new appreciation for butterflies." *And other things that are beautiful and free.*

The corners of her lips tugged upward into a dubious grin. "Is that so?"

"Yes," he said in all seriousness. "Of late, I have learned an entire new realm of appreciation."

Her smile faltered, hesitated, and then it brightened in all sincerity. Standing in a field of wildflowers, Rose appeared not a visitor to the wonders of nature, but rather, a part of it. She was Gaia, personification of earth. She was Inanna, goddess of love, wisdom, war, fertility, and lust. Rose was all of that and more.

Burke died a thousand deaths, knowing he'd hurt her, that he had not only shunned her tender heart, but had done so in the cruelest of manners. He'd crushed her spirit with his vicious bile at a time when she needed him most.

"We should go now," he said, clipping his words to keep from unleashing his self-loathing in front of her.

Without further conversation, without touching her any more than was necessary, Burke returned Rose to the house. He secured her promise she would remain inside. As soon as the door closed behind her, Burke leapt onto his horse, tugged on the reins, and gave the horse his head.

He rode, as fast as his stallion's long strides could carry him, across fields, through the beaten trails of the woods, along a brisk-running stream. He rode hard, as if he could outride his grievous wrongs and find fresh ground on which to start anew. He rode until fear of pushing his horse too far forced him to slow.

****

Coffee-colored eyes peered through the shrubbery. It had been two days of waiting, waiting for that whore to take one of her walks. Frustration tightened dirty fingers around the wooden handle of the knife. It was a fine knife. The blade was as clean and as sharp as it had been when grandfather owned it. Soon, Rose's blood would cover the shiny steel. The thought was calming.

Today was a good day, for it was the first sighting of Lady Rose Sennett. *He* rode as her private guard, but eventually, that would change. They would all grow more comfortable with their perceived safety out here in the country, with their stupid guards on patrol. People were foolish that way. They knew naught of patient danger.

Lost in satisfying images, the knife had been plunged deep into the rich earth. Upon withdrawal, damp soil marred the well-honed blade. Cleaning it would not be a problem at the small camp erected not far outside the property of Lord Burke Darington, third Earl of Blackwood, keeper of whores.

Chapter 21

Rose took a long, critical look at herself in the standing mirror. She was dressed appropriately for dinner, if the main course was seduction. She slanted a questioning glance toward the amber pig on her bedside table.

"Well?" she asked.

Getting no answer, she faced the mirror again to make her own assessment. Cora had styled her hair up in a mass of soft curls, with several left out to hang long down her back. It was an elegant style. One she'd never worn. She wondered if it made her appear more mature, more…womanly. Cora had said so. Rose was going to have to take her word for it.

Her gaze shifted downward then, at her brazen dress.

Ashton had designed and commissioned the silver gown. The last time she had it on was so he could see the fit of the finished product. No matter how many times he and Lewis told her it was a glorious gown and flattering beyond compare, Rose never wore it for anyone but them, and just the one time. She thought it would molder in her wardrobe because she would never have the courage to wear such a thing out in public. She was surprised Cora even brought it.

The neckline plunged dangerously low, especially the way the fabric cinched under her breasts, forcing them upward for shameless display. The snug fit of the dropped waist gave a clear view of her form. Starting at her hips, the seamstress had sewn to the skirt countless swatches of silver gossamer layers. The flounces were so light they floated with even the smallest movement.

Ashton had wanted her to wear the gown the night of their soiree, the night he'd introduced her to Burke. At the last minute, she'd not been able to summon the daring needed to wear such a garment. Even now, with what she had in mind, it took great effort.

"My lady," Cora said, freezing in place as soon as she entered the room. She held in her hand the cup of tea on a saucer Rose had requested. "You look lovely. Claude could serve empty platters and his lordship wouldn't even realize it with you at the table wearing that gown."

"You don't think it's too…provocative?"

"Well, if you don't mind me saying so," Cora said, setting the cup and saucer on the dressing table. "Unless I miss my guess, provocative is the look you were striving for."

Shocked at the obviousness of her ploy, Rose stared at her maid. Cora sent back a knowing expression with a hint of sympathy.

"Is it so evident?" Rose asked, second thoughts about the evening poking at her.

"From the moment you met him."

Rose plunked down on the padded stool at her dressing table and sipped her tea, too embarrassed to face her maid.

"Oh, now, you're a lovely young woman, he's a fine gentleman. With the way you two peek at each other when you think the other isn't looking, it's clear even to your little pig over there."

Rose glanced at her stoic pig, and then set her cup back in the saucer.

"I had no idea," Rose said to Cora. "He truly looks at me so?"

Cora nodded her head. With a warm smile she said, "You both have the same besotted longing in your eyes."

Rose faced the mirror once more. The idea of seducing Burke had come to her last night. Yet this morning when he'd taken her out for a ride, she was at a complete loss as what to do even when the opportunity to make her desires known presented itself. If he did indeed find her as appealing as she found him, it would make things much easier.

Well, she would find out tonight. This afternoon she sent a message to Burke while he was out on patrol, requesting he join her for dinner. She'd not received a reply and doubt picked at her. Chances were, she'd be dining by herself tonight. She dressed for the occasion anyway. If nothing else, it helped set her state of mind. But if what Cora said were true, perhaps she would not be dining alone this evening after all.

Her fingers fluttered a nervous skim along the gown's plunging neckline before squaring her shoulders and smoothing down the gossamer flounces. *Be bold.* Well, the gown was a good start. Burke said he wouldn't touch her unless she said different. Tonight, she would say different.

****

Burke stood at the dining room window staring out into the night. In the distance, trees ascended like towers, darker against dark. The mere sliver of a moon gave but a trace of stingy light to the great expanse of his land. For all he could see, anything sinister could be prowling about this night.

It was very possible the villain, likely Edwina Rutherford, had slipped from her home as well as the authorities and followed them here. Was Rose's sister lurking there in the mass of growth around his property at this very moment, watching him stare into the night? Or had she paid an assassin to see to the ugly task for her?

Perhaps they were wrong in their assumption of guilt, and someone other than Edwina had committed murder and assaults. There were several viable suspects. There could be others with ill intent they'd not even considered. The array of possibilities and worries was maddening.

Though he couldn't see them, Burke knew his guards were patrolling. He'd personally interviewed and chosen each and every one. Still, a determined killer could always find a way. He drew in a steadying breath, scanning the darkness yet again. Fear for Rose's safety plagued him beyond reason.

Earlier, he'd sent a missive to Arness. He hadn't heard from the constable and he insisted the man kept him apprised of the goings-on. And then he received Rose's message requesting he join her for dinner.

Making an excuse would have been easy enough. In an instant, he conjured up half a dozen. He discarded them all. Rose should not have to eat every meal alone. As it was, she spent all of her time indoors and most of it in solitude. And as far as his appetites for other than food, well, it was just a meal shared. They both had to eat. He would excuse himself as soon as they finished, though. There would be no card games tonight.

At the sound of rustling skirts, Burke turned around. If his chest was tight with concern a moment before, he must be close to losing consciousness now. For whatever breath his lungs held, left him in a rush of desire so powerful his entire body went rigid.

The gown was audacious. Rose wore it with equal defiance. His gaze scanned her from top to bottom, and then he took his time on the return climb.

The skirt appeared covered in a thousand silver butterfly wings. Her bodice fit so snug, it begged for the sensuous glide of a hand. The neckline, designed to suite the bewitching approach of a temptress, plunged to heavenly depths from which no man could look away. Rose was a vision in silver with spun gold atop her regal head.

"Rose," Burke said, his voice a distant sound to his own ears.

There were compliments due, a litany of praises. It was all lost in her intent. Yes, he understood she meant to do this night what she had not been able see through this afternoon, or last night. The design of her dress was naught but for seduction.

And he was but a man.

"Rose. You are…exquisite."

"Thank you," she said.

A slight blush added a touch of innocence to her look. It only aroused him further. Burke gathered his manners as best he could and seated her before taking his own chair. Timmons served their artfully prepared dinners, which sat before them with little more than a bite or two taken. If asked on a hundred-pound wager, he couldn't have named a single item on his plate.

They talked about the weather, even though it was clear neither one cared a wit what the skies offered this night. Rose told him she spotted the blue holly again through the library window. Mention of the butterfly had him lost in remembrance of the feel of his hands on her waist. From there it was but a short leap to thoughts of what they once shared in the bed of his London home.

Burke picked at food that would not slake his hunger. He surrendered his weak effort to eat and set down his fork. Rose did the same.

"Would you care for some wine?" Burke asked her after Timmons removed their plates.

"I believe I would enjoy a brandy."

They withdrew to the blue room, a cozy parlor with blue-cushioned furnishings. The draperies matched the cushions, tied back with broad swatches of gold damask. A middling fire burned in the hearth. Along with several candles, it provided a low, serene flow of light.

Burke poured fine brandy into two crystal snifters and handed one to Rose. She raised the glass and sniffed, and then set it down on the polished table. Almost immediately, she picked it up again and took a gulp. For a moment, she froze. Her eyes widened and she commenced a rough bout of coughing.

Burke took her snifter and set it on the table along with his. At the sideboard, he poured a glass of water and put it in her hand. Rose managed to swallow some. He took the glass and set it with the others. Her coughing subsided, but she still appeared to be a bit stunned.

"Are you all right?"

Glaring at the glasses on the table, she said, "That's vile."

He laughed, and then his brow furrowed. "I just remembered, you told me you don't drink. In fact, I believe you told me you've never had a drink in your life."

"Yes. That was my first. I believe it shall be my last."

"And what made you change your mind tonight?" he asked, knowing, teasing. Lightening the mood might relax them both, and perhaps the brandy would muster her courage. He would give her no more liquor, though. He needed clear consent from her, and he wanted it to come from her soul, not from the brandy.

Rose opened her mouth to say something, but then she appeared to change her mind on that, too. For a moment, they stood surrounded by silence and firelight. She caught him by complete surprise when she lunged toward him and stretched up to kiss him. Her arms wrapped around his neck. Burke kept his at his side. At his lack of response, Rose backed away.

"Am I...am I doing something wrong?"

"No," he said, his taught body held still, his voice rough. "In fact, you're doing everything exactly right."

"I don't understand. You..."

"I gave you my word I wouldn't touch you unless you say different."

Her smile grew in a slow revelation, lit by a mischievous glint in her eyes. At his return grin, she said, "Burke?"

"Yes?"

"I'm saying different."

Burke spun around and strode to the door. He

closed it tight and turned the lock. When he faced Rose again, he said on an exhale, "Thank the heavens."

They met in the middle, lips merging, arms clasping around willing, wanting bodies. Buttons popped at the yanking of eager hands, fabric ripped, and a host silver gossamer flounces tore loose from their stitching. The scraps of fabric sailed an aimless drift until they joined the rest of their clothing in a chaotic heap upon the floor.

This was no slow seduction. This was desperate need. This was wild desire unleashed.

Once he'd relieved Rose of every bit of her clothing, Burke backed her to the settee, where he laid her down to stretch out before him. He lifted one of her knees so her bent leg rested against the cushioned back. He dragged her other leg until her shin dropped over the edge and her bare toes touched the floor. And then he took a step back for the sheer pleasure of gazing at her.

Firelight played upon her creamy skin. Her breasts rose and fell with her heavy breaths. The only thing more glorious than Rose in that temptress gown, was Rose bared to him so, naked, open, wanting.

Burke knelt beside her, taking her breast in his mouth, letting his hands go where they wanted, where she wanted.

The urgency tore through Rose like a thunderbolt. Gripping his strong shoulders, she yanked herself up to wrap her body around him. Burke shifted them as he sat upon the settee and positioned her atop his lap where she straddled him. He helped her, guided her, let her take what she wanted, and took all she wanted to give.

Chapter 22

Rose awoke in Burke's bed to her own sleepy sigh of contentment. Her eyes opened as she rolled on her back. Burke stood a few feet from the bed, a virile, consummate male, wearing his trousers and shrugging into his shirt.

"Good morning," he said, gazing down at her with a smile warmer than the bedsheets they'd heated throughout the night.

"Good morning."

"You look lovely with your hair mussed, wearing nothing but my sheet."

Rose smiled and rolled on her side to behold this man while he finished dressing. She gazed with no small degree of loss as each fastened button took from her the sight of dark hairs over hardened muscle.

She giggled a bit before saying, "I hardly even remember coming up here."

"Neither to I," he said, almost as giddy.

"Where are you off to so early?" she asked.

"Early? My dear, it is almost ten o'clock."

"Ten o'clock!" Rose shouted, sitting up straight.

The sheet dropped to her waist. In an instant, she snatched it up to cover her nudity. Silly, really, after he'd seen and touched every inch of her throughout the night. In the morning's light, however, her modesty had returned.

"Rose," Burke said in a deep, breathy timbre. If you do that again, you'll not leave this bed until ten o'clock tonight. Possibly not even then."

Rose laughed and resisted the temptation to drop the sheet. "It's no wonder I'm abed so late. I don't think you let me sleep more than an hour last night."

"What's a man to do when he's in the clutches of an insatiable woman?"

"Burke!"

"Mmm," Burke said, pausing before he stuffed his feet into his boots. "I do love it when you shout my name."

Rose gasped through her smile and leaned toward him with amused accusation. "You're shameless."

Burke chuckled. "You make me so. And eager. I've a feeling the servants will be finding silver flounces about the house for months."

Rose slapped a hand to her mouth, and then giggled through her fingers.

Burke bent to press a kiss to her forehead. "I'm going to take a quick ride around the grounds, speak with the guards and such. Meet you for breakfast in, say, forty-five minutes?"

"Sounds perfect. I'm famished."

"I must say, I've worked up a bit of an appetite myself."

His gaze turned hungry as it lit on her bare shoulder. His hand floated over to allow his fingers a reverent touch of the soft skin on her neck, and then dragged down to where the sheet lay atop the sensuous swell of her breasts.

"Breakfast first, Burke."

He sighed aloud, eliciting another giggle from her.

"Very well. I suppose at some point one does need sustenance."

Burke bent to her again, this time kissing her shoulder before pivoting away. He closed the door behind him.

Breakfast was a quiet affair, eaten over shared smiles both sensuous, and at times on her part, shy. Just the remembrance of the things they'd done last night heated a blush, as well as a rekindling.

It amazed her how freedom befell her in his bed. A mere touch of his hand formed her into a sensual woman. And with her own hands relishing the feel of his masculine body, she experienced the potent power of her femininity. She reveled in wielding it to bring him equal pleasure.

Rose set down her fork and stifled a yawn. Burke grinned without looking at her, causing her to face to heat again.

"I have some work to do in my study," he said. "Why don't you have a nap? We can take a short stroll outside this afternoon."

"That sounds perfect."

They stood and Burke walked her to the foot of the staircase where he kissed her with the promise of passions to come. Rose sensed his eyes upon her as she climbed the stairs. She glanced back. Yes, he was there, gazing at her with a heated grin that tempted her to run back down and jump into his arms.

Later she would revisit the pleasures she'd learned to give and take. Yes, she would. Rose spun around and floated down the corridor, as light as her lost flounces. In her room, she fell asleep almost as soon as she lay atop her bed.

****

Burke stared at the papers atop his desk, just as he'd done for the last twenty minutes. He shuffled a document or two. It didn't matter. Wherever he focused his eyes, he only saw Rose. He was so infused with her, he could swear her sweet scent lingered about his head.

He pushed back from his desk. No, she needed to rest after the long night they'd shared. He scooted his chair back in again and made another attempt at reading a document. At the bottom of the page, he laughed out loud, as he had no idea what it was he'd just read.

"Sir?" Timmons said, poking his head into the study. The butler's stare was wide as he made a quick scan of the room before directing his gaze toward his employer. "Is everything all right?"

"Yes, Timmons, of course it is. Why..." Ah, he didn't need to ask Timmons why he thought anything was amiss. Thinking back, Burke could almost be sure enough to swear in a judicial proceeding his butler had never heard him laugh.

"Everything is fine," he said to Timmons. He almost laughed again at the concerned expression on the man's face.

"Can I bring you anything, my lord?"

"Thank you, Timmons, but not right now."

The butler gave him a wary nod and a short pause before going about his business.

Burke shook his head and grinned. He dropped his attention back to his desk, determined to get through at least one document before he went to Rose.

****

"Ow!" Rose shouted at the sharp sting in her arm. Her eyelids popped open and in an instant, she was focused on the figure standing over her.

"Shut up," said the voice in an angry whisper. "I didn't hurt you. I just wanted you to wake up. I don't want to kill you in your sleep."

Chapter 23

After setting his desk in order, Burke sauntered into the kitchen. Through the window he saw Claude, his new cook, picking at the herb garden. He looked forward to trying the man's fare. Rose raved about the man's cooking, swore he was the best. It's a shame he couldn't remember what he'd eaten last night. Sitting across from Rose in that dress, it was a miracle he remembered his own name.

From a bowl on the wood-block table, Burke chose a couple of apples to take up to Rose's room. They would serve well for later, as his plan was to work up their appetites.

He stepped toward the main kitchen door which would take him to the corridor leading to the front of the house, and then stopped. The service hall led to the back stairs. That route would be quicker. He didn't want to wait one second more than he had to before he held Rose in his arms again. If she still slept, he would lie beside her, and perhaps nap himself. And if she awoke when he slipped into her bed…Burke smiled as he rounded a corner.

The breeze against his face surprised him two seconds before the broken window. He reached it in three urgent strides. Glass crunched beneath his boots. His heart pounded an alarm in his head. This wasn't an accident of one of the servants passing through. The window had been broken from the outside.

By the time the apples hit the floor, Burke was already at a full run.

Chapter 24

Rose slapped her hand against the cut on her arm at the same time she jolted up to a seated position on the bed.

A thin rivulet of blood seeped between her fingers. For several seconds, all she could do was stare in bewilderment at the crimson flow. Then, she raised wide eyes to the woman standing over her holding the long knife, the tip red with her blood.

"Lady Hortence? You...It...it was you all along."

Prudence stepped back and flicked the knife. "Get up."

With movements stunned into sluggishness, Rose dragged her legs around and stood beside the bed. She gaped at Prudence Hortence.

The elegant woman was now almost unrecognizable. Filth encrusted the many wrinkles of her gray, once fine, gown. Dirt smudged her face and caked her hands. Most of her hair had come loose from its pins and hung in tangled disarray. Her unwashed body produced an odor that permeated the room, emphasizing her crazed demeanor. The gleeful rage in her eyes was nothing short of savage.

"Why?" Rose asked.

Prudence sneered at her. "It wasn't enough you had Lord Sennett for a husband, a man who couldn't be brought up to scratch by the best of us. You had to have

Burke, too?"

Ignoring her question which was more an accusation, Rose asked, "If you hate me so, if you wanted me out of your way, why kill Ashton? Why not kill me instead?"

"Killing you was my original plan," Prudence said, sniffing and raising her dirt-smudged chin. "I missed and hit Lord Da Ville. That's when the idea struck me. If I killed Lord Sennett instead of you, if I made it look like you'd committed the murder, Burke would turn from you, not mourn you. And you would know my suffering. You would know what it's like to lose a man like him."

For a moment, Prudence appeared as if she would break down in tears. Her bottom lip quivered. Her nostrils flared. But then her face lifted, as did her brows over a flash of pure insanity. "And," Prudence said, snickering. "You would live out the rest of your days in Newgate, or maybe even hang."

Prudence covered her mouth with her dirty hands, muffling a burst of laughter.

"How did you get her pistol?" Burke asked from the doorway.

Both women swung their gazes in his direction.

"Burke," Prudence said. At first, warm hope softened her, and then her expression hardened.

Rose answered the question. "You stole it at the theatre, in the ladies retiring room. I set my reticule down to press a damp cloth to my face."

To Rose, Prudence said, "I followed you in to get a look at you. When I saw your reticule sitting there, I thought to take your money, to cause some imperfection in your perfect little life. I took the pistol on a whim. It wasn't until later that night I decided what I was going to do with it. The way Lords' Da Ville and Sennett whisked me off to stargaze so you two could have a bit of privacy, you think I didn't notice?"

Prudence cast disdain down her nose before rotating until she faced Burke. She kept the blade pointed at Rose while she spoke. "You discarded me for this little stick of a woman?" She then thrust out her bosom. "Tell me you don't miss me."

"This is over, Prudence," Burke told her, holding out his hand. "Give me the knife."

Prudence narrowed her eyes to a savage glare. Her lips twisted into a snarl. "It's *not* over, not yet."

Still pointing the knife at Rose, Prudence used her other hand to dig into the pocket of her skirt. When she removed her hand, she had a pistol clasped in a firm grip.

To Burke she said, "I wasn't going to use this because I didn't want to draw your attention. I guess it doesn't matter now. I've lost you for good anyway. Pity," Prudence said. Her face fell from the height of anger to the depths of a consuming sadness. "We could have been so good together."

"Prudence, don't do this," Burke said.

Prudence glanced down at her gown, appearing to notice her condition for the first time. She drew in her arm holding the knife, inspecting the back of her hand, and then rotated her wrist to take in her dirty fingernails. Her anger returned, full force.

"I hate you, Burke Darington. Look what you've brought me to. *You* did this to me. I hate the *both* of you!" She pointed the pistol straight at Burke's chest.

"Pru…"

Before he could say another word, Prudence dropped to the floor in a solid heap. Rose stood over the inert woman, her golden amber pig in her hand.

Chapter 25

"What will happen to her?" Rose asked.

Sitting beside her on the sofa downstairs in the blue parlor, Burke inspected the white bandage wrapped around her arm. He'd cut off the sleeve of her gown to tend to the cut inflicted by Prudence's knife. Fortunately, the wound hadn't needed stitching. Still, he fussed with the bandage, making sure it was tight enough, yet not too tight.

"My men are taking her back to London where they will turn her over to the constable," Burke said. A wave of fury and fear washed through him, leaving a residue not soon to bear away. "I've also instructed them to notify Lord Da Ville as to who is responsible for Ashton's murder."

"Thank you for seeing to it that Lewis knows. I miss his friendship. Though, I don't think it could ever be the same as it once was."

"Lewis's grief overwhelmed his knowledge that you would never harm Ashton. Emotions can send a person's words and actions to the wrong. I know. Perhaps your friendship is not altogether lost."

"I hope you're right. Burke, my arm is fine."

He didn't cease his gentle ministrations. He stayed focused, his gaze intense, as if she'd sustained a serious injury, and her life was in his hands. Rose clasped onto his hand and squeezed until he raised his eyes to meet hers.

"It's not that bad, Burke," Rose said. "She only poked me with the knife so I would awake."

"She should never have gotten so close to you. It's my fault, as I should not have let you out of my sight for an instant. I didn't do enough to protect you."

"You saved my life, Burke," she said.

A wry smile touched the corner of his lips. "I think it's the other way around. If you remember right, I was about to take a ball to the chest. If it hadn't been for you and your handy pig…"

"When I saw her point the pistol at you," Rose said. She stopped talking then, tears choking off her words.

Burke drew her into a fierce hug, careful of her injured arm.

Speaking into her ear, he said, "I'm never letting you go. Could you be happy here, spending your days in the country, reading, walking the land, and the nights loving me? Could you envision this life for yourself?"

"Oh, Burke, it sounds like heaven. But what about your business dealings?"

"We'll go back to London, occasionally, but much of it I can handle from here. His face rested against hers and his smile rubbed her cheek. He said, "I'll see the banns posted at once."

She eased back then, her fingertips on his chest. "Burke, I can't marry you."

His joy dissipated as his hands came to rest upon his thighs.

"The scandal is fresh, and I'm newly widowed," Rose said. "Society won't let what's happened pass without judgement."

"They won't touch us out here. Besides, when have either of us cared to be a part of that crowd?"

"Your business dealings—"

"Will be fine. I've explained all this to you before."

"And the foundling home. I can't abandon the children. I have to go back. With Ashton gone, and the committee disbanded—"

"I haven't forgotten them, Rose. Most of the funds were already in the foundling home account. I'm more than happy to make up for any shortages. The building will be erected, and soon. I've already commissioned a draftsman."

"You have?"

"And I've informed him he'll be working with you on the plans," Burke said. "With Ashton gone, you are to head the committee, even if the committee now consists of just the two of us. The new home *will* be built, Rose."

Rose lit up like daybreak after a long, dark night. She was his daybreak.

Most men would never permit their wives to work so. But he was not most men, and Rose was not most women. He would be a fool to try and change her.

She possessed a sharp mind. She produced viable ideas. He saw no reason whatsoever to oppose her seeing this project through. In fact, he rather liked that aspect of her. Her uniqueness fit well with his. Burke smiled from the inside out. Even marrying, he could still thumb his nose at Society. His title and wealth would protect them both. This was all too right for it not to happen.

There was just one more matter to see to. But it wasn't a small one. In fact, this blossoming garden might well die from it.

"Rose," he said. "There is something you need to know about me. It might affect your decision."

"What is it, Burke?" At his hesitation, she said. "Please, tell me."

How he wished he could erase this part of his history. But if she is to pledge herself to him, to bear his children, she had a right to know.

"The second earl, he was not my legitimate father. My mother, she…knew other men during their marriage. Other than my friend Drew, no one in Society is aware of this. If that helps."

"It doesn't help," she said, and he deflated near to nothing. Until she finished her meaning. "It doesn't help, because it doesn't matter. I love you, Burke. I accept all that comes with you, just as you do me."

He wrapped himself around her then.

"I love you, too, Rose, forever and always. No matter what."

"Forever and always. No matter what," she repeated.

Leaning back a bit, he said, "How does this sound? We'll go back to London and marry in a quiet ceremony as soon as possible. We will see the new home built and the children settled. In the meantime, we'll work on making some children of our own. That is, if you'll consent to be my wife."

Rose's smile dominated her face. He caught her joy before she even spoke the words. "It sounds like a perfect life."

"It will be a perfect life," Burke promised as he took her into his arms, where he intended to keep her for the rest of their days.

A Scandalous Request

A word about the author...

I lived most of my life in the wondrous city of Las Vegas, Nevada. For ten years my husband and I traveled several months of the year in an R.V., and I was fortunate to see every state in this amazing country. Now I live in beautiful Michigan, where I've learned about layering clothes and that boats don't have brakes.